Rose Way

By
C. L. Glass

Published by C. L. Glass
Copyright 2010 by C. L. Glass

Edited by Michael Glass

Thank you for choosing this book. For over three years, I wrote and rewrote *Rose Way*. Your support and respect for my hard work and property rights as an author is appreciated.

Reading appropriate for ages pre-teen and above.

Dedication

To my wonderful family,
Michael, Alisha, Andy, and Patrick.

To Jake and all my incredible furry companions
over the years... too many too name...

I Love You All, with all my heart!
Thanks for sharing the journey with me.

~~~~~~~~~~~~~~~~~

Prologue

Will Grant (a young police officer) and Emily (a college
student) uncover the truth to the town's tragedy and
recent deaths?

Most towns have tales of mysterious tragedies. Is a
past sinister force at play in this small town? Will a
young police officer and a college student uncover the
truth in time?

What key does an eccentric elderly lady hold in the
search to unearth the cause behind strange behavior and
afflictions that have befallen some of the town's residents?

Table of Contents

Chapter 1

Who Goes There?

Moonlight cast ominous shadows across the silent parking lot. A crumpled ball of newspaper tumbled by an isolated old beat-up car. Several yards away in a dark corner, two supply trucks were parked on the edge of the rough asphalt. The asphalt stretched into the darkness meeting a straight row of small, connected stores. Each shop sat like a square box connected to the next, a sidewalk spanning the entire strip. Along the sidewalk, eerie wafts of mist drifted, curling and flowing treacherously.

A faint light flashed in one of the dark stores, Hal's Pals. The flickering caught the attention of a passing police car. The marked car circled back. Slowly, it pulled into the lot and stopped far enough away to avoid danger. The random lights disappeared. But, the full moon's glow unveiled three shadowy human-like forms darting about inside the store.

Metal chings rang out as coins, hitting the hard tile floor fell from the opened cash-drawer. An ear-shattering alarm sounded. As the store alarm wailed, indistinguishable figures raced towards the rear of the store. Several large glass aquariums were knocked from their shelves by the apparitions rushing past.

Some of the containers shattered, spraying out particles of glass as they crashed to the floor. Metal cages were disrupted from their regular abode, overturned, and doors thrown open. Pet food, uncontained, littered the aisles, counter tops, and shelves. Pet toys, collars, leashes, and other items were scattered everywhere in the invaded shop.

A troupe of rabbits hopped about wiggling curious noses into the air. Nervous mice and rats scurried up and down the aisles, countertops and shelves. Hissing snakes slithered towards anything resembling shelter as freed birds fluttered their wings and screeched loudly, excited by all the upheaval.

Back outside in the parking lot, a patrol car idled with its headlights shining on the store. Behind its wheel, Officer Kratz sat with a police radio clutched in his hand. Krazt reported into the radio, "Dan here. Looks like we have a burglary in progress at Hal's in Cedar Plaza. Thought I saw three in there. Probably should send at least two officers to assist. Over."

A voice radioed back, "Bill and Grant are on the way. Wait in your car. Over."

A few minutes later, a second patrol car swerved into the lot. Two policemen emerged from its doors. The older officer, Bill was a bit robust. As he strolled towards the waiting patrol car, his gait revealed an odd limp and his bald head glimmered strangely in the moonlight giving him an alien-like semblance.

The other officer, Grant, was taller and much younger, only twenty-three, with a strong, muscular build. His confident stride revealed inner resilience. His thick wavy black hair tussled slightly in the night breeze as he surveyed the area for trouble.

Grant had joined the force right out of high school. His father had been a cop. Even after he was offered a full scholarship to MIT, Grant still decided to become a cop. It was in his blood, he thought. His dark blue eyes glimmered in the night's light reflecting what some would say was an old soul.

Thinking to himself, Grant shook his head in disappointment. Another senseless crime. How sad and unfortunate that some people couldn't find better things to do with their time than hurt others.

As Bill and Grant reached the awaiting car, an officer with ghost-like features sprang out. His short black hair and black eyes contrasted sharply with his pallid skin. Excessive thinness made him look smaller and weaker than he was. His every moment exuded nervousness.

The nervous man raised his thick black caterpillar eyebrows. Uneasiness resonated in his voice as he began, "It was probably some of those college kids again. I think they ran out the back. Every since they built that damn school, our town has gone downhill. As if those uppity teachers aren't enough to deal with..."

Grant interrupted, "Well, let's do it. Can't stand around all night." If he didn't cut Dan off, they could be here for hours listening to Dan complain.

Cautiously, he moved towards the store. The other two tagged behind him. He beamed the flashlight through the large windows searching for intruders. No signs of burglars, only unrestrained animals, scattered merchandise, open cages and shattered aquariums.

Reaching into his front pocket, he found the master key he had brought. This wasn't the first time he had to check in on this store. The key slid into the lock without effort and the front door pushed open.

The alarm was still bellowing out. Grant leaned to his left and flicked the lights on. Stepping through the living, moving chaos, over things that the storeowner characterized as pets, he arrived at the alarm's location.

After hitting its shutoff, Grant commented, "That's better." In a louder voice, he announced, "I'll close the back doors. Call Hal and let him know there is a horrendous mess to pick up. This time the perps were pretty destructive. It's going to cost a lot to replace all this destroyed merchandise."

Bill nodded and stepped back out the front door into the parking lot. Dan stood frozen only a foot within the entrance, staring at two enormous snakes intertwined on the floor. Their long thick bodies slid erratically against each other. Dan's horrified expression communicated his fear.

Making his way back to where Dan stood petrified, Grant joked, "Do you want to put those snakes back in their cages, Dan?" He thrust a snake catcher towards Dan.

Dan shuttered, "I don't get paid that much. I'll help catch the bunnies as soon as you've got those things locked up." He pointed to the pair of snakes.

"Why in the world anyone would want that kind of pet is just weird. Weird, weird, weirdoes.... It ain't normal!" Dan's voice squeaked.

Grant extended the snake catcher and gently untangled one of the massive snakes so he could return it to a nearby aquarium. Out of the corner of his eye, he saw Dan's narrow face twist with terror.

He chuckled, "These here aren't the bad ones Dan. I think the ones that are really dangerous like to hide in dark places underneath stuff. Hal probably kept some in those over cages there." Grant pointed to some open, empty, overturned containers to the left of Dan. "But, like Hal always says, Treat them with respect, then they will treat you with respect... unless of course, they're hungry ...then throw food or run fast."

Dan stumbled backwards toward the store's entrance, glancing for any signs of deadly invertebrates as he moved. "I'll, I'll just go outside... and look around to see....

4

huh.... to see if any entry attempts have been made at the other stores." He stepped back a little further and vanished; the glass entrance door banged shut with his departure.

Grant continued scooping up the unconfined critters, returning them to the safety of their cages. He had often helped out here after school when he was younger. Learning to handle animals was something he had taken too quickly. Hal had said that Grant had an extraordinary way with animals. Grant thought it only took a little patience and a keen eye to manage pets.

The front door eased open. Grant turned to see Bill returning with Hal, a kind, eccentric old man, who had a passionate adoration for all creatures. There wasn't one animal that Hal thought badly of. He admired them all.

Hal's eyes surveyed the store. He paused, "I just don't understand why my store. This is the second time this month. It's not like this is a jewelry store. Why would someone..."

He cautiously began stepping over the wreckage, up and down the aisles. Looking through his collection, he mentally checked off who was present and who was not. "Oh my, my, my-my, my. It'll take a while this time to see who is missing. Did you see Lona?" His kind old eyes widened with concern. "I will have to find her before her babies are born."

Grant pointed to a large aquarium further back. "I had to put her in that one. It was one of the few aquariums still intact."

Hal rushed towards the indicated cage. His wrinkled hand reached inside, calming the large snake. He murmured, "Oh Lona, I hope you weren't too frightened. There, there, I'm here now..."

Standing across the room, Bill rolled his eyes and twirled his index finger close to his temple. He mouthed the word, 'Cuckoo'. Bill was not one to hide what he thought, especially about this odd little man.

Bill's raspy voice complained, "They've busted up the place real good this time. I hope too many of your friends aren't missing Hal. Last time Shirley had a fit when that boa decided to hang in her front tree like some damn lawn ornament. And, it took months to catch those baby alligators."

His voice got a little deeper and sharper, "You have got to stop ordering unusual pets. Just sell regular ones... dogs, cats, turtles... you know, normal ones. Be a regular guy, like Grant here."

Ignoring Bill's dislike of his selections, Hal crackled optimistically, "Well, good thing it's spring. At least anyone who got out won't die from the cold."

With escalating glee, he added, "Maybe they'll run free, find happiness, finds mates, have lots of babies!" A smile beamed across his face.

Grant commented "Well Hal, you can't sell them and make any money if they run free."

He handed Hal a form sheet. "List all the missing pets and items on here... and try to get it to us as soon as possible so we know what we are dealing with."

Hal took the sheet, laid it on the counter. His demeanor changed as he looked around again. All the destruction to his precious animal paradise settled in. "Still don't understand why my store... my precious pets..."

Grant reminded him, "You know, times have changed. Town is getting bigger. More and more crime is headed this way. You just have to be better equipped to deal with it. Call Dave and pay him to install a better security system on those back doors. Maybe some heavy duty deadbolts."

Hal's voice took on an agitated tone, "Well, if that stupid, greedy Senator hadn't retired and wanted to build a university in his name so all his relatives could go to college for free, life would have stayed the same here for us a while longer. Waste of taxes if you ask me."

He restacked a few boxes. This mess was overwhelming. What was the town coming to?

"Crackpots are even tearing down the old Windel mansion behind the university to add a new student-housing complex," Hal complained. "Windel's mansion is a historical landmark, been here since the town has. You know some even say that mansion is cursed, and I wouldn't be a bit surprised if terrible things start happening once those idiots disturb it. Mark my forewarning... Anyways, need to preserve some land, not build on every inch of it. Good thing my late wife Julia didn't live to see her hometown destroyed like this. People just need to stop coming here." Hal shook his head in protest as his grayish brows frowned together forming a continuous line.

With a roguish smile, Grant patted Hal on the back. "The Indians probably felt the same way about you, Hal, when you moved in. It's a good thing you're arrow proof."

"I'm not that old, you young snot," Hal glared affectionately.

The front door popped open, interrupting the friendly banter. Dan screeched, "Hey, you guys all done in there?" He stood nervously on the other side of the threshold. "I'm going back to the station. My shift's up in about ten minutes." He lifted up his thin boney, wrist, and flashed his watch as though it could verify his statement.

Grant picked up another rouge bunny and placed it gently in a cage. "I've gotta get going, too. I'll have to leave the rest of the roundup to you. Be careful and keep an eye out. Call down to the station if you need anything."

He glanced over to Bill who was dusting for prints. "Bill, guess I'll see you back at the station."

Bill nodded. Grant made his way to the door and left.

Hal eyes fixed on the door, "I always liked Grant. He's such a fine young man; a son that almost anybody would be proud of, except.... Can't see how that awful mean-spirited horrible man was Grant's father. There was something dark about that man."

Bill added, "Yep, hard to imagine how Grant's mother was ever fooled into marrying such a demon. We were all astounded when she returned home from college married to a fellow like that. Don't know what she saw in him. But that's women for you. They don't make much sense." Bill stooped over and picked up a snake that slide across his foot and offered it to Hal.

"Oh, there he is!" Hal exclaimed as he accepted the retile.

While putting the thin black snake in a nearby cage, Hal shook his head again remembering Grant's father... "Thank God Grant turned out okay. An unselfish, caring boy. You know, he used to stop by after school just to see if I needed anything... Never expected a thing for it. I hate to say it, but it was a good thing Grant was so small when that evil man died so he didn't have a chance to corrupt Grant."

Bill interjected, "Yep, he was a strange man. Stranger though, was how his blood- drained body was found on the Windel Mansion's overgrown lawn. Never found out what caused the death or should I say who. Guess every town has its mysteries.

Chapter 2

The Arrival

On the way back to the police station, Grant drove past the old Windel Mansion. Slowing down, he came to a stop at the edge of its grassy lawn. He stared out the car window at the old familiar place. The tattered, wooden, three-story dwelling was huge and daunting, especially in this moonlight.

The mansion had been only two stories when it was first built. The first and second story vaulted up higher than an average home, at least the height of a story and a-half. Construction of the first level and a half was stone and rock, whereas, the second story had both wood and stone work. Shallow carved relief and spiral patterns adorned the wood and stone. Molded figurative bronze accents decorated the exterior. Miniature figures such as dragons, elves, fairies, were depicted as playfully dancing and hiding throughout the leaves and vines of the bronze embellishment.

Displaying a great variety of openings and arcades, including wheel and rose shaped windows along with many small ornate windows, the features were reminiscent of a European Cathedral. Three castle-like domed spirals pointed into the sky, one on each side of the home's roof and one in the middle. The domes with their tiny windows provided a view stretching for miles.

Or, if the windows were opened, clean fresh air to percolate through the building. Lightly shaded red-colored wooden shakes covered the roof repelling the sun's summer rays making the mansion a little cooler on steamy hot days.

The third story had a myriad of curiously shaped, kaleidoscopic stained-glass windows. They were incongruously placed around this third level and each displayed a different image. It was easy to understand how these exotic images coupled with the idiosyncratic arrangements gave most people an uneasy feeling.

Rumors were that the images told a story, but no one knew what the story was except that it was about witches. His mind drifted back to when he was about seven years old. His Godmother, Dotia Hazell was warming up dinner.

He could smell the fresh baked bread and meaty stew. The small cozy kitchen was the place he liked best inside Dotia's home. He knew some of the kids at school thought she was a witch or something, but all Grant knew was that she was the kindest, smartest person he knew. He looked up at her gently etched face bordered by soft dark black hair shimmering with silvery flecks. Her blue eyes radiated like enchanted dark sapphires. He decided to ask her.

"Nana, are you a witch?" Grant's young voice held an innocent inquisitiveness.

Dotia smiled, "Why do you ask?"

"The kids at school say you're an evil witch," he murmured. He didn't like saying those words. Each one stung as it left his lips.

"Do you think any of those kids are smart enough to know a witch if they see one, much less know an evil witch from a good one?" she soothingly inquired. She understood it pained the child to be teased at school over such things. It was only natural for a child to need the security of a verbal answer.

Many people talked about her behind her back. They always had. Dotia didn't mind anymore because sometimes it gave her an advantage. People may not think twice about harming or taking advantage of an old woman, but they weren't likely to cross a witch.

"Are there good witches?" His eyes grew big with imagination.

"Sure. You saw the Wizard of Oz and Sleeping Beauty."

"Ohhh, those are just stories."

"Maybe not," she gave him one of her wise looks. "Anyways, you tell those kids I'm a good witch, unless there are children who are being unkind or bad.... Then I turn into a bad witch." She laughed as his faced scrunched up

Grant wasn't sure it was a good idea to say that. The kids might decide to *really* torment him. Or worse, they may be so afraid that no one would ever play with him again. No more kickball, baseball, soccer, basketball ... He shuttered at the thought. He wouldn't ever be picked to play on anyone's team.

Dotia placed his plate in front of him as he pulled up to the kitchen table.

Since asking about the witch thing had went so well, Grant decided to press Dotia for answers to something else people whispered about, The Windel Mansion.

"Some of the kids at school were talking about that old house again. What really happened? Is it haunted?"

She settled beside him at the table. "Do you really want to hear the legend?"

Grant nodded as he attacked the food on his plate.

She began, "The Windel family was the first high-society European inhabitants of this town. They came from Europe somewhere in Romania. Mr. Windel was the first to arrive. Striding into town with shoulder-length wavy black hair, crystal blue eyes, and wearing a long dark bronzed gentleman's coat with a fashionable fold down collar, he was quite the curious sight.

Several foreign workers came with him to assist with the construction of what was imagined to be a marvelous two-story house. The design was very unique and exquisite. No one had ever seen anything quite like it. Once the task was completed, the workers all returned to their homes far away. Mr. Windel stood alone gazing in awe on the seemingly enchanted structure awaiting its masters."

Dotia's soothing voice transported Grant back to a time long ago... It was as though he was there, standing on the dirt street staring at the finely crafted house.

******

In the misty morning, two stage coaches slowly traversed through town and halted in front of the two-story house. An elegant dark beauty, Mrs. Windel, gracefully ascended from the first coach. Her long softly twisted charcoal hair shimmered in the early morning sun, emphasizing her deep blue-grey eyes. On her thin long purple cloak, a crest was embroidered that would further fuel the rumor that she was from royalty.

Into her arms one by one, three delightful young black-haired girls and a small black-haired boy bounced. The children ranged in ages, a few years apart from each other. The youngest girl was around ten years old and the small lad, six years of age.

Out of the second coach, four more charming young maidens appeared. The oldest girl appeared to be about sixteen. Each possessed the same enchanting black shiny tresses, falling down the length of their backs. The sisters ran over to the fidgeting boy. Each girl gave him a huge hug. It was clear to see, the entire family lavished the small tot incessantly.

As the days passed, more belongings and furniture arrived. Little by little, the family settled in and accepted their new environment. Not so accepting, were the town's people. The locals were standoffish towards the family. The Windels spoke with an odd accent and their clothes were a bit unusual. When the family would venture out for a stroll, the town's people avoided eye contact and didn't return the Windel's polite greetings.

But even with the unfriendly social setting, it wasn't long before the Windels had several businesses up and running successfully. Mr. Windel was a genius when it came to business. First, there was a new gigantic General Store. Then, they built a Grain Mill, Lumber Mill, and new Stables with an iron smith. Mr. Windel talents were revealed in every financial venture he took. His fortunes increased several hundredfold.

As the Windels became more and more prosperous, the town and the townspeople gained from this prosperity. Mr. Windel was a very generous man. He made sure to pay the highest wages and share his wealth through philanthropic gifts to the community. He funded a new school for the town's children that included an elaborate library.

At the ground-breaking ceremony for the library, the mayor gave Mr. Windel a ceremonious key to the city. The mayor proclaimed, "Our small town is honored that you choose it as your new home. We humbly offer this key to the city to show our appreciation for all you and your family have done."

Mr. Windel continued his humanitarian efforts. He was the first to offer assistance anytime the town was in need. The Windels even gave money and gifts to the community church, although they didn't attend the religious gatherings.

Still, some of the local people shunned them, not inviting them to private social gatherings or allowing their children to play with the Windel children.

Finally, one Sunday, the local pastor remarked, "Our little community is growing. My prayers are that this church would grow too and be an example to all. We all need to embrace those different from us, those who may hold different beliefs. When God clearly shows us he has favored someone, it is our obligation to treat that favored person with respect. How can we tell one is favored by God? When they are blessed with many offspring, like the Windel Family with seven girls and one boy. Or, blessed with wealth. Who here can deny the Windel's success in every business venture? Yes, fruitfulness can be a sign of blessing from God, just as sickness, ill fortune, and death can be a sign of God's curse. Of course, though, we must remember the story of Job and not ever jump to conclusions. Good people can suffer evil and evil people can be bountiful. However, it is my belief that in our town we are fortunate to only have good people among us."

Thus, in time, with the coaxing of the town mayor and local pastor, the family was more accepted. Seems that most people can learn to forgive peculiarities and differences when that forgiveness continues to profit them.

******

Years passed. The Windel children grew. The young Windel boy became a handsome lad, a pre-teen adored by the whole town. His smile could charm a snake. He was always had a kind word and a ready hand to help.

The Windel girls, as well, had become stunning young women. The oldest stood in front of a long old-fashioned mirror, a partial wedding dress draped loosely on her body. Her mother patiently measured and analyzed the dress.

"Stand still, please," Mrs. Windel tenderly lectured.

"Mother, are you sure it will be good to marry a man I do not remember?" the young woman asked with a quiver in her voice.

"Yes. It is our family way. This marriage was agreed to upon at your birth. I know you have not seen him in several years, but he is from a wealthy family and a noble. You will see; he is well mannered and polished, beside handsome and clever. In time, you both will be bonded in love."

Before the young lady come muster more objections, in through the door, the youngest daughter bounced over waving a white envelope. "Mother, a letter," she squealed.

Mrs. Windel laid her measuring tools down. "Let's see." She held out her hand to accept the letter from her young daughter. Carefully, she scored along the top with a near-by letter opener. Both girls tried to look over her shoulder as she unfolded the paper.

"It says... your finance will be arriving by ship not this coming fall but the one after. Thus, we should see him in less than two years time. That will provide us plenty of time to plan a grand festival to honor his arrival and then shortly after the wedding." Mrs. Windel held mixed emotion. It was good to know that he had scheduled the trip. But, it seemed like so far away.

"I miss the old country sometimes," she reminisced, glancing out the window to the new world in which she lived. The townspeople bustled about, tending to daily tasks.

"But why mother? We have so much here and everyone is very nice to us now," the elder girl stated.

"We had much there as well. And the people were my people. But, you are right. We have so much to be thankful for and so much to look forward to." Mrs. Windels eyes alighted on a magnificent Blood rosebush that she had planted. The deep red blooms were almost as plentiful as the deep green leaves. "At least I was able to bring a few Blood rose roots and get them grow."

"Yes, it has grown into such a lovely shrub. You have what the townspeople call a green thumb, mother."

"That is a strange saying. Now, let us get back to designing your dress. We must make a list of what more must be mail ordered. Your dress shall be the most stunning wedding dress in history."

The females giggled with delight thinking of the pleasant tasks ahead of them and the ever-increasing happiness befalling the family.

******

A siren wailed in the distance breaking Grant's daydream of Dotia's story. Still sitting in his car, Grant surveyed the outside of the once inviting home. The solid fence had been taken down years ago, but the rest of the place had remained untouched.

His eyes were drawn to an aged, rambling Blood-red rose bush blooming near a dried-up granite fountain. The dark, intense color of the blooms was extraordinary. The massive flowering bush had continued to grow throughout the decades. Now, it beckoned to Grant with its Blood roses.

He opened the car door and got out. Like in a trance, he wandered over to the tall iron rod gate, which guarded entry onto the overgrown path leading to the formerly glorious mansion. Taking a small key from his pocket, he opened the large padlock unbinding the gate.

Running his hand over the intricate designs of the gate,

he commented aloud, "This was definitely remarkable craftsmanship. I could see how people back then thought magic played a part in its making. Truly remarkable." His large steady hand pushed the stiffened gate open until it was wide enough for him to enter.

Again, Dotia's voice invaded his mind, continuing the alluring tale. "Definitely, the Windel's present days were joyful. But sometimes, even the brilliance of the sun is eclipsed by the moon, and only darkness can descend. This was one of those sometimes for the Windels. The coming years would cast tragic darkness on many."

Chapter 3

Truth or Lies?

Everything had indeed been going smoothly for the Windels. The day began like so many others; Mr. Windel was accepting a shipment at his delivery store. A group of townspeople stood in the store gossiping loudly. The main speaker was a rather large stout woman, who was loading her basket with groceries. The listeners were a few of the local townswomen.

The stout woman warned, "Terrible sickness passing through the country. You ladies better stock up goods in case it strikes the town. If the sickness is spreading that means it's contagious. I won't be out and around if it hits here. I plan to have enough on hand to wait it out, in my home. No sense in taking chances!"

A petite woman with fancy clothes retorted, "Don't listen to such untruths. My husband says the stories are just rumors started by a band of traveling gypsies so they could pawn off worthless medicines and fake charms. Gypsies are known to be vivid storytellers and 'traveling thieves'!"

An old woman wearing a solid-colored conservative dress added, "She's right. You know Gypsy women wear those flamboyant billowing skirts to distract people. Heard tell they called them *Banjara*. There are hidden pockets sewn right into the folds. You know what they are for? I'll tell you, the pockets free up both hands for more skillful pocket-picking. That's where they hide their ill-gotten gains."

A younger girl, who wasn't more than twenty-five years old couldn't wait to jump in with disparaging words. To be viewed above others, empowered her. In a sassy voice, she added to the hatred, "Yes, yes, and gypsies speak a demonic language. I heard them once when Marshall took me to the city. Scared me to death. I thought they were going to set a curse on me or something." She paused to make sure that she had the group's attention.

Then, she dramatically continued, "Cityfolk say gypsies sacrifice animals to the devil, practice black magic and drink blood of virgins to fend off aging. That fortunetelling comes from packs made with demons. And everyone knows demons require blood or souls as payment for any covenant. That's why they can't stay in one place too long, cause good lord-fearing people catch them doing those things after awhile. People can't hide what they really are."

The stout woman not to be out done piped up again with a new wave of horrors, "What's more that you don't know is that gypsies steal children to increase their numbers, cast spells upon non-gypsies, and rob from the naïve. Gypsies are really half-human... no one knows what the other half is ... and who dares to imagine ...."

Mr. Windel had heard enough. Differences often build barriers leading to people not liking each other, sometimes hating each other. In this case, it led to most people fearing gypsies and the gypsy way of life. He causally strolled over to the gossipers with an array of the European necklaces he had just received in a shipment. Although the jewelry wasn't real expensive the pieces were attractive and well-crafted. Displayed on a velvety maroon boxed tray, the necklaces mystically shimmered.

"Ladies, good afternoon. It's not often I am privileged with such a wonderful gathering of beautiful women in my store. Since I have the opportunity to serve you today, is there anything I may assist any of you with?"

All the ladies smiled at his complement.

"Well, I got what I need and can't afford what I don't," the large stout woman quipped chuckling at her own humor as she enviously eyed the jewelry Mr. Windel was holding.

"Excellent adage, my charming maiden," he smiled as he tilted the tray. "It appears five of my most wonderful patrons are standing before me and I have five necklaces ...."

Cutting off his sentence, the oldest woman sniped, "Well, we aren't going to buy them!"

"Oh my dear sweet lady, you misunderstood my intentions. I would be pleased to offer each of you one as a gift in honor of today being the Gypsy holiday, Iubitor Prientenie."

"Oh my!" one of the ladies gasped.

"What does Iubitor Prientenie mean?" another asked.

"It means day of Loving Friendship," he replied. "In my old country it is told that gypsies bring good fortune because they are such hard workers as to please the heavens. The Gypsy women even sew small pockets into their skirts to serve as pocket purses, so to always have two hands ready for hard work. They are Tinkers of metals and Crafters of woods. Some travel in caravans from town to town making and selling specialty items like jewelry, copper pots, brass ornaments.... Never a finer good, will you find, then one handmade by gypsy hands."

Pointing to the necklaces, he revealed, "In fact, these were crafted by a tribe in Romania. Please take one each."

The youngest of the group, who had been silent until

now, asked "How should we choose?" She couldn't wait to get one. The metal glittered. It was all she could do to keep from reaching forward and snatching one.

Mr. Windel, being remarkably clever, sensed that the oldest lady in the group really controlled the group. So he answered, "The best way is from oldest to youngest. We should always celebrate the wisdom that comes with each year of life. That is a Gypsy saying too," Mr. Windel disclosed.

"Did you ever know any?" The youngest girl was enthralled with hearing stories about other cultures and lands. In truth, she had never been anywhere but the nearest big city, and she had never met any gypsy folk.

"Why yes. They were everywhere in my country. Wonderful people. The women are experts in herbs and medicines."

"Did you ever have your fortune told?" The inquisitive girl's eyes glowed with excitement.

"I do not take too much stock into fortune telling or pen dukkerin, in Gypsy tongue. I believe it is up to the man or woman and God to set or find fortune. But, the gypsies tell a fine story, probably more entertaining than true."

The ladies each selected a necklace. They helped one another clasp the shimmering treasures around the corresponding necks. Mr. Windel didn't know what shined brighter, the jewelry or the women's smiles.

******

Soon after, a gypsy band arrived in town with whimsical painted wagons, which they called *vardos*, trained carnival animals, and odd musical instruments playing foreign melodies that pierced the sadness of the soul yet lifted the spirit. The townsfolk's apprehension rose as superstitious rumors increased.

A town council meeting was called. On the date, the

mayor, town council and some of the town's people gathered in the town hall. Mr. Windel was there in the small audience as well.

The meeting began with the mayor beating a small mallet on the large rectangular table where he and the council were seated. After the small crowd silenced, he stated, "Folks we are gathered here to surmise what to do about the gypsies."

From the middle of the audience, Mr. Windel stood up tall and raised his hand for permission to speak.

"Yes, Mr. Windel, please address the council," the mayor invited. He was glad to have someone interject. This was not an easy issue. If someone had to go out in tell the gypsies to leave, he didn't want to do it… gypsy's curses were the worst. Maybe he could get Mr. Windel tricked into it.

In a soothing, calm tone, Mr. Windel rationalized, "These extraordinary craftsmen are to be admired. Everyone knows the fables of thievery and child-stealing are just malicious gossip. Gypsy life may be carefree, untethered by societal class restrictions or governmental regulations, but that doesn't make them evil. But Gypsies do abide by rules, it just a simpler system of Gypsy societal order."

He truthfully elaborated, "In Europe, it is a prize possession for a Royal family to have several Gypsy families within their providences. Royalty without Gypsies are social outcasts."

The town council nodded being seduced by the ideas of royalty. Even people in the small crowd seemed appeased. Mr. Windel had their attention.

Sensing the growing positive reception, Mr. Windel continued his speech, "With help of such skilled craftsmen, I could even afford to provide funds to build a new town hall. I would allow them to stay on my property outside town if my fellow town's people, my friends will allow my humble offer."

The group whispered among themselves. Finally the mayor spoke out, "All in favor of allowing the gypsies to stay if Mr. Windel conducts all interactions required say aye."

Resounding 'ayes' rang out from the committee. There was only one or two who shook their heads in protest. The non-committee spectators clapped with approval of the council's decision.

"The ayes have it. Mr. Windel, we will concede for now and allow the Gypsies to stay outside of town on your land. But, the first sign of trouble, *you* must make them leave. Also, you will be responsible for any harm or damage the gypsies cause the townfolk. Do you agree?"

"Yes, I agree to your terms and appreciate your trust in me." Mr. Windel shook several hands as the meeting dispersed and the townspeople went off to their respective homes.

In the end, Mr. Windel's charm and more likely, the promise of town hall funds, had convinced the Mayor and town council to permit the Gypsies to stay.

******

That evening Mr. Windel rode out to where the gypsy tribe had set up a make-shift camp. They agreed to hold a meeting with him. Fortunately, he had learned enough of their language as a young man to speak almost fluently.

Speaking in their language, he invited, "My friends for no money I lend you my humble pastures. Please be my guests."

"How do you know of our words?" the old Gypsy Matron asked. "Our words are held dear and special for only Gypsies. We do not allow regular folk, *Gadje* to learn our tongue."

"I mean no offense. Please accept my apology. I only wanted to communicate in your tongue to honor you. My family was prosperous in Romanian, my homeland. It was our tradition to host Gypsy tribes. I often worked beside my fellow gypsies and called them brothers," Mr. Windel explained.

After some discussion and a tribal vote, the gypsies agreed to camp in the Windel's large fields a few miles outside town. The Gypsy set up areas for their animals and each Gypsy family had an area of its own. The small encampment soon resembled an unusual make-shift settlement.

******

Thud! The metal gate snapped shut behind Grant as he released it, moving past its iron clutches. The moon was bright tonight... brighter than he had seen it in a long time. The roses swayed in the gentle breeze. Grant scanned the area as he walked towards the giant old house.

High up on the house's exterior, the multitude of mosaic windows reflected the moon's light. It almost seemed as if there were lights emanating from behind the glass panes. The windows were magical-looking, making the house appear alive... he gazed onto the illustrative images.

A young maiden, in a flowing gown, knelt beside a wolf, which was baying at the moon. A magnificent waterfall cascaded down a mountain cliff, as fairy-like images hovered in the air. Hosted tents with waving banners dotted the imaginary landscape. Bushes, vines, and flowers interwove throughout the glass artistry.

One window featured a Romanian castle on a jagged mountain cliff. Lightning bolts and torrential rain menacingly pounded down upon the fortress. There was nothing as magical as the energy of a thundering rainstorm.

As his eyes traced along the different mosaic sections, it struck him how much the kaleidoscope of colors reminded him of a circus, no a carnival. He wondered what the gypsy carnival Dotia told about in the Windel story had really been like... It seemed like she had just told him about it yesterday, Dotia's story entered his mind once again.

Chapter 4

Carnival

Dotia soft voice continued the Windel's tale of happiness and tragedy, "After many months, the town's people seemed to become at ease with the new inhabitants. Some of the men would sneak down to buy Gypsy wine and whisky. The Gypsy's were even invited to put on a show for the town. Soon signs were all over town announcing a Gypsy Carnival in the downtown square.

The day of the event, the town was elaborately decorated with Gypsy flare. Colorful cloth banners and ribbons were strewn up on every building and gas lamp pole. A variety of children's games occupied make-shift booths, such as throwing a ball into one of three hoops for a small prize. This one was popular with the adults as well. However, of all the games, the men liked the dart throwing game the best. Most of the local men weren't very good at it, but they lined up to get a chance at it.

The children's favorite was the Fantasy Booth. Children could have theater makeup applied to their faces. Facial foundation colors ranged from white, red, blue, purple, and green. Then, intricate designs were painted on top of the foundation. Some chose fancy designs with flowers and spirals. Others wanted more of a clown like style, with rosy cheeks, colorful eyes, and a big bulbous nose.

For the main show, the gypsies orchestrated a

theatrical of animal tricks. Their collection of performing pets consisted of parakeets, monkeys, ponies, dogs, and two bears. They also had entertaining skits with unicyclists and jugglers. During the show, people could purchase special flavored drinks, meatball sandwiches, popcorn, a variety of baked sweet breads, and cookies.

But the highest drawing attraction was the Fortune Teller's Den. There were so many wanting fortunes read that appointments had to be made. Most of the tales were of good fortune and happiness. Gypsies knew that people only wanted to hear good news. So, it was seldom wise to disclose any negative impending events. And of course, the future was always changing with each decision that the person or people around the person made.

It was Mr. Windel's turn to have his destiny revealed. Although he didn't really believe in it, curiosity and his daughters' hounding for everyone to have their fortune read, got the better of him.

The heavily draped, dimly lighted room was filled with smoky incense that swirled around a small table with a crystal ball in its center. At the gesture of the old Gypsy Seer, Mr. Windel sat into the chair across from her. "Sărut mâna," he said offering a formal Romanian greeting to the gypsy woman.

With the mystical darkness playing tricks on his senses, he almost didn't notice the young gypsy girl, maybe an apprentice, off to the side, sitting on the floor. *Gadje* wouldn't have known that it was customary to have another person in the room to serve as protection for the Seer, from human or sometimes non-human visitors.

"Place your hands on the table please, so your energies can be read by the crystal," she directed with a theatrical flair.

Then, she started to recite her usual good-news spiel while circling her palms above the crystal and pretending the glass globe was sending messages. *"For' shava.* The Gods have favored you. Great things lie ahead. Ask what you will."

She placed her hands on his and turned his palms face up. Suddenly, the old woman swooned in her chair, as though under great strain. True visions aren't gathered through a fake crystal ball, but invisibly stream through unseen psychic links to the person who truly has the gift. And, although this particular old woman usually gave fake readings, she truly had the gift or curse, as some might say.

Most of the time she was able to block images or voices that tried to flow or push themselves into her conscious. But, the connection of Mr. Windel's hands to hers sent an abrupt chaotic and disturbing vision flooding into her mind before she could react.

To the Gypsies, Mr. Windel had become a *te' sorthene* (heart friend). Adopted as *familia* (extended family), her Gypsy honor obliged a warning to him. So, she permitted the images to continue into her mind's sight.

"Terrible," she crowed in a long drawn out voice, *"Terrible. To such an honorable man, tragedy awaits to sink it black teeth into the kind-hearted flesh. In many months to come, you will suffer great loss. Yes, great loss. Dark days, a struggle ensues, your family dragged from your house, into the square. You must prepare for the day. Fortify your wits."*

Abruptly, the woman collapsed head first onto the table as a result of the spiritual drain. Channeling took enormous energy. The young gypsy girl, who had been seated on the floor, flew over to her. Her incredible swift speed surprised Mr. Windel.

"Should I call for help?" he asked.

"Naght, sheee'll be fit," the girl stated with a thick dialect. "Putta sign out, mulțumesc?"

"Oh, yes, I'll put your break sign up outside so she can rest. You're welcome. Are you sure everything is alright?"

Using a few pillows strategically placed in the chair, she had adjusted the old woman to a slightly reclining position. Thin multicolor blankets wrapped the lady firmly.

"Yah," the girl gave him a reassuring soft smile as she sat on the floor at the woman's side.

"Let her know, I appreciate and honor her." He set several gold pieces down on the table, turned and left out through the heavily draped entrance.

Seeing the coins, the young girl called out loudly "Mulțumesc, mulțumesc!"

******

The night air chilled Grant's face and exposed hands. The temperature had dropped since he had been out here. Rubbing his hands to gain some warmth, he lifted his gaze from the enchanting windows. Walking around the side of the house, he entered the back courtyard area.

"I imagine this place must have been grand in its day." His voice resounded loudly against the empty night.

The back area was as overgrown as the front. The few magnificent stone statutes left appeared out of place. He maneuvered around the back windows shining his flash light to make sure there were no signs of vandalism. The boards on the windows were snug in place. One boarded window area was huge, almost as large as a dual patio doors. This was the spot that Dotia had told him about. The spot the young Windel daughter had learned about the letter that was to change their lives.

He remembered repeating to Dotia, "So after the carnival was when Mr. Windel got the letter from the old gypsy woman... the witch!"

Chapter 4

"Now Grant, don't call the Matron a witch. A witch has such a bad condemnation to it. Instead you can think of her as a wise woman with a magical touch."

Yes, it was a few days later, when a Gypsy appeared at the Windel Mansion with a sealed letter for Mr. Windel. A servant accepted the letter and delivered it promptly to Mr. Windel who was resting on a day-couch in the back courtyard.

Mr. Windel quickly retreated to his study room inside the home. Once in the safety of his study, Mr. Windel opened the letter. The odd Gypsy language looked like ancient script. It took him a few minutes to decipher it. The note was from the old woman who had read his fortune. She was the highest ranking matron of the gypsy tribe, a very esteemed and respected position among the travelers. Her message warned of impending danger to the Windels and offered to perform protection rites for no expense.

He hid the note away in his desk drawer. It would be best, he decided, to not upset his wife or children with the dark message. In the past, he had thought that gypsies held strange powers, but he was a modern man and had learned to ignore such old-way beliefs.

Thinking the letter safely hidden away, he headed back out to work. Unbeknownst to him, his youngest daughter, Oana was playing outside. The strange way her father reacted to the beige paper in his hand ignited her curiosity. Spying from the outside window, her deep blue eyes watched him hide the mystery in his desk drawer. Oana knew papa wouldn't approve of her snooping, but she couldn't restrain herself.

Soon he left his study. Oana waited a minute and then entered the house through the back patio entrance. She had to make sure Papa was gone before she continued her stealthy plan. She strolled inconspicuously up to her eldest sister who was busy painting a portrait in the main living room.

"Is Papa off to work again?" she asked the artist.

"I suppose so. Why?" The elder girl applied a bit more paint on the tip of her brush and dotted it onto the canvas.

"No particular reason. Thought I'd see if he needed help with anything. He is always working so hard. I'll go see about Mama." She twirled around playfully as she exited the room. It was true that Papa worked far too hard. She had not seen much of him this year. But she was not really going to see her mama.

Repeatedly glancing in each direction to avoid detection, she snuck down the hall and into the study, closing the door softly behind her. The grand desk beckoned her. She rushed over. It had been the third drawer. She was sure. Clutching its handle, Oana pulled. Inside the drawer lay her conquest, a folded beige paper. Swiftly, Oana grabbed it and then manipulated it into a smaller square. As she tucked the small square down into the top of her dress, she kept her eyes peeled for intruders.

Once up in her bedroom, Oana gently uncreased the paper. "There's no way I can understand what this says," she complained out loud to herself as she tried to understand the strange text. "Maybe I can sneak down to the Gypsy camp and get one of the women to tell me what it says."

She grabbed some paper and a pen quill. Carefully she transposed the strange markings onto her paper. After she completed her task, she re folded her papa's letter, tucked it back into her blouse, and headed back down to return it.

Oana skipped down the stairs and swung into Papa's study. Papa was sitting at his desk working. Had he noticed the letter gone? How would she get it back into the drawer? Never before had she done anything against her parents. What had possessed her?

"Oana, my child, are you looking for me?" Papa asked. His voice was so kind. Tears brimmed in Oana's eyes. Guilt surged up, paining her heart.

"Oh Papa, I've done something very bad. I'm so ashamed and sorry," Oana blurted out before she could stop herself.

"It can't be as bad as that. Close the door, come here and we shall talk about it. I'm pleased that you trusted me enough to come to me Oana." Papa soothing voice calmed the ache in Oana's chest.

Closing the door, Oana inched over to her papa's side. She reached inside her blouse, pulled out the burden and handed it to her papa.

"I see." His hand reached out and gently accepted the letter. "Oana, why did you sneak away with something meant for me?' The voice was not angry, or contemptible. It simply questioned.

"Oh Papa, please do hate me or tell Mama. I didn't mean to spy. I was outside and could see you from through the window. I was going to tap on the window to wave to you, but when I saw your face as you read the letter ⋯, I knew something was not right. Something inside my heart stirred me to find out what was wrong. I thought I could help. But I realize now I should not have done such a thing." Tears fell down the young girl's face as she told her story.

"Did you understand the letter?" Papa softly asked.

"No. What manner of writing is it?" The ache in Oana's chest had lessened somewhat having relieved her spirit of the wretched injustice she had measured against her Papa. She had learned a valuable lesson. The guilt of one's actions can weigh down a spirit into darkness and pain.

"It's old Gypsy script and nothing to be concerned about. I will tell you the truth on one condition. You are not to tell the others. I do not want our family ruled by superstition. Do you agree?" Papa's voice had an edge of sternness to it.

"Yes, Papa." Oana threw her arms around his neck so happy to have such a wonderful loving Papa. "Will you also teach me Gypsy script?" She whispered.

"Well, it is very difficult and I do not have a lot of time. My businesses are keeping me busier than I have ever wanted. Sometimes I feel guilty about the time I spend away from you children," Papa confessed.

"We understand Papa. I could help out more at the store. I can stock shelves and take orders. We would all be very happy if you would let us help. You work too hard and are wonderful Papa. Please let us help." Oana's eyes shined with admiration.

"My daughters have grown while I was not watching," He chuckled.

"Yes, I will accept your help and your sisters' as well. We shall discuss this at a family meeting after I have seen to the details." He kissed the top of head. "Off you go for now while I finish my work."

"But Papa, you have not told me what the letter said," she boldly reminded. Her curiosity was still intact, though she vowed to never use subterfuge against those she loved to satisfy her inquisitiveness.

"It said that ill fortune was coming. The Gypsy Matron volunteered to cast protection spells for our family. See how silly it sounds? Even if the Gypsy Matron meant well and I am sure that she did, we should never allow superstitions to interfere with practical thinking," Papa confidently assured her.

A few nights later after supper, the family gathered for a meeting. Papa led. "As you all are aware, Oana requested that she be allowed to work at the family's store. After reviewing all of the details, I have approved Oana's petition. She will begin working at the store tomorrow."

Mr. Windel glanced around to take in the reaction of his family. They all seem mildly surprised, had the appearance of approval

He continued, "She can assist with orders and deliveries. However, I do not want my daughter traveling alone delivering orders. Thus, I seek to know if any of you would accompany Oano in deliveries." Papa's eyes glanced from one daughter to the next to appraise the reaction.

The oldest daughter spoke. "I would Papa. I don't know why we didn't start helping you before now. What a clever idea, Oana." The sincerity in her voice flooded Oana with relief. She had been a little unsure about her sisters' reaction to her asking to work like a commoner.

While Oana thought it would be an exciting adventure, learning about business and people, she had been afraid some of her sisters may consider it undignified. It was all going to work out better than she could ever hope. They spent the rest of the evening going over work plans and tasks that each child would assume.

Soon the Windel girls were working happily at the supply store, while the boy assisted his father in his managerial responsibilities. Each Windel daughter was polite and respectful as they accomplished daily tasks. The local townsfolk were pleased to see that the wealthy girls were not strangers to common manual labor. Their unpretentious attitude endeared the Windels further into the hearts of the locals.

The task that Oano loved most was delivering orders out to the Gypsy camp. She especially didn't mind when her oldest sister came too because her oldest sister loved to spend time there also. While her sister was learning about dying fabrics and sewing, or training animals, Oana learned the Gypsy language, folklore, herbal practices, and what some would call Gypsy magic. Oana became a favorite of the Gypsy Matron. The crafty old woman even referred to Oana her beloved adopted child.

******

The wind whipped by Grant's face, stinging his cheeks and eyes. As the wind grew stronger, the boards on the old mansion creaked, making it sound like the house was groaning in rebellion against its impending fate. Even vagrants were afraid to stay at the ill-fated manor. Nope, there were no indications that anyone had dared to take up temporary shelter here.

Grant walked back around to the front of the once magnificent home. He sauntered over to the swaying rose bush. He pulled out his pocket knife and flicked its blade open. The metal gleamed in the moonlight. Selecting one of the gorgeous deep red blooms, he ran his knife through its thorny stalk. As he heard its thick stem snap, he thought about all the herbs that Dotia had taught him about.

"I guess most people never think about a rose being an herb. But, you are probably the mother of herbs. European people in ancient days even thought you had the power to ward off the plague." He said to the bush as he cut another blossom and laid it on the ground next to the first.

"Would have been nice if you could have saved all those people here years ago." Again, Grant's mind drifted back to the Windel story and the tragedy that befell the town.

Chapter 5

Sadness Comes

About a year or more after the arrival of the Gypsies, just when all had settled and most of the townspeople had accepted the nomads, an unknown plague arrived. It wreaked havoc upon the small town. Almost no one was spared the misery of contracting the dreadful disease. Several people died.

Sickness even struck some of the Windel family. Mr. Windel sat downstairs resting on the couch. Stillness pervaded the once lively home. Oana laid a cool cloth that she had been soaking in a herbal mixture on his forehead.

"Papa, I know you do not believe it, but the reason I am not sick was because of the Gypsy magic," Oana insisted.

"Oana, I agree that some of their herbs have almost magical properties, but they do not hold magic."

"But none of them have been sick in the slightest. Also, the herbs they have shared seem to be making Mama better faster. But I worry so about my sweet dear brother. Please let me take him to their camp." Oana redipped the cloth, twisted out the herbal water and returned it to her father's forehead.

"Oana, I know you mean well. But I do not believe in magic. If the townspeople hear wind of your stories, we will be run out of here or killed for witchcraft. No more talk of Gypsy magic. I cannot risk such rumors. Your brother's health must be left up to God." Her father's eyes closed as the illness exhausted him.

Tears streaked Oana's cheeks as she leaned forward and lightly kissed her father on the top of his head. She knew it was useless to argue. She couldn't, wouldn't go against her father's commands.

As for Mr. and Mrs. Windel and the girls, they all recovered rather quickly. However, the charming boy was unable to endure the wretched illness and fell into prolonged unconsciousness. His weak, frail body was rumored to lay virtually motionless upon his bed in the Windel home.

It was then that the family constructed the mysterious third story onto their home. Mr. Windel hired the gypsies to expedite the project. With the Gypsies involved, construction of the third story with its mystifying windows only took a few days to complete.

Stained glass windows with bold deep hypnotic colors dominated the story's features. The fast completion and odd design unsettled the town. Although no one said anything to the Windels, among themselves, the townsfolk whispered disapproval of the strange addition and the noticeable uncommon friendship between those gypsies and the Windels. It was whispered that only magic could have created such a sudden achievement.

Shortly after the Windel Mansion's transformation, the town called for a meeting. All, except the gypsies, were notified to appear at the town hall for an important community discussion. A special notice was sent to Mr. and Mrs. Windel demanding attendance at the scheduled meeting, but there was no mention of the topic to be discussed.

The town hall was a stately wooden building lining one of the streets in the town square. A broad flight of wooden steps stacked higher and higher until ending at several large wooden doors leading into the town hall. On its outside walls, several small circle windows decorated the upper most part.

The doors were opened wide as the people poured in. The assembly gathered in an inner room large enough to hold a hundred people. All the prominent leaders, including Mr. and Mrs. Windel were present. The meeting's narrator began the meeting.

"This meeting has been called to order to vote on whether the Gypsy folk should be asked to move on. Many of us here believe that misfortune follows those who are not Godly. Gypsies are known to practice dark arts. This plague is our suffering for allowing ourselves to befriend patrons of darkness.

A forceful male voice from the crowd broke in, "It was the gypsies who brought the sickness. They can't be trusted."

Another man's voice shouted, "If the gypsies don't leave on their own accord, let's burn them out."

Mr. Windel stood up and tapped the table in front of him loudly. "Now friends. You are all good decent rational people. Let us not be rash and full of superstition. They are only simple folk who have a few different customs from us."

The more he tried to reason with hostile crowd, the louder the cries of protest became.

Mr. Windel's waning influence could not persuade them otherwise. Finally, he conceded to the mob. He shouted loudly above the roar of the scared townsfolk,

"Ya, Ya, I shall support your decision. On behalf of the town, I volunteer to be the one to travel to the camp and demand that they leave immediately. It's the least that I can do for you good townsfolk since I was the one who let them stay on my land. My only thought is for the town's safety and happiness."

A rumbling went through the crowd and many shook their heads in agreement. After all most of the town were afraid of the gypsies and did not want to confront any of them. No one wanted to become the victim of a curse. Let Mr. Windel suffer the consequences. After all he had let them stay on his land.

The narrator rapped his mallet heavily on the table several times. "It has been decided then. Mr. Windel shall notify the vagrants that they are to leave immediately or face punishment."

That very night, promptly after the meeting, Mr. Windel saddled his horse. He rode out to the Gypsy camp to warn them of the town's growing animosity. He hoped the troupe would understand this tragic situation and forgive his failure to be their champion.

Upon seeing Mr. Windels horse approaching, music began playing, women began dancing, and outside tables were bristly covered with food and wine. The Gypsies always greeted their friends with a joyous reception. But after Mr. Windel relayed the dreadful recent event, the Gypsy King clapped his hands in a strange rhythmic pattern. The travelers swiftly packed their possessions into their *vardos.* All the creatures were gathered and harnessed to form a long caravan. The flamboyant procession was pulling out, leaving, within what seemed only moments from Mr. Windel's arrival. Silently, almost magically, the gypsies disappeared into the dark night.

With the gypsies gone, things still did not settle down as Mr. Windel has hoped. Days went by. The Windel boy's health steadily became worse. Although Mr. Windel kept his routine schedule, the rest of his family became withdrawn. The girls were seldom seen. No longer did they help out at the family businesses.

At the town store, a few women gathered outside gossiping.

"I heard the sisters are practicing gypsy witchcraft, desperate to save their beloved brother," a younger lady in a modest dress informed the others.

Another older woman offered her rendition of the unfolding events. "That's not what I heard. Mabel said she had personal knowledge that the Windels have sent for a necromancer. As told by the Gypsies in one of their stories, a necromancer is an unnatural creature deceptively appearing to be a handsome man. There is a very special Necromancer living in Europe who has found a way to be immortal. The Gypsies say he can turn others immortal through his blood. According to Mabel, a man is supposed to be arriving this Fall. Mark my words, it's that Necromancer."

A lady in a flowery dress agreed. "Yes, that is more than likely their course. After all, they are rich and will do anything to save that boy."

However, months after the gossip began, the Windel lad did not become immortal, but instead died. The Windel maidens did not attend his funeral and the coffin remained closed. Most of the townspeople came, not to really pay respects, but out of curiosity. It was hard to imagine the lively lad dead behind that wooden barrier. It was even harder to imagine that any hardship had befallen the Windels.

As soon as funeral was over, people started more rumors. A man at the local pub told the man next to him, "Bet the coffin was closed because there wasn't no body in it. Heard them girls were practicing magic, casting obscene spell after obscene spell over his corpse." He took another swig of his beer.

The other man, with a large hat on, nodded and then added his mischief to the story. "Yep, heard that and more. Have you noticed those girls have stopped coming out of the house during the daytime? That's because dark magic infuses into a witch's body making daylight unbearable. A few people have told me that if you keep a watch out late into the night, you may catch a glimpse of one of them. Maidens of darkness are what they are now. Wait till the full moon. I'd keep my family clear of them, if I were you. Luckily, all I have is me to worry about." He cackled thrilled with himself for being able to send shivers down the back of his drinking companion.

The barkeeper standing close to the pair added, "Nope, heard that they sent for an evil creature that drinks blood, but in return it can make someone immortal. Could explain why Mr. Windel has became so pale and he acts so strangely lately. Maybe, he will be the first to mix company with that creature. It's enough to make me want to start attending church."

The large hatful man chuckled, "Yep, better get your crosses and bibles out."

******

On the first full moon after the Windel boy's death, strange things indeed began to happen. Some animals were found dead, all the blood drained from their bodies. Most thought it was the girls' doings.

"I saw them girls dancing in the woods around a bluish fire chanting foreign words," a young boy told the preacher. "Bet they was the ones who stole the animals' blood. I heard from the next town over, them kind of creatures are vampires... spawns of Satan."

The preacher looked down at the excited young boy, "Now, Son, I'm not denying what you are saying, but these are very serious accusations. It could mean people wanting to kill the Windels. Please be careful and take time to think about things before you share these words with others. I will speak to the Windels and make sure they are not committing such sins. If they are, I give my promise that I will be swift to stop such evil."

The preacher doubted the truth of the boy's stories, but if he called the boy a liar, it might spurn the boy to tell these tales all over town. He didn't want to get in the middle of such things. Hearing all the rumors sweeping through town, he knew that a witch hunt could easily ensue.

Later that evening, the preacher knocked on the Windels door. He had to make a good show of it for the sake of the town. Maybe it would put people at ease if he was seen visiting them. The Windel servant ushered the preacher into the home and down to a guest sitting area. Promptly, Mr. Windel appeared. The two sat for a short time and discussed the rumors. Of course, Mr. Windel denied all of the accusations.

In spite of his visit to the Windels, the preacher's attempts to quash all of the gossiping were in vain. The community had become frightened and one thing led to another.

One dark night when madness was at its height, the townsfolk stormed the Windel mansion. Inside were exotic dried roots, leaves and flowers. Someone screamed, "Look, dried animal parts harvested for evil rituals." The mob cried, "Demons, witches! Death to the witches."

Struggling against their capturers, the entire family was dragged out of their home into the center of town. Mr. Windel tried to fight valiantly but was beaten unconscious.

His limp body was tethered to a large upright stake. One by one, each Windel was strapped to an adjacent stake. The townspeople threw firewood around each hostage's stake until on all sides were mounded by the wood.

Mrs. Windel pled tearfully for the lives of her children. "Please do not harm my children. They are good girls. Take out your wrath and anger on me and my husband, but spare the girls. They are just children."

The girls cried out, "We are innocent! Please someone save us! Do not commit this evil!"

The screaming and roars from the raging crowd could be heard for miles. But, there were no other towns for miles and no other townspeople to rescue them. The pleas for mercy beseeched blackened, callas hearts. The mob leader lit and threw a torch on the wood surrounding Mr. Windel. The flame licked the dry thicket slowly. Thick smoke wafted up around Mr. Windel bound, unaware body. In moments, the fire would reach his trousers.

The oldest girl shrieked, "I did it! I did it! I, alone, stand guilty of the crimes! Kill only me! I'm the only guilty one!" She thought they might spare her family if she confessed.

But the madness and crowd only grew wilder. Shouts erupted, "Death to them all! Death to the Gypsy-loving witches! They've sold their souls to the Devil!"

The oldest girl again cried out, "You will all be cursed if you continue with this madness. I will curse you all with financial ruin. And... All from this day forward who dare place feet on Windel soil will fall dead, drained of blood. Beware! My death will be avenged!"

But her rant did not deter the crowd's indomitable course. Madness had indeed befallen all. Evil reigned.

The mob leader grabbed another torch to toss onto the next Windel victim. Before the leader's torch could go flying through the air, a woman in the crowd screamed, "The youngest girl has vanished!" Silence fell.

The stunned, anxious mob froze. "Where had she gone?" the question lingered in their minds. The pole... where the young girl had been bound... stood... empty. Confused, the mob standing like statutes visually scanned the vicinity.

The mob's angry eyes all halted and became focused on a dense bluish-grey fog rapidly seeping up from the backside of the huge stakes holding the other Windels hostage. None of the town's people had ever seen anything like it. It grew thicker and thicker as it surged up covering the tied Windels and progressing threateningly towards the crowd.

A smell like a sickly sweet perfume, a mixture of petunias, daffodils and jasmine permuted the air. The strange, impenetrable fog swelled up until all visibility was limited. The blazing flames, consuming the murdered Mr. Windel, turned into an eerie glow behind the fog's opaque blanket.

Burning flesh mixed with the overwhelming odor. The strong pungent stench filled the balmy night air making people cough and gasp for fresh air. Strange ominous howls erupted from the nearby forest. The howls intensified sending shivers through everyone. Panic ensued and the once fearless multitude crumbled. Each ran towards the safety of their own homes, terrified by the unnatural sounds and the relentless engulfing haze.

******

With the rising of the sun the next morning, the citizens regained some courage. A crowd reconvened where the previous night's episodes had taken place. They searched the area for answers as to what had happened. None could figure out the mysterious events.

Each of the wooden stakes stood empty. There was a pile of ashes where Mr. Windel had been held captive, but it was only a pile of wood ashes. No bodily remains were found anywhere. The Windels had disappeared.

Fear struck the hearts of the townspeople. They erected a solid fence around the Windel mansion because they were afraid to burn it down or set a foot on the property.

A few days after the incidence, the majority of the town's livestock came up missing. Pets, such as dogs and cats disappeared as well. Then, several people in the town became very ill and died. The symptoms were always the same.

First, the sick person would act very bizarre. Next, he or she would turn very pale. Within days, the person would be dead. The superstitious townspeople decided it would be best to burn these dead, just in case. Fear from these strange occurrences drove all the residents to move out of the town to other towns and cities in less than a year.

Dotia's voice flooded into Grant's mind as the story was coming to an end, "But, the town didn't stay vacant for too long. Eventually, brave, new settlers arrived and moved into the vacant houses.

Shops were reopened for business and the town lived once more. The new residents knew about the terrible bloody ordeal because other towns keep the story alive. Plus, some of the story was logged in the town's history books in the town hall. Out of superstition, fear, or maybe just to remember how fragile life could be, the fenced-in Windel Mansion was left untouched and unoccupied."

******

Grant stared up at the bold home as her voice continued. His breath formed smoke in the cold night air. Mist circled along the ground and around his feet

******

"Of course, throughout the years many fables and stories were told about the Windel mansion. Some even true. Bats dwell in the mansion's eves and have been spotted flying around the place at night.

And once in a while, on the darkest of nights, an odd

glow would radiate from behind the opaque stain-glass windows. The best by far is the tale that a curse awaits anyone who dares to enter on the mansion's grounds."

******

The story came to a halt in Grant's mind. Grant gathered his stolen Blood roses from the ground and clutched them firmly in his hand. With his bouquet secured, he walked back around to the front of the mansion.

As he neared the front pathway, he paused and knelt down, resting his free hand on the ground. This was the spot where his father had been found, lying face up, unmoving, with his eyes wide open.

"Guess I'll never really know the truth, huh Dad. Guess it really doesn't matter anymore. Just like the Windel brother.... gone is gone." He laid one of his red roses down on the unmarked site. Then, he rose back up from his kneeling stance, wiping a tear from his cheek.

Grant made his way back to the car, and back to his present task of being a policeman. Placing the blossoms on the seat next to him, he settled in behind the steering wheel. He closed the car door, and cranked the engine.

Staring back at the house, Grant wondered about the past and the future. In the fading moonlight, the old mansion's stained-glass windows shimmered, like lights flickering out the windows. Grant whispered, "It's sad that no one will shine another light out these windows ever again." He turned his attention back to the road in front of him and drove off.

Chapter 6

Ms. Hazell

A light-blue pickup truck drove down the street, which was bordered on each side by quiet neighborhood homes. It slowed and came to a stop at the end of the road in front of a cottage. The quaint cottage seemed a little out of place in the conservative neighborhood. Hundreds of different kinds of flowering plants and herbs filled its entry courtyard. A medley of colors and textures like this would ordinarily only be seen in a classical painting of an imaginary land, not a real place. Adding to the transcendental aura, butterflies and birds fluttered around snatching nectar from the variety of blooms.

The truck door opened. Grant slid out. Hidden behind his back, he carried the earlier confiscated roses, wrapped at their base by wet newspaper and a layer of plastic. Following the winding patio stones, he reached the cottage door. His bare knuckles thudded several times on its wood.

The door opened slowly. The gap revealed a small older woman dressed vibrantly in a multitude of colors. Her gold dangly earrings touched the edges of her puffy blouse, which draped around her shoulders. The blouse was the perfect match for her long flowing skirt. Large twinkling dark blue eyes complemented her wavy silver hair stylishly pinned back by big colorful barrettes. Recognizing her visitor was Grant; her soft wrinkled face glowed with delight. Her tiny thin lips curved up into enormous warm smile.

"I knew you were coming. I made you a small dinner. It is in the kitchen ..... What did you bring me, I couldn't make it out," she said. "I saw something in my thoughts..."

Grant presented his hidden gift in an effortless flowing motion, "These... for you, the ever-so-beautiful Ms. Hazell. At least you don't always know everything."

She clutched them in her delicate hands. Looking adoringly at the roses, she whispered, "Blood roses. Rare." Then her voice became a little louder and slightly scolding, "These came from the mansion?" She knew the answer.

"Yes. I figured they were going to waste away there with no one to look at them. I know they're your favorite. I would have taken Mom a bunch too, but I wouldn't have heard the end of it if she knew I was in that yard. Every time she catches wind that I was there, she goes on and on. You'd think the place was haunted." Grant mischievously smiled.

Dotia smiled back, "I won't say a word. I'm just very glad that her cough is better. I was barely able to talk her into taking the remedy I made for her."

She motioned for him to follow her into the home. Sweet aromas emanated from inside. The front entrance opened into a quaint living room. Candles accented the walls and furnishings. Pet beds scattered about on the wooden floor were occupied by oversize sleeping cats. A winged chair harbored a smaller orangey cat that stared intently at the new arrival.

Perched on a lofty shelf with no reasonable means of access, a monstrous black cat with orange eyes, stared down upon the room as though keeping watch. A speckled cat lay sprawled out on a sofa at the far end of the room. Each one seemed to be in its own coveted spot.

All were undisturbed by the entering visitor.

As Grant took another step, a sleek white feline bounded in front of him. She pressed affectionately against his leg, purring loudly. Grant scooped the cat up and looked into her mesmerizing blue eyes.

"Hello, Princess. Have you been talking good care of Nana?" Grant inquired.

Princess meowed as though she understood his question. Grant stroked her soft fur for a few seconds and then gently placed her back down on the carpet. She scampered off as though she had other things to attend to now that she had formally welcomed her guest.

"I swear that cat can talk," Grant said.

"I keep telling you that. Is it too hard to grasp that animals could learn our language? Here... everyone goes on about how bright you are...," Dotia teased.

Grant smiled, "Well, it was probably all that strange food that you fed me growing up that made me a little slow. Not everyone has an auntie like you!"

Dotia pulled his arm, "Speaking of which, I have a concoction made for you in the kitchen."

Dotia and Grant strolled into the kitchen. Dotia grabbed a large flower vase from the neatly arranged cupboard. Rows of glass jars containing dried plant parts lined much of the shelves.

"Sit and eat before it gets cold," Dotia commanded.

A plate of food awaited him at the table. Grant pulled out the chair and sat down. After a quick prayer, he wasted no time in shoveling the mouthwatering meal into his mouth.

Dotia arranged the roses in the vase. She placed her beautiful bouquet in the table's center and sat down in a chair across from him.

Staring at the flowers, Dotia remarked, "They are just as beautiful as the last batch. I should go over and dig up some of the roots sometime. I keep thinking about it, but haven't managed to do it all these years. It is such a sad place."

"Well, you better hurry. They are going to be tearing it down in a week or two," Grant reminded her. "I would do it for you but I never acquired your touch with plants.... I would probably kill it.... Let me know when you want to go and I'll take you. Maybe I can do the digging without killing it if you are there to tell me how."

"Okay, we will have to go Thursday. The full moon is tonight. By Thursday it will be at a good descent phase. Roots should be ready then. Will Thursday work for you?" Dotia asked.

"Sure," Grant stated just before taking another bite.

Dotia's eyes began misty. "I wish the old place could have come alive with the joy it once held. Guess the time has come for it to sleep forever."

Grant reached over and comfortingly patted Dotia's forearm. His eyes met hers, "Everything eventually changes with time, good or bad." His hand slide down and gently squeezed her hand.

Her voice changed into a firmer tone. "And speaking of time isn't it time you find a nice girl to settle down with. Has anyone caught your eye lately? I could make a love potion for you. I have a recipe," She offered.

Grant grinned, "I'm sure you do. But the town couldn't take your voodoo. Everyone in the area would be hooking up. I'd be putting tons of people in jail for being over friendly..." He laughed envisioning all the people running around, the effects of a love potion in full swing.

"Anyways, I don't know why you and Mom are always thinking about getting me settled. I've got you two to keep me straight and to make sure I eat right. Neither of you have any other man in your lives. So, what would you do without me to fuss over?" He joked.

"Well, I wouldn't be losing you, but gaining another someone to fuss over," Dotia responded.

Dotia sprang up from her chair. "I almost forgot," she berated herself as she moved towards her seated prey. "Speaking of taking care of things, is your amulet on? It better be."

She tugged at his shirt collar. Around his neck hung a leather braid with a curious walnut-sized trinket attached. "Let me see it so I can refresh it. Remember, it's only good for about three months. It won't work so well after that. I don't know what you'll do once I'm gone. You'll forget to refill it," She sighed at the thought of having to leave him one day. He was the child she never bore.

He lifted it from his neck and laid it in her open hands. With the treasure in her hands, she walked over to a small wastebasket. Above the basket, she twisted the small, attached amulet in a strange manner. As it popped open, grayish-brownish dust puffed up from its hollow chamber. She flipped its contents into the wastebasket and then laid the emptied necklace on the table.

She slid a wooden stool over to the cabinet. Stepping up on the stool, she grabbed a few jars from the cupboard and set her collection on the table. Dotia grabbed a small wooden bowl and a wooded spoon. Measuring each ingredient as it went into the bowl, she hummed a tune. Listening to the tune, Grant finished his meal not really paying any attention to what the little old woman was doing.

After her additions were complete, she ground the concoction into a coarse powdery substance. Carefully, she scooped the fresh mixture into the trinket making it full once more. With another twist, Dotia snapped it closed again, then wiped the outside off with a cloth.

"Here you are. Freshly done," she pleasingly crowed, handing the necklace back to him.

Grant jested, "Only because it makes you happy. You know I don't really believe in all that hocus nonsense. On the other hand, some of your home remedies work better than modern medicine and don't cost me a thing." Grinning, he replaced the charm around his neck.

She swatted him gently on the arm to show her disapproval of his comment. She hoped it was not what he truly believed. "If you only knew about unseen dangers like I do," she admonished. "I'm glad you placate a senile old woman for it might be the only thing that protects you one day." Her lips pursed tight reflecting her concern.

He knew not tease any further. She took this stuff seriously, and down deep he knew she had a gift of some kind. He couldn't deny all the times she had seen things before they happened. When he was younger, it sometimes scared him; but it sometimes had kept him from getting in trouble.

He was never sure if she would know what he was doing, which often made him think twice before he acted. As he grew older, he understood that her gift was limited. But by then he pretty good at making choices based on what was right in his heart, and what Dotia would say was right.

Looking at her now in the pale kitchen light, he realized for the first time, just how tiny and fragile she was. Her once silken black hair was now silver, speckled with black, and although her spirit was still vibrant, age had tired her body. He couldn't think of her not being here.....

Somehow sensing his thoughts she compassionately

smiled, "You must always remember that this is not our ending, just another step on our journey, and my journey will someday meet back up with yours. You know that I love you as much as your own mother, and that love will forever be with you. Now enough of this melancholy, you've best get on your way. Aren't you going fishing tomorrow?"

It was easy to figure out where she was going with this. "Don't worry I couldn't possibly forget. I'll remember to bring the cats some fish."

He turned and headed towards the front door. She followed.

Reaching the door, Grant turned towards her, leaned over, and kissed the top of her head. "I'll stop back by tomorrow with lots of fish. Don't forget to lock your doors."

She stroked his arm affectionately. "Don't worry about me. I've got all my cats to protect me." She smiled as though she held a secret.

She watched him stroll back to his truck. It reminded her of when he was a little boy. They had walked that path so many times together, his little hand clinging to hers. Time had passed so quickly. Dotia knew she only had a few more years left.

Her thoughts invaded and the words flowed under her breath, "If only before my passing he finds someone to share his life with.... maybe there is time for another little child to hold my hand as we walk the path together. But Grant is always so busy. None of the girls so far have been the right one. Must interfere."

There was always a way to speed things up. Sometimes these ways had consequences though. But, she would be gone soon and then it would be too late. Dotia knew the only way would be the old way, the ancestral prayers and rituals.

"Yes, that is what I will do...I'll find a spell and deal with the consequences later," she whispered to herself as she watched Grant drive away.

She closed the door, walked over to a bookshelf, and removed a tattered old book from it. Cradling the book she glided over to the couch. A huge brown brindled cat lay curled up on it with his green eyes slightly opened. She settled down beside him and patted him on the head.

"I'm glad to see that you have graced us with your presence, Jacque," Dotia cooed. The large cat purred and stretched out his massive claws. Dotia opened the book and began reading.

Time sped by. Dotia glanced at the clock. It was just before midnight. She closed the book and returned it to the bookshelf. Dotia went back into the kitchen. Determined to set her plan into action, she aligned the stepping stool below a set of cabinets. The top doors had a small inset lock in each of them. Reaching up, she inserted a small key from her pocket into the lock, and turned it.

The door clicked open displaying several small jars. Some of the jars were multicolored. A dark red one and a sky blue sat close to the front. There seemed to be one of about every color. She grabbed two of the multicolored ones and the dark red one. Returning to the table, she measured some of the contents of each jar into the wooden bowl. Then, she walked over to the vase of Blood red roses on the table and tore two petals from each blossom.

In a singsong cadence, Dotia chanted, her words not making any sense. Several of the cats wandered into the kitchen. They watched as she dropped the rose petals one by one into the bowl, crushing them into the mixture. Still chanting, Dotia carried the privileged bowl out the kitchen door into her back courtyard, the luminous moon lighting the pathway. A parade of cats followed her, at times almost surrounding her.

The mosaic of colors and textures created by the sundry of trees, shrubs, small bushes, herbs and flowers was even more spectacular then the display in the front courtyard. In the garden's center, a small feminine statute resembling a wingless fairy stood in the middle of an open patch. The statute's delicate hands held a stone platter raised towards the heavens.

Dotia sauntered up to the statute. The full moon shone brightly as she emptied the bowl's contents onto the platter. She struck a match and tossed it onto the mounded mixture. The concoction burst into flames emitting swirls of strange reddish grey smoke. The smoke became thicker and thicker as it rose up into the gentle night breeze. A sweet peculiar odor filled the air. The cats meowed and purred with approval.

Smiling very contented, Dotia retreated back into her cottage. As she entered into the living room Princess pranced up to her. Dotia swept the feline up into her arms. Stroking the soft white fur, Dotia glided over to a plush velvet chair and softly reclined. Princess meowed knowingly and closed her blue eyes. Dotia leaned back and closed her eyes as well.

She felt so sleepy. Maybe that smoke wasn't the best thing to have been around. Her mind began to swirl. Images darted in her mind. She saw a girl running... a girl with long brown hair running. The girl was in great danger and she was very afraid. Dotia had to help.... Who was she? What was she running from? What was the danger?

The house....there was the house and the rose bush.... Something white.... bluish.....the images were all jumbled and Dotia was so tired. Grant....blood....Her mind flooded with images.

Everything went black.

Chapter 7

Three Things

Long dark brunette hair covered the sleeping girl like an exotic fur mantle, as she lay curled up into a ball on her bed. The soft lilac frilly bedspread made her hair appear darker and wilder than it really was. The adjacent walls were covered with pictures of cats; kittens playing with balls of yarn or other toys, cats dressed in cute outfits mimicking people, and cats involved in everyday activities, walking, sitting, sleeping, or cuddling with other cats. Every variety of feline was featured somewhere. It was the girl's way of trying to fill a gap. She had always wanted a cat, but her mother had been allergic to animals.

Two feet away was another bed, empty. It was covered somewhat untidily with a lacey white bedspread and two small matching pillows. Bordering walls were plastered with pictures of male movie stars, heartthrobs of the moment.

The dorm room was small. It barely contained enough space for all the furniture that inhabited it; two beds, a little night table, an undersized black frig, microwave, a sink, and a small, fat, roundish pink chair.

The slumbering girl had tossed and turned all night. Finally, sometime in the early morning she had managed to fall asleep. The phone rang, wakening her. She rolled over and grabbed it.

"Hello," she answered sleepily.

She hesitated and then continued, "No! I was not out too late last night! I just didn't sleep too well. I kept having odd dreams, but I can't remember them now."

She sat passively for a few seconds listening to what the caller was saying. Subconsciously, she twirled a lock of brown hair around her finger, "Mary, it'll be fine. Ria and I aren't moving off campus till after spring session is over." Her voice paused for a moment. As Mary talked on the other end, Emily rolled her sparkling green eyes and smiled.

"No, it will only be the two of us, no guys. I can't believe you would kid about that. I need peace and quiet so I can study, not love fests." She laughed thinking about the hippy images those words conjured in her mind.

She listened intently for a few seconds as the caller spoke. This voice on the other line was very soothing.

"That would be great Mary! I'd love it if you could come down next Christmas. .... Yes, I have to work to help pay for things, but they should let me have a few days off then. After all, the school is closed for the holidays." She paused once again listening. "I really miss you too."

Mary, an extrovert with many acquaintances had been Emily's only friend in the area she grew up. Although Mary was ten years older than Emily, she and Emily got along pretty well. She always was giving advice whether it was wanted or not. Emily didn't mind though. It was nice to have someone who at least cared enough to try to interject.

"Okay, love ya too. Talk to you next week. Bye," she ended the call.

The silent phone lingered in her hand, cradled just below her ear as though the conversation hadn't really ended. After a few minutes, she returned it to its base.

She reached over to the night table and picked up the

small picture of her parents. Stroking their faces with her finger, she whispered out loud, "I wish you both would have lived to see me graduate next year. Maybe, you might have been proud of me or finally held some kind of affection towards me. I wish I knew why...."

One year back her parents had been in a car accident. Her mother died instantly. After a few days in the hospital, her father passed away too. She suffered deeply from the loss even though her parents had never really been close to her. They had never wanted children, but unfortunately, for them and Emily, it happened. A child was born.

They had not been actually cruel towards her, just neglectful. Neither parent had been involved in Emily's school functions or even looked at her grades. They never held a birthday party to celebrate her birth. Like a visiting neighbor's child, with only bare minimum contact with her parents, her childhood years passed by.

She had always thought the day would come when they would look at her with sincere affection and love. But, it never had.

"You know I didn't just lose the both of you, but I lost any chance of ever having a loving relationship with either of you. That is the greater pain ... almost unbearable at times." She tried to hold back the tears brimming in her eyes.

Remembering the revelation that had hit her back then she reflected on it again. "Guess, I'll never truly 'get over' it; I'll just have to try to learn how to live with the loss, and adjust to the emptiness in my heart. I still believe that there is something after this, Heaven, Hell, or maybe rebirth."

It is often said that death has a way of changing lives in many ways, but Emily's life pretty much stayed the same. She was still working her way through school with a campus job and trying to borrow as little money as possible on student loans.

Her parents had never paid off anything they owned. They hadn't bought life insurance either. Emily had just barely enough from their estate left to pay probate fees and provide a modest funeral. Not many people had appeared to pay respects anyways.

Tears swelled in her shimmering eyes as she stared longingly at the picture. As a single teardrop escaped down her cheek, a key wriggled in the door lock to the room. The door flew opened. Emily quickly returned the picture to its spot, and brushed away the tear.

A slender girl with pixy-cut reddish hair and big brown eyes burst into the room excitedly fanning some papers in her hand. Her matching shirt and shorts exercise outfit reminded Emily of a Tennis player. The girl slung the door shut behind her causing a loud thud.

In a light, bubbly voice she said, "Emily, look! I got the papers for our new apartment. It will be ready in about ten weeks, round the end of May. I can't wait!"

Amused with the intruding girl's contagious enthusiasm, Emily giggled "I hope it has real strong doors with heavy duty hinges cause you're worst than a little kid, Ria."

"Am not!" Ria said pouting slightly.

She plopped down in the small pink chair next to her bed.

"Aren't you ready yet, sleepy head?" Ria asked half-impatiently.

"Almost, I only need to throw some clothes on, put my tennis shoes on, and braid my hair real quick," Emily answered.

From her small dresser, Emily grabbed her bra, a pair

of thin sweat pants, and what looked like a cross between a tee-shirt and exercise shirt. To be polite as she was changing clothes, she turned her back towards Ria. Ria had plopped down on the bed with the white bedspread and was now absorbed in reading through her lease papers again.

After she was clothed, Emily moved over to the other side of her bed and faced Ria. She gathered her long silky brunette hair and began spinning it into a braid. Ria looked up from her papers stared with amazement.

"I don't see how you can do that. You must have a spider gene or something," Ria said.

"Oh, it becomes easy with practice. You should grow your hair long and try it," Emily suggested.

"No way. I don't have that kind of patience. You know that. You're the designated patient one," Ria remarked stroking her own short reddish hair backward.

Emily patted the velcro strip down on her tennis shoes, grinning. "Okay, I'm ready, Ms. Impatience, Ms. Impractical, Ms. Impulsive, Ms. Imagination..."

Ria teasingly interrupted, "Okay that's enough, Ms. Prude, Ms. Almost Perfect, but not ever ready on time ....."

The pair strode out the door. "Wait a sec." Emily pushed her key into the dead-bolt, clicking it to lock. "Can't be too careful."

Ria knew not to tease about this precaution. With sincerity in her voice, Ria said, "I'm glad you remember. I keep forgetting. The other day when I came back, the door had been left unlocked. I was a little bit nervous walking in."

Emily joggled the knob to make sure the lock had caught. "Yep you should get more than a little nervous. You should be terrified! I don't want either of us to end up like that girl who was attacked a month back."

The girls started down the hall.

Ria didn't like it when Emily scolded her. "Well, that *was* very unusual and I don't think we have to worry about some crazy guy who thinks the devil told him gather fresh virgin blood. Also, he got in through the window cause the girl had left it cracked. Plus, they caught the nut and the girl ended up okay."

"Still Ria, I don't think we should take any chances. That girl was cut-up pretty bad from what I heard."

They proceeded down the barely lit stairway to the first floor hall. The building was silent as they made their way.

"I can't believe the term is almost over. It's too quiet with everyone gone for spring break. It's creepy," Ria said. Her voice echoed down the passageway.

Reaching the outer doors, the girls stepped out into the bright sunshine. The day was beautiful. Taking a second to get accustomed to the bright light, the pair scanned the campus's manicured lawns. The young university's modern architecture dominated the picturesque landscape.

"Yep, first year more than half-way done!" Emily chirped. "I still can't believe I got a full ride. I didn't think I would ever be able to go to college."

"Well, you did have top scores at your high school," Ria reminded her. "You were a shoe-in for somewhere. Good thing it was here with me. Of course, I wouldn't be here unless someone hadn't felt sorry for poor people. Good thing they have partial scholarships for underprivileged kids. I'll be the first in my family to get a degree. Probably the only one too, besides my children one day... if I decide to have some."

The girls skipped down the dorm steps and continued

along the concrete sidewalk in the direction of the field track.

"Do you want children?" Ria asked.

"Not sure yet, maybe. But there are more important things to think of now," Emily stated. "Like school work and exams. Do you have your class work caught up? It'll be final's week before we know it."

"Yes, and I'm scheduled to join the next crew on their mission to Mars," Ria replied raising her eyebrows up and down. "My astronaut suit should be here any day."

"Ohhh Ria, how are we going to graduate together if you are not more serious?" Emily's tone reflected her concern.

"Well, I guess I'll have to take classes this summer," Ria complained. "What are you going to take? I bet you have yours all planned out," she teased.

Emily's demeanor changed into a more philosophical stance. "Actually, I've only got one that I'm really sure of. It is an experimental social class .... seems very interesting. The basis is to find a person over sixty-five and spend a minimum of twenty hours a week with him or her. You've got to keep a weekly journal and at the end, turn in a fifteen-page single-spaced report. The object is to expose how valuable older people can be as a unique resource." Emily seemed fascinated by the prospect.

The chatting pair passed another new building freshly landscaped. This was the half-way point to the track and they hadn't crossed a single person. The vacated campus stood deserted like a forgotten church waiting for the Sabbath to arrive.

"What do you mean a unique resource?" Ria inquired, puzzled by the description.

Emily explained, "You know, like, an old person *must*

have acquired something special over a period of sixty-five years. Society usually doesn't recognized or know about special skills or hidden talents that seniors have developed. The professor wants to bring awareness to the untapped potential of this particular age group. He says they could be and should be the next hottest sought after group."

Interrupting, Ria laughingly said, "Oh ya, I can see a hot, steamy sixty-five year old posing on the cover of Vogue."

Emily frowned, "That's so not what I meant, and sex appeal is not the only thing someone should be praised for. Just wait you'll be old soon, too."

Ria quipped, "Okay, so how do you find your old geezer? Do you go to the old folks' home and try to latch on to a sane one?"

"Ria, I don't think that is funny. This is *exactly* what I was talking about - misconceptions!" Emily continued sharply, "I know several older people, who are not only physically fit, but brilliant. Older people should be celebrated!"

Again Ria cut in, "My grandma couldn't figure her way out of a wet paper bag, and my grandpa... well he was just mean. He was meaner than a rabid dog. It's no wonder someone didn't shoot him long before he got old. Would have done the world and me both a favor." The bitterness in Ria's heart bled into her voice.

Emily's heart ached for her. "I'm sooo sorry, Ria. I couldn't imagine what you must have been through. It's hard to believe that any mother would just take off, leaving a baby like that, not telling anyone who your father was."

Continuing, Emily's voice was filled with kindness and sincerity as she put her arm around her friend, "Every child deserves to be loved. You deserved more, much more."

"Please don't pity me, Emily. I want you to be my friend because you like me, not because you feel sorry for me." Ria's voice had a hint of anxiety in it. What if people couldn't like her?

Emily softly coed, "Oh Ria, you are my bestest friend! I adore you. You are like a ray of sunshine everywhere you go. I wish I could be more like you. Confident and carefree."

Ria was relieved and elated that her friend thought so much of her. But, she was also slightly embarrassed by the deep show of emotions. She was unsure as to how to react. Her grandparents had never been kind or loving towards her. Instinctively, she turned to humor to ease her pain.

"If you were more like me, you'd have to retake your classes, and would have never ever made it out of calculus," Ria giggled.

"That's true!" Emily said laughing.

Reaching the deserted track, the girls began their stretching routine. Last year, the girls had decided to try to go jogging at least once a week. Unfortunately, they had only managed to reach the track about every three weeks. Classes mandated a lot of sitting around studying. They both had gotten a little out of shape.

After jogging about a quarter of the way around the track Ria asked, "Do I look any more fit yet?" The girls continued jogging, but their pace slowed down a little

"Why? Are you trying to attract that guy in your science class?" teased Emily.

"No, but speaking of dates, are you going to go out with Stan?" Ria inquired.

"No," Emily firmly stated, her voice a little rushed,

"He's not my type."

"Do you have a type?" Ria continued, "I mean no one ever seems to live up to your standards. You've never been on a date yet."

"It's not my standards that are a problem. It's got to click. I have to know it's right, *before* I get involved," explained Emily.

"What if it is never clicks? You're not getting any younger. You'll be a lonely old maid," Ria over-dramatized.

Emily pitifully inquired, "But won't you come and see me? Or will you be too busy with all your many old, sexy, over-the-hill suitors?" Cackling cattily Emily took off running around the track.

Ria hollered out to her, "That's not funny, Ms. Prude."

Ria stopped for a second and retied her shoelaces. Then she took off in hot pursuit around the track.

After jogging a few laps around the track, the two girls collapsed on the ground under a large Magnolia tree. The whitish blossoms filled the air with a sweet, mystical fragrance. Rays of sunlight glittered through the opening of the branches.

The earth was alive, rejuvenated after a long winter's rest and rainy spring. The girls, on the other hand, were not. Tired out from their run, they laid propped up by the trees massive trunk.

Breathing heavily Ria said, "I'm not cut out for exercise."

"Me neither," Emily enjoined, also breathing heavily.

"Well, at least you girls look great exercising," a male voice said.

The girls looked up. A sandy-brown mossy-haired guy

was standing to their left. He wore a striped shirt that hung crookedly off his wide shoulders and non-matching track shorts. His smile was nice though; it made him look trustworthy.

"I guess I should introduce myself. I'm Brad. Brad Richards. I was in American Lit with you Ria," he said. He hoped that she remembered him. It had taken all of his courage to walk over to the girls. He had heard that she broke it off with her boyfriend a month ago, but he could never catch her alone. He figured catching her with only one other person around was about as good as it would get.

Ria remembered him all too well. If she hadn't had a boyfriend, she would have found a way to introduce herself. "Yeah, you were pretty quiet, sat in the back toward the windows," she said.

"Yeah, I was trying to avoid the professor calling on me. I never understood anything in that class," he confessed.

"That made two of us," Ria admitted.

They stared at each other not sure what to say next.

Emily interjected, "The two of you sound like a match made in heaven." It was obvious that they really liked each other, and this one might actually be good for Ria, unlike the bad boys she usually ended up with.

Emily volunteered some more, "Ria's favorite food is spaghetti, and there is a real nice place on Fifth Street that I'd recommend."

Brad took advantage of the information and shyly asked "Would you like to go there Friday, Ria? I mean, uhhh, could I take you out to dinner?"

"That would be great. I could meet you there around six," Ria answered.

"Okay, I'll see ya there then. It's a date." His cheeks blushed a little. His hand waved bye awkwardly as he darted off. He didn't want to give her a chance to change her mind.

The girls looked at each other and grinned. As soon as he was out of earshot Ria said, "Wow! I can't believe what a great day this has been. First the apartment and now a cute guy. He's a nice guy, too. Not like those losers I keep ending up with. I don't know why I'm attracted to bad boys; They always end up to being such jerks. Bad boys are nothing but trouble and heartache."

"Yep," Emily enjoined. "A good guy is what you deserve. Someone who knows how to love..."

"Ria Richards." A dreamy gaze appeared in Ria's eyes. "That might work."

Emily giggled at her friend's sudden marriage plans. "Maybe you should take it a little slower. But, I think it will be a good thing for you to date him." She paused for a moment as she pondered something she had once heard. "I wonder if good things happen in threes, like bad things. If so, you've got one more coming,"

"Too bad it's not like a wish, cause then I'd wish for a thousand more wishes," Ria wistfully sighed.

"Well, that would just get us both into trouble," Emily chimed, amused with her friend's intelligent observation.

Rested, Emily stood up and stretched. "What do you want to do now?"

Ria looked up at her lazily. "I'm not sure. How about go to the store and get some ice cream, creamy, cool, ice cream?"

"You are a bad influence..... I'm in," Emily said. She extended her hand toward Ria who was still relaxing on the ground. Ria grabbed hold and leaped up.

"Let's take the back way. It's a nicer walk. Hardly any cars ever use it," suggested Ria.

The two girls bounded off toward the small grocery store in Cedar Plaza several blocks away.

Chapter 8

The Walk

The walk was comfortingly peaceful in the warm afternoon sun. Since there wasn't a sidewalk, the girls had to walk on the edge of the payment. Luckily not too many cars came down this way. This stretch of road was mainly vacant land owned by the university. The plan was to preserve it until future school buildings were needed. Here and there, an old shed or utility building interrupted expanses of wildflower fields and thickly wooded clusters.

A yellow Pontiac sped by breaking the soothing lull of the breezy field. The car braked and then turned around, driving back to where the girls were walking. It slowed almost stopping, its window parallel to Ria.

A man's voice echoed out. "Hey, you wanta ride, pretty things?" The voice had a disturbing tone to it.

Neither girl looked over at the man. If they didn't make eye contact with him, maybe he'd leave. The girls stepped further over into the grass away from the car.

The car persisted. "I said... Do you want a ride?" The voice was louder, deeper this time and slightly edged with anger.

"No thanks, we live one street down," Ria lied trying to discourage him.

Ria whispered to Emily. "He gives me the creeps. If he tries anything I think we should run. You take off and I'll follow you."

The man grumbled, "What did you tell your friend there, honey? It's not polite to whisper."

The girls didn't reply, but both changed direction, veering away from the road into the vacant field hoping to discourage any more communication attempts by the man. The car sped off, squealing tires conveying the man's displeasure with the girls' actions.

"My God, he was scary!" Ria announced. She patted her gym shorts. "I can't believe I left my phone. That's the last time I leave without it. In fact, since they come so tiny now, I'm going to have one put on a necklace. Do you have yours?"

"I left mine too. I didn't think about it, cause we were only going to the track. I did bring some change for the snack machines though." Emily confessed.

Ria's heart beat faster anxious about the evil possibilities. "If he comes back I think we should run through that patch of woods. On the other side there are some houses. We could bang on doors till we find someone at home."

"Boy, you are skittish today aren't you? That's not like you. He was scary, though. But, he won't bother us anymore," said Emily trying to reassure herself as well.

A loud thud erupted from behind them. It was the car. It had jumped off the road and was headed through the field like a mad bull charging a red flag. Emily grabbed Ria's hand as they raced across the open field into the camouflage of the trees. They could hear the car spinning circles in the field behind them. Still running, they disappeared into the thick green haven. A briar ripped open the skin on Emily's leg left leg. We must keep going, she told herself trying to ignore the searing pain. She could hear Ria's breath quickening. Her own chest was heaving and her heart was racing. They were almost through the woods.

A row of houses lay on the far side of the woods, like a sanctuary to terrified girls. If they could only get there in time, all would be okay. Continuing their frantic pace, they ran up to the nearest house and pounded on the door. No one answered.

"I don't think it's any use. Look at the houses, no cars. Everyone's gone off to work or something," Ria's voice quivered as she tried to catch her breath. "The fences are too high to jump, so we can't hide in the back yard. We've got to hide, somewhere. We're in plain view if he drives around this side, or worst... walks through the woods after us."

The girls both shivered at the thought of that man finding them. Their eyes searched the area for a place that offered more protection than the woods they had just abandoned.

"Do you see that huge old house over there, Emily, sitting all by itself? The one with the windows boarded up? Maybe, we can hide behind it. He wouldn't be able to see us from the road. He probably wouldn't look there. We could wait there till someone comes home to one of these houses," Ria calculated.

"Okay, that might be the optimum plan. We best move quickly." Emily was surprised by Ria's quick thinking, but very grateful for it.

Watching cautiously for any signs of the villain, they escaped across the vast road expanse, scrambled over the waist high fence, bolted through the overgrown lawn, and dashed around to the back of the old house, praying to be safe.

Emily whispered, "Do you think he saw us?"

"I'm not sure," Ria admitted.

The girls were just beginning to catch their breath

when they heard a car squealing on the road. It was the same sound made by the Pontiac earlier. Emily saw Ria tremble. Emily edged up to a nearby window on the corner of the house. The covering of the thick plywood boards would make it next to impossible to get into the house. She took her fingers and pried hard at the edge of the boarded window anyways. Ria caught on to what Emily was thinking. So she inched over and tried the door. It was shut up tight. There were boards on the inside over the glass areas, so breaking in was not going to be an option. They were stuck. The only option seemed to be to move around the outside of house and stay out of his view if they heard him coming.

The tire squealing got louder and louder, and then stopped. The girls looked at each other in an effort to calm the overwhelming feelings of panic. Desperate, Emily tugged on the plywood covering the window again. She glanced around to find something, anything, to assist her in prying the wood off the window. Maybe someone dropped a screw driver or knife, or something. It was all she could hope for at the moment.

The high grass wouldn't reveal any hidden treasures easily. She got down on her hands and knees. Gently raking her hands through the grass, Emily felt around on the ground near the house wall. She didn't want to pat the grass down flat for two reasons. One, it would be a tell-tale sign that they had been here. Two, the padded down thick grass could cover any concealed items.

As her hands swept in front of the second boarded window, something drew Emily's gaze to an odd rectangle wooden panel directly under the window. The rest of the outside of the house was stone, but this was wood and it was made to look like stone. If someone was a bit farther away, they would never make out that it was wood. She felt something compelling her to the panel.

The panel looked stationary, but for some reason, it

reminded her of a large odd-looking pet door. "In," she thought she heard a voice whisper. She looked over at Ria. Ria was a few feet away. Emily firmly pushed on it. No budging.

The she ran her hands over the protruding design features on the wooden panel. They reminded her of the stories she read in the Wizard of Oz series when she was a child. Maybe one of them opened this panel. She pushed everyone. Nothing.

A sound like something had slapped a piece of wood echoed from around the front of the house. Had he climbed over the lawn's fencing? Was he at the front of the house? Grass crunched as if something heavy was moving around on the other side of the house. A wave of nausea swept over Emily.

She tried hard to refocus. This must opened, she thought. A row of roses set above the top of the wooden panel, in the stone section. Each of the stone roses emerged about two inches from the stone's background. They looked like they were stuck on, sort of like decorations on a cake. One to the left of the panel was slightly bigger that the others. She twisted it back and forth. On the twist to the left, it turned. The wooden panel's bottom part stiffly tilted inwards toward the house, exposing a small opening. Maybe it was large enough for her to slide her body through.

She motioned to Ria. Ria had give up on a finding a way in. She had been watching Emily trying to figure out what Emily's fascination with that area was. She slid over close to Emily. As Emily held the mysterious panel partially open, she whispered, "Look. I think it leads inside. I'll go first; you follow. Be quick, 'cause I think he's around the front side of the house."

Ria nodded.

"This is freaky. Something better not grab me." Emily

was almost tempted not to do it, but the alternative was facing the crazy Pontiac Guy. She took a deep breath and slid her feet in through the dark void.

Cool air from inside wrapped her legs. She looked one more time at Ria and then shoved the rest of herself into the hole. She had to twist and turn her body to progress further into the blackness. Emily couldn't see a thing.

Somehow, she knew she was to press her hands up. Her lifted palms met with something that felt like wood. Pushing a little harder, the wood lifted like a hinged lid. Up above her was the ceiling to a room inside the house. She felt Ria's feet pushing on her. Emily hastily sat up and scampered out of what appeared to be a long rectangular window seat located inside the dining room of the house.

Although the lower windows were boarded up, smaller stained glass windows, placed about 15 feet up from the floor, were unboarded. Sunlight streamed through these high windows making it bright enough to easily see across the room. Emily gasped. "What a beautiful place this must have been once," she said softly. She helped Ria straighten up and crawl out of the box. They both sat on the floor next to the window seat.

"What is this?" Ria said in a hushed tone, being very aware that *he*, their pursuer might be in hearing distance.

The girls glanced around in amazement. Although it appeared like no one had lived here in a very, very long time, the place was incredible. A magnificent pedestal dining table stood elegantly in the center of the room. Its dark wood was engraved with a mystical scene composed of roses, fancy carriages, castles, dragons, knights, and maidens. The chairs had matching engravings. The other furniture in the room also had similar cravings. Neither girl had ever seen such exquisite furnishings.

A car door shut loudly. The girls snapped out of their trance.

Emily whispered, "Did you shut the panel tightly behind you?"

Ria whispered back, "Yes. Let's find something heavy to put over this window seat though."

Looking around, they spotted a big chest a few feet away. The girls creped over and each took one side. It was heavier then it looked. Any other time curiosity would have gotten the better of them and they would not have been able to resist opening the trunk. But, now was not a time for such indulgences. Safety was more important. Covertly, the pair placed it on top of the window seat. Then, Ria grabbed a chair and placed it on top of the chest. She angled it so that any movement of the chest would cause the chair to fall to the floor.

"The chest should help keep him out if he figures out about the panel. But just in case, the noise of the chair hitting the floor will let us know someone is trying to get in. It would buy us time to figure out what to do next." Ria explained in a hushed tone. "We should pick up anything see that can be used as a weapon too."

Emily faintly suggested, "Maybe if we go upstairs we can see out one of the windows to see if he is still out there. The stairs are probably on the front side near the front door."

"Great idea." Ria nodded in agreement.

The girls made their way, almost tiptoeing, towards the front of the eerily silent mansion. Cobwebs hung from every corner and a thin layer of dust covered the beautiful furniture and floors.

The walls contained no pictures, but discolorations revealed outlines of where something, probably pictures once hung. Lacking also were any small decorative items like candles or vases. Without those finishing touches, the place appeared incomplete and sad.

Finding the stairs, they gently trotted up the carpeted steps. As they proceeded, the front entrance door thudded. Someone was trying to get in it. The girls shuddered. It had to be him. Fortunately, both the back door and front door were braced on the inside by large planks of wood running horizontally. Each end was fitted into medal brackets, which were secured into the concrete wall. It reminded Emily of the thick bars across castle doors in movies. Once everyone was inside, the bars went up keeping all the bad invaders out.

The thudding noise moved from the door to the wood covering the downstairs windows. The disturbing sound continued echoing from various directions. He was moving from one window to the next trying to get in. The girls continued their journey up the stairs seeking an advantage point.

At the top of the third floor, they turned left and followed the hallway to the end. There was a small room with windows facing both the front side of the house and the left side. At least they would be able to see two sides.

Before entering the room, each girl descended down on all fours. It was important not to expose themselves to anyone who might be able to see them from the outside.

Emily and Ria crept over to opposite sides of a stained glass window and peered out. Emily's heart beat wildly. There was the car, but where was the man? The girls looked at each other. Both were trembling inside. Emily sank down to the floor and crawled over to Ria.

"I saw the car, but I didn't see him in it," Emily whispered.

Ria scooted over to the other window that faced the side yard, and peeked out. She dropped and returned to her pervious spot next to Emily. "I don't see him anywhere," Ria confirmed softly, the nervousness in her voice radiated through.

"What now?" Emily asked, still using hushed tones.

"Well, the noise seems to have stopped. I haven't heard anything that sounds like a window or door opening. Hopefully, if he is outside somewhere, he won't be able to get into the house," Ria suggested.

"I'll look again," Emily volunteered.

As Emily started to rise back up, a car engine began revving. Cautiously, she peered out to catch sight of the creep. The Pontiac was driving off down the road.

"I think he's gone," Emily sighed with a deep breath of relief. "I can't believe this. I've never had anything like this happen. Do you think we over reacted?"

"No way!" Ria exclaimed. "He was a nut, I'm sure of it. Good thing we got away. Anyways, what is this place? It's really neat looking. Look at these windows." She held her hand up to the window and ran her finger along the etching.

"I hope we don't get in trouble for being in here. That was really odd.... that secret way in. Who would have ever thought about something like that? I wonder if the family who used to live here used it. You wouldn't have to worry about forgetting your house key," Emily said.

"How did you discover it anyways?" Ria inquired.

"I'm not sure. It was strange... like someone told me it was there. Probably my imagination," Emily confided.

"Let's hope so. I'd be worried if you started hearing voices or something," Ria joked trying to use humor as a bridge to help herself overcome the nervousness still lingering in her stomach.

"When do you think it will be safe to leave?" Emily asked, ready to leave the enormous peculiar house.

"Well, I guess after we see a few cars pull into some of the houses over there," Ria said. "Do you want to explore the house?"

"Not today. I've had enough surprises for one day. I mean what if there was a dead body in here. I don't think I could take it," Emily told her.

Ria thought about it for a moment and then said, "You're probably right, but I have to, you know ... Do you think there is a bathroom here?"

Emily laughed, "I can't believe you have to pee! What's even funnier is I have to also."

The girls giggled about their predicament. Emily stretched up to look out the window to see if any neighbors were home. She saw only one car at a house at the far end of the road. But, it seemed promising to her. She wanted to get this over as soon as possible.

"Okay, I think we can head out," Emily informed Ria.

A car revved again. Ria peered out the corner of the window and then collapsed back down beside Emily. Still keeping her voice under normal tone level, she croaked, "OH MY GOD! He's back. What are we going to do? What if he knows we're here?" Her breathing became very rapid. She threw her hands up to her face as if she were going to start sobbing.

Emily grabbed Ria's hands and pulled them down. Forcibly, she stared into Ria's eyes and whispered in a stern voice, "Get a hold of yourself! He doesn't know we're here. But he will if you start bawling. That sound will carry down the street and we'll be dead meat! Remember, we have to keep our voices down and try not to make any noises."

Ria nodded and tried to take slow deliberate breaths. It was going to be okay she told herself. Panicking would only put them at risk.

Seeing Ria had regrouped and gotten her emotions under better control, Emily commanded in a low sound, "Now, let's crawl around to find a bathroom to pee in and find some weapons to protect ourselves with like you thought about earlier. Then, we'll figure out the rest... even if we have to stay the night here!"

Chapter 9

Is Anyone Home?

The girls crawled out of the room. Once in the hallway, they stood up and stretched for a moment. Resuming their bathroom quest, the duo traveled down the hallway checking out each doorway. They peeped in, door after door making sure not to accidently make their presence known to anyone on the outside. Unfortunately or maybe fortunately, most of the rooms were bare.

In one room, a huge antique wooden desk stood pressed up against a wall. The windows in that room, like nearly all in the house were stained glass. Afraid her body might cast a shadow that could be seen through the window, Ria crawled on her hands and knees over to the desk. Methodically, she investigated each drawer.

Most of the drawers were empty. But, in one drawer, there were a few long fat candles and old long stick matches. She had never seen matches like those, but they looked like they would light. She tried to stick them in the front pockets of her shorts for later use. But, the candles and matches were too large for her tiny pockets. She placed the new found items into her blouse.

Her shorts reminded her that it would be a chilly in a few hours. Next time she skipped outside for a 'quick run', she would either wear pants or bring a jacket. Maybe there was a blanket or coat somewhere in the house. She remembered the trunk downstairs and wished they would have had time to look through it. Maybe they could later.

Finally, after combing the third story looking for a bathroom, the girls descended to the second floor. A few minutes of searching revealed a spacious bathroom. The girls peeked in from the hallway. Inside was a large old-fashion free standing tub, a small wood burning stove, a tall linen closet, a marble double-sink, which was fitted on top of a hand crafted cabinet, a few bare towel racks, and, thankfully, a commode.

Oddly, the sink had a small hand pump on it where a set of facets would normally go. The tub didn't have any facets. Emily assumed that the previous tenants had gathered water from the sink using the hand pump and then distributed to wherever it was needed. The stove must have been used to not only heat the bathroom, but for heating bath water as well.

The walls were bare other than the towel racks. There were three small opaque windows located on the upper outside wall. That was good, no one could see in, but some light still shone through. The girls entered.

"This toilet looks really... strange. How old do you think this is? Do you think it works?" Ria asked Emily continuing the tradition of speaking in a hushed manner.

The toilet had a water tank abnormally higher than any model either girl had ever seen. There was a pull chain attached instead of a lever. The toilet bowl was odd too. It was very round, like a donut instead of oval or elongated.

"Not sure on either question, Emily answered. "But, it has water in it, so it might work. I think we have to refill the tank from the sink. Anyways, I don't think we have a choice but to use it. I can't hold it all night and I'm not going outside till we know he's gone. We will try flushing it once we see his car gone from out front just in case it makes lot's of noise."

Emily reached down to the cabinet below the sink and opened its small rectangle door. "Thank God! There's toilet paper in here. It's still in the plastic from the store and looks new. Someone must have been here recently. I hope no one shows up while we're here. We could get arrested for trespassing or something."

"It's not like we plan on damaging anything. We were forced in here for our own protection. Surely, the owners wouldn't press any charges once they heard our story." Ria predicted with uncertainty.

"Yeah, but maybe they wouldn't believe us." Emily added. "Anyways, you keep a watch out and I'll try the commode out first."

Ria stepped out into the hall and waited for Emily to announce it was her turn.

"Okay, all yours," Emily said peering through the doorway.

As Emily stepped out, Ria stepped in.

A few minutes later, the girls were back to the mission of peeking out windows to spot Pontiac guy and scouting for items that may be useful as weapons. As for weapons, the girls found a heavy candle stick holder on the second floor and some screwdrivers on the third floor.

In one of the hall closets, Ria found a few thin multicolored blankets. She shook them out and then folded them back up.

"I'm going to keep these blankets with me. They might come in handy if we have to stay here all night. Which based on the fact that Pontiac guy left again, only to return again, looks like a reality. How long do you think he was gone?" Ria asked clutching her find in her arms.

"Probably a little over an hour. It's hard to tell without a clock, but looking at the sun, that's what I'd surmise," Emily answered. "He's probably been back for two."

Down the street at the edge of the woods, the ominous Pontiac was parked. The girls weren't sure what the weird guy was up to or where he had went. For now, they tried to content themselves by moving silently through the house, staying alert to any noise that would signal an invasion into their current haven.

Room after room, they explored the second floor. But most of the rooms were pretty much bare. There were a few pieces of furniture here and there, mostly chairs. However, the girls did find an additional large candle and candle holder to add to the collection.

Clutching her borrowed blankets, Ria remembered the hall closet in the center of the third floor. "Do you want to look for more blankets in the closet on the third floor?"

"Okay," Emily nodded.

They snuck back up the stairs and opened the large panel closet doors. Neither girl had peeped in the closet earlier because they were too busy trying to find a bathroom. The deep shelves inside had mostly empty wooden boxes on them. Emily started with the boxes on the floor below the lowest shelf, while Ria stretched up to explore the top shelves.

After exploring the first wooden box she had pulled out, Emily shoved it back in, across the floor, into the bottom of the closet. Sometimes Emily didn't realize her strength. The box slid in, made a large thunk, and kept going till she could barely see it.

Getting down on all fours, Emily stretched into the closet and pulled the box back out. The wooden back of the closet behind the area had disappeared. Now, there was a large open space. Looking closer to determine how much damage she had inadvertently caused, she noticed small hinges on the floor attached to wood. The back panel had collapsed flat to the floor. The backing hadn't fell out, it had hinged down. Was this space to store larger items?

She scooted back out and tapped Ria on the shoulder. "Okay, I found another weird hidden thing. There is a fold-down back on the bottom of this closet. Is it like that on the other shelves?"

Ria bent down to see what Emily was trying to explain. Yep, there was a fold-down hinged door there. Ria stood back up and pulled the boxes off first shelf directly above the floor. Emily catching on helped her. They pushed on the backing. It didn't budge. Methodically, they examined each higher shelf backing to see if it moved. No success.

"I guess the only one with extended storage area is the bottom," Emily commented.

"Let's light a candle and look in there to see how deep it goes," Ria suggested pulling out a candle and some matches.

"Do you think you can do it without catching the house on fire?" Emily was especially concerned with the closet being wood.

"Sure, I'm good with fire. When I was sent to camp by the local church, I loved building the fire and tending to it. Bet you didn't know that I'm a wiz cooking over an open flame!" A wide impish smile spread across Ria's face. "Oh those were fun days at camp. Churches can be so cool sometimes."

Taking the match, Ria struck it rapidly against the wooded hallway wall. It lit with a flash. She maneuvered the candle into the flame. Once the candle was burning confidently, Ria blew the match out. "Okay, you hold this one and I'll light another one. That way if one gets blown out somehow, you can hand me the backup."

"Ria, you know, you are a natural planner and thinker. I would have never thought to do that. If there was ever anyone to be stuck with in an emergency, I want it to be you from now on." Emily admired Ria's skill in forethought. She took hold of the candle that Ria had thrust towards her.

"Camp again," Ria credited. She pulled out the back up candle from her shirt and lit it as well. Once the flame was consistently burning, Ria stooped down and flattened herself against the floor.

With the candle clutched in her fist, she stretched her fist out as far as she could in front of her, and she scrunched forward. Good thing she had short hair. It would be hard to do this with long hair like Emily's. But still, she loved Emily's beautiful long hair even, if most of the time she liked her own short hair better.

Surprisingly, the strange expansion was a bit larger past the initial opening. It was about four high and three feet wide. That was large enough to crawl on one's hands and knees. Someone, who wasn't too tall, like a child could probably walk upright in here, she thought.

The area kept going like a mini-passage way. She pulled her feet across the hinged panel. Her whole body was in past the opening now. Ria glanced around nervously. No spiders or bugs. There weren't any spider webs either. She really hated spiders. They were so gross. She pushed the images of spiders out of her mind before she terrified herself.

"Ria, is everything okay?" Emily called softly into the closet.

"Yeah, all fine," Ria confirmed. "It goes much further in here. I'm going to check just a little bit further."

Continuing into the passage, she entered into a small windowless room. There were a few wooden crates and a couple of long bare wardrobe racks. This must be some kind of storage room. She went back to get Emily.

Emerging back out, Ria excitedly announced, "You've got to see this. It's like a mini-room in there. We can fix the exterior so no one knows we're in there."

The girls situated the hall closet so they could close the doors behind them after they squeezed into the passage way. This would conceal their hiding spot. They lifted the hinged bottom closet back panel up and noticed that there were latches on this side. No one could get in from the other side if the latches were bolted.

"Wow! Who knew people had panic rooms back when this house was built," Emily exclaimed. "This is too cool. I've heard of hiding in the basement under a trap door, but a secret room. Too Cool! It's the 'Situation Room'!"

"You watch way too much T.V." Ria giggled. Emily always got excited about the weirdest things. But she had to admit, this was 'too cool'.

Once secured inside the hidden room, the girls placed all the items they had collected into the center of the room. Sitting down next to the meager supplies, they glanced around. The light of the two candles illuminated the whole room.

Ria picked up the larger candle holder and matching candle. "We can set up this candle holder over there on top of that crate, and push another crate over there, and put the other holder there. That should be good."

Emily nodded. She proceeded over and pushed the crate, Ria had designated, to its proper spot. The crate was a little heavy. Curiosity got the better of her and she grabbed a screw driver. Firmly prying at the lid, Emily was able to open it. There were framed pictures in it. No, they were paintings. Emily gently lifted one out.

"Ria, look. It looks like a family portrait that's painted." Emily held it up so Ria could see it too. "This lady is gorgeous. I wonder if she really looked like that."

She continued, "I heard that in older days, painters would take great pains to paint ladies very favorable or they weren't likely to get paid, or much less get any future work."

"That sounds like air brushing... guess today's photos and videos don't have nothing new. Wow, learn something new every day," Ria confessed.

"Hey, this young girl here looks familiar. Wonder where I've seen her? Do you think she was someone famous?" Emily questioned.

"Nah, this small town would have hooped up anyone famous coming from here. There'd be caps, hats, and tee-shirts for sale. Probably just looks like someone you saw at school or in a local newspaper or something," Ria responded.

"Gosh, I'm getting hungry." Emily rubbed her belly. She put the painting back and closed the crate's lid.

Ria set the largest holder on it and secured the unlit candle in. She held the lit tip of her candle on it until the unlit candle's wick was ablaze.

After her latest task was complete she commented on Emily's realization. "Hungry? I'm starving, but figured it was easier to try to ignore it. It's not like there would be any food in this house."

"Well, if we are real quiet we could go down stairs and look. It's worth a try. Anyways, we need to peek out and see if pervert is still hanging around," Emily suggested

.

Chapter 10

Any Thing to Eat?

The pair left the large candle burning in the center of the hidden room and ventured back out without making a sound. Before heading down to the first level, they peered out one of the third floor windows. The car was still there and the sunlight was fading fast. That meant not only were they still prisoners, but with night coming, their jail cell would have to be the panic room.

Traveling slowly back down the stairs, they took in more of the dwelling's characteristics then they were able to earlier. The walls had sculptured crown and base molding. Scarring on the walls, indicated that items, maybe candleholders, had once been attached. Definitely wealthy people had once lived here.

As she was taking the last step off of the stairway, Emily saw something glimmer across the room in a corner beside a chair. She walked over and moved the chair. It wasn't imagined. Emily bent over and picked up the shiny thing.

"What is it Emily?" Ria asked in a whisper as she walked over to where Emily was standing. Both knew that their stalker was still around, which mandated still speaking at beardy audible levels.

"I'm not sure." Emily turned it over in her hand. "It looks like ...... a large locket, no it's a golden amulet."

Ria stared at the fascinating piece of jewelry in Emily's

hand. She had never seen anything like it. "It's beautiful!" Ria commented. "You should keep it."

"But it probably belongs to whoever owns the house," Emily said.

"Look at the house, Emily! No one has been in here for years. I don't think anyone will miss it much less care," Ria justified.

"I'm tempted, but I can't. Plus, you can't tell me that no one's been here for years when there's toilet paper upstairs in a newer type of packaging." The amulet felt warm and comforting in her palm. The dining room table looked like the right place to leave it. She walked over and gently laid it there.

Ria tagged behind her. "You're right. It should be left. It might bring bad karma or something," Ria said.

Quietly, they continued the search for the kitchen. Finally, it was discovered off to the right side of the house towards the back. But, by now it was really getting dark. Only the rising moon shed visibility for them.

"I know there's not much chance of food, but if there's toilet paper, maybe there's food," Emily chimed. It wasn't time to give up as the kitchen had dozens of cabinets and drawers. Emily noticed that there was the same type of hand pump at the sink here as upstairs. This one was just bigger.

Emily heard a few crackles like plastic being crumpled. She jumped. Then she realized how silly her reaction was. The sound had come from Ria who was holding a packaged bag of something. Emily strolled over. Ria was smiling.

"It's a big bag of shelled pecans. It wasn't opened either. Hopefully they are still edible. I can't see the expiration date."

After looking through all the cabinets, the pair relented

to the obvious that the only food was possibly the pecans, if they were edible. They would be able to see better in the panic room since the lit candles were up there. Emily grabbed two large glasses from a set on one of the shelves. There was also a ceramic pitcher. She carefully stacked the glasses inside the pitcher. Hopefully, the sink on the second floor would pump drinkable water. Her throat felt dry. Until now, she hadn't realized how thirsty she was. Oh, to have the comforts of home, she thought.

******

Once back up in the secured in the panic room, the girls found the expiration date on the pecan bag. It was next year.

"Okay, that's scary. That means someone comes here for sure." Ria shuddered.

"Well, I guess we can look at another way.... Angels are watching over us. Look edible pecans, fresh water that looks and smells drinkable, and a safe warm hiding place with lights and blankets. What else could two girls hiding from a perverted stalker want?"

Ria knew she should feel grateful, but down deep she was still scared and awfully hungry.

"Alright, let's divide these up and have dinner. If you pour the water, I'll divvy up the nuts on our fancy toilet paper plates." She laid out a few sheets of clean toilet paper for her and for Emily to use as plates. The pecan bag was easy to tear open. After that she just shook some out on each of their plates. Her mouth watered. At least it was healthy stuff.

After eating and drinking, the girls spread the blankets out into a make shift bed.

"Okay, who's going to take first shift?" Ria asked.

"I guess I will," Emily volunteered.

"Are you sure, cause I can do it if you are too tired."

"No, go ahead," Emily insisted.

Ria snuggled down into the soft blankets. She was so tired that she didn't even mind the hard wood floor underneath her. In a few minutes, she was fast asleep.

Emily scooted over on the blanket bed and sat cross-legged next to Ria. Since it was getting a little chilly, she draped one of the blankets around her shoulders and pulled the corners across her front forming a wrap.

She stared around the room trying to stay awake. How was she going to know how much time had passed? As hard as she tried to fight it, her eyes flickered and finally closed. Her head bobbed downwards. Within minutes, Emily had slumped over onto the bed, across Ria and was fast asleep. Both girls were unknowingly exhausted from the day's commotion.

When Ria woke up, she saw Emily culled up in a ball, sleeping soundly. Emily fell asleep, Ria thought. Good thing we were boarded up in here. Ria wondered what time it was. Gently she shook Emily's shoulder.

"Emily, get up. Emily... Remind me not to let you take first watch ever again." As much as she wanted her friend to get enough rest, she wanted to go home more.

Emily's eyelids opened and she gazed hazily out. "I'm sorry I fell asleep."

"That doesn't matter now. I think it's morning. We need to go see."

"Okay," Emily muttered as she sat up.

The girls ventured out from the safety of their lair taking a lit candle with them. It was unneeded. The morning sunlight streamed through the stained glassed windows painting magical rainbows on the walls throughout the house.

Once again, they peered out from a third floor window; neither girl could spot the Pontiac or the stalker.

"Finally, we can go home." Emily sighed. "We need to pick up and not leave any signs that we were here. I don't want whoever is tending to the house or at least whoever is coming and going to find any signs of out trespassing."

Ria nodded in agreement. "But, of course, we can't replace the pecans we ate, because I don't want to come back in here."

"I'll leave the change I have in my pocket on the table downstairs, next to the amulet." Emily decided that was the least they could do.

They scurried back into the panic room and picked everything up. Ria returned the blankets to the closest, and the candles and matches to the dresser. Meanwhile, Emily put the screwdrivers back, and flushed the toilet plates down the toilet. Then, the two scampered down to the kitchen with the two drinking glasses and the ceramic pitcher.

After the kitchen items were placed back in their proper spots on the shelf, Ria asked "Do you think we can go out the door this time?"

"I think the back door would be okay if we can open it and lock it back behind us," Emily said. "Oh no, we almost forgot to put the chair and trunk back."

The trunk felt heavier the second time lifting it. Ria wanted to look inside, but noticed a lock on it. Oh, well, she would have to quash her curiosity this time.

"Okay, let's go to the nearest house with a car and use the phone to call a taxi. I don't want to chance walking all the way back to school with that creep out there," Ria stated.

Emily nodded.

The two girls left through the back door, locking it behind them.

Glancing around cautiously as they turned the corner of the old mansion, the girls headed to the closest house with a car parked outside. The pair walked up to the door and knocked. A woman opened the door slightly and said, "Yes?"

Emily said, "I'm sorry to bother you but can I use your phone? My friend and I forgot our cells and ran in to a bit of trouble and need to call for a ride."

"Just a minute, I'll go get it," the woman said. She returned a few seconds later and handed Emily the cell. Emily dialed a number.

"Hello. Yes, I need a taxi at..." (She looked up at the woman as to ask for the address).

"2110 Rose Way," the woman volunteered.

Emily repeated the address into the phone, then handed the phone back to the woman.

"Thank you. Do you mind if we wait right here for the taxi?" Emily said.

The woman looked at Emily and Ria suspiciously. "Are you girls okay? Did your car break down?"

"Actually, we were walking to the store and some creepy looking guy stopped us on the road and scared us so we ran through the woods to here," Ria's words rushed out. The stress of the whole ordeal was still controlling her. Somehow though, she managed to stop before she confessed to breaking into the old house and spending the night there.

"Oh, you poor dears. Maybe we should call the police and file a report," the woman proposed.

The girls hadn't even thought of that. They were just tired, and wanted to return to the familiarity and safety of their dorm room.

"That's a good idea. We'll file one later," Emily said.

The taxi pulled up. A man's voice called out, "Are you the ones waiting for the taxi?"

"Yes," Emily called back.

"Thank you again," both girls voiced in unison to the woman.

The woman nodded as if to say you're welcome. The girls got into the taxi and safely returned to their dorm.

******

The long unusual ordeal had come to an end. After baths and a full meal, the girls lay snug in their beds watching the end of a movie on TV. A local news flash broke in, "This is a special report. Right here in our quiet sleepy town, a suspected serial killer was almost appended while trying to drive off in a yellow Pontiac from the scene of a brutal attack on a young woman in her home. Neighbors heard suspicious screams and alerted police......"

The news story continued for about thirty minutes. The girls watched with in horror and dismay.

After the report was over, Emily said, "I guess that was your third blessing Ria. Who would ever thunk,....... being saved out of the hands of a serial killer?"

Both girls slept uneasy that night knowing Pontiac guy had almost cornered them. Heaven had watched over them keeping them safe. But, the Pontiac serial killer was still out there... hunting.

Chapter 11

The Holdup

"What's the holdup Sam?" a large burley-looking man stomped towards the desk shaking the office trailer walls as he moved.

Sam, a seasoned construction superintendent, sat behind his desk reviewing a set of plans. He stood up and extended his hand in a welcoming gesture towards the half-giant.

"If it's not the devil himself. Glad to see you, Mr. Faraday," Sam said.

The man shook Sam's hand roughly and growled, "It might take the devil to get this job completed on time. It's already two weeks behind."

"Yeah, I had a time trying to find good help around here. We've had to hire a company from outside the state to tear down the old mansion. They should be here anytime."

"What do you mean?" puzzled Mr. Faraday questioned.

"Well, it seems there is a local legend or something. Everyone's afraid they'll be cursed if they get near the old place," Sam informed him. "Everyone knows about it for miles away."

"That's the dumbest thing I've heard yet. Are they all retards?" Mr. Faraday griped. "How come you didn't just rent some equipment locally, have your boys demo it, and haul it off?"

"I tried that approach," Sam said. "No one will even let anything they own get near the place. As it was, I had to get with a dump two counties over, and arrange to dispose of the scrap there. It seems the local folks didn't want the old ghost house laid to rest in the local county fill."

Mr. Faraday's eyes widened with disbelief, "What?"

"I know, it sounds incredible, but it's the truth. I've never encountered anything like it. You'd think that place was the Amityville Horror House," Sam complained.

"Why didn't you threaten to sue?" Faraday's growled.

"I did... and I even called the governor to see what he could do. No good. But, got it settled now." Sam knew this bit of news infuriated Faraday. Faraday was used to always getting his way.

"How much extra is this going to cost?" Mr. Faraday barked.

"I'm not sure yet," Sam answered.

Mr. Faraday grumbled, his face turning slightly red, "I can't believe we are going to be so far off budget over a stupid house. Somebody else is going to pay for this one, not me. Is that clear?"

Sam, trying to reassure him, promised, "I'll make up the cost somewhere. I've been looking at the plans to see what we can cut. Some of the finishing around the dishwashers and heating units can go. We can put in cheaper cabinets, too. That would make up a little more than half of the extra costs."

"Just remember Sam, this complex is the foundation for two more in other cities. You'd better hide any cuts so they don't cause me problems. I want those other jobs," Mr. Faraday directed.

A loud semi-truck horn sounded. The two men walked

out of the trailer door onto the construction site. A big rig loaded with a couple of bulldozers idled in front of second truck, which was packed with graders and other equipment. Behind those were five dump trucks.

Out of the cab of the first truck jumped a tall skinny guy. "Where do you want this stuff unloaded?" asked the guy.

"Right over there. That'll be great!" Sam said, eager to get started.

Turning to Mr. Faraday, Sam assured, "Now we'll get it moving."

"Okay. Jump on it, because it's your feet in the fire, not mine. Remember that!" Faraday warned walking towards his shiny new truck. He turned just before getting in and wagged his finger at Sam to make sure his point had gotten across. The shiny truck sped off leaving Sam to deal with the challenge.

Sam helped unload all the equipment and shouted order after order. Everything was lining up to bring the old Windel place down. Finally, the wrecking ball was ready.

"Clear the area!" Sam shouted through a blow horn. "Repeat. Clear the area immediately. The wrecking ball is in place. We are starting demolition in five, four, three, two, one."

The huge metal ball swung forward and struck the old mansion creating a huge hole in the wooded wall. Loud eerie shrieks echoed through the air. The unnerving sound seemed to emit from everywhere and nowhere. Sam shuttered. His mind questioned, "Could the curse be real? Nonsense Sam! Get a grip! That stuff isn't real! Only idiots believe in that junk." However, Sam singled for the ball to stop. The screeches lessoned, growing fainter and fainter, until Sam could only hear the loud diesel engines of the wrecker.

Sam lifted the bright orange blow horn he held in his right hand and instructed, "Let's take a quick break."

The crew dispersed, some using the time to grab a bite to eat, others a chance to rest their tired body. Sam was bewildered by what he had heard. He inconspicuously scavenged the area for about ten minutes, but there was nothing unusual.

"Probably the machinery," he said to himself.

Through the horn, Sam's voice sounded again, "Break's over. Let's get back to taking this monster down. Clear the area! Repeat! Clear the area!"

The gigantic metal ball struck the wooden walls, again and again. Under the pounding siege, the old place collapsed into a massive broken heap. The crews continued to work hard until dusk. All that remained were a few splintered boards and shattered fragments of glass.

The other newly built three story apartments, about fifty feet away, could easily be seen without the mansion obstructing the view. The buildings had an elegant air about them even though they were not completely finished.

Sam gazed proudly over at them. He had done well running this project, until that house got in the way. But now, he could pick back up the pace.

"I *will* get the last unit finished on schedule, come hell or high water," Sam said out loud to himself stressing the word will as if that would invoke miracles.

******

Two weeks had passed by and Sam was standing in front of the last completed unit where the old mansion had once stood. Mr. Faraday stood beside him. The crisply painted structure was surrounded by a simple, but captivating landscape. A large welcome sign invited renters to check out the luxurious apartments at special prices available for a limited time only.

"Well, didn't think you'd pull it off Sam," Mr. Faraday confided.

"To the day. Told you'd I'd do it!" Sam bragged.

"And almost within budget," Mr. Faraday added. "Now if you just survive the curse," he taunted. His eyes surveyed the surrounding area. Several older type homes lined the street about a block away. Looking at them was like stepping back in time at least fifty years.

He looked back at Sam. "Hard to imagine that these ignorant people believe in such nonsense as curses and demons. What next? If you ask me they just don't want to see progress come. They need to step into the twenty-first century."

"And you want to profit at every step they take, don't you?" Sam remarked.

"You got that right. Business is business. And new buildings are my business. This project is going to add nicely to my portfolio. With its success, I'll get at least two more projects." He paused a minute. His face scrunched up. "Those corners you cut... to make budget... better not come back to haunt us." Mr. Faraday strolled over to his truck, Sam following.

"No one will notice. I'll wrap up a few lose ends and meet you at your office next week," Sam confirmed.

Mr. Faraday nodded, then closed his truck door. Within seconds he was driving away.

Sam got into his own truck and cranked it. A few feet from Sam's truck, a small car occupied by two girls pulled up. The young girls bounced out of its doors, as Sam drove off.

"Which way do we go, Ria?" Emily asked.

"It's up that way," Ria directed.

The girls walked up the exposed steps leading to the third floor. Reaching the balcony, Emily leaned over and glanced down.

"My...what a drop!" she said. "I'm glad there are high guard rails."

Ria stared out into the open view, "Look how far you can see."

"Wow!" Emily gasped. "Look at that beautiful rose bush. It's gorgeous."

Ria commented, "It's huge. Those roses are so red.... blood red... amazing. I wonder if we could sneak down and pick some to put in the apartment. Surely, if we only took a few no one would care."

"Probably not. I wonder if it was already here or if they planted it," Emily said.

Continuing down the balcony Ria counted, "609, 611, 613.... Here it is. Our very own apartment."

Ria slipped the key in, turned the knob and pushed the door open. The door, offset and positioned to the far left, fully exposed the living room. Sunlight streamed in from the two, large front windows illuminating the entire space. New light-grey carpet matched the off-white walls, which had a silver sparkle integrated into its finish.

Further into the apartment, a breakfast bar separated the living room from the kitchen. Beyond the bar, a black refrigerator towered in the far corner of the kitchen. Small, modern-looking fans hung from the ceiling. The vacant, unoccupied space beckoned to the girls.

"Okay, now we have to cross over the threshold together, at the same time. It's good luck," Ria instructed.

"Okay," Emily said nodding her head in agreement.

The pair lined up, raised their right legs simultaneously and stepped in unison over the threshold into the apartment.

"This is gorgeous!" Ria exclaimed as she bounced across the living room. "A couch could go here, a TV there, chair there....What do you think?"

She didn't wait for Emily's answer but disappeared down the hallway. "Which bedroom do you want?" she called out.

"Either one is fine," Emily answered from the kitchen. Scanning the interior, she mused that the black handles and door hardware contrasted nicely with the white cabinets.

The dishwasher was black as well. However, the expanse of bare walls made the place feel a little cold and uninviting. That would have to be remedied. Selecting decor to liven the place up might be fun.

Ria popped into the kitchen having already explored the rest of the place. "Time to buy some cheap stuff to liven this place up.. needs a little color in here!," Ria chimed. It seemed that she and Emily had the same idea.

Emily was still investigating the kitchen, analyzing storage space. She was amazed at Ria's quick once over through the whole apartment. Opening the bottom cabinets below the sink, Emily shuttered, "Ewww yuck!"

"What?" Ria wondered what could be wrong.

"There's a big hole in the cabinet behind the dishwasher, and around the pipes, there are big gaps as well. It's just kind of gross looking. I guess it's okay, though. Probably like that in all apartments. We'll have to put some kind of tape over the holes."

Ria peered over Emily's shoulder, "It is kinda of spooky looking. Good thing we can close the cupboard doors."

The girls retreated into the living room and sprawled out on the carpet.

"I'll bring my stuff over tomorrow. When will you be able to get yours?" Ria inquired.

"Hmmmm," Emily mumbled as she ran through the list of things she had to accomplish this week. "Probably Tuesday night after I meet my selected senior."

"Okay, then I'll change moving in till Tuesday too. Now, which room do you want? The back one is slightly bigger but has the heating unit in the closet," Ria told her.

"I'm fine with either one,.... like I said earlier," Emily giggled.

"Okay, I'll take the back one because the front bedroom faces the east and the sun streams in early in the morning," Ria chirped happy with the thought of being able to sleep in now and then.

Chapter 12

The Introduction

Emily adjusted her backpack as she strolled sown the neighborhood sidewalk. She glanced at each house's number as she progressed.

The street ended up ahead. At the street's ending stood a tall block wall. About three hundred feet before reaching the wall, Emily veered left towards a cottage-like home. The large stepping-stone winding path towards the door reminded her of fairy fables. Dominating the path a few steps in was a large flowery bush; she reached out and cradled its limb in her hand. Emily examined it thoroughly, admiring its leaf structure and gigantic pink blooms.

"Meeoow, Meeoow". A huge brown brindled cat stood in the path in front of Emily.

"Wow! You are gigantic!"

"Meeoow," echoed the cat.

"I'm not sure if I should run! I hope you don't bite. Are you a cat or ...?"

"Meeoow, Meeoow," the cat replied as it flipped over onto its belly.

The cat wiggled and flopped around, etching closer to Emily's shoes.

"Do you want to play?"

"Meeeooooow."

Emily cautiously reached forward as she knelt down. Her fingers gently stoked the back of the large cat's ears. "Oh.. my.. your fur is so thick and soft. I always wanted a cat just like you. Okay, maybe smaller, but Mom was allergic."

The cat purred loudly, making a sound like a saw cutting a log.

"I hope you are not growling at me," Emily stated as she ran her hand over its back.

A women's voice sweetly echoed, "He really seems to like you. I've never seen him take to someone like that."

Looking up, Emily blushed. "I'm sorry. Is he yours?"

From the cottage where Emily was headed, a dainty elderly lady sauntered towards her. The lady's billowing multi-colored skirt reminded Emily of a gypsy she had seen once in a movie. The lady's silver hair was loosely pulled back into a French braid allowing her gold dangling earrings to flash as she moved. A gold necklace and several jingling bracelets accented her attire.

"Hi, I'm Dotia Hazell," she offered gentle voice. "You must be Emily."

Emily nodded. "Yes, I'm Emily!" She awkwardly stuck her hand out. She was a bit embarrassed to be caught talking to a cat. She thought Ms. Hazell might think her odd. "How do you do?" she chirped trying to recover.

Dotia tenderly clasped her palms over Emily's extended hand. "Very well, Dear" Dotia reassuringly replied. "My, what exquisite positive energy you have. No wonder Jacque is enthralled!"

Dotia amiably released Emily's hand and motioned for Emily to follow. Jacque jumped up and bounded against Dotia's calf.

"Yes, Jacque, she is wonderful. She's our new friend. Do mind your manners."

Emily couldn't help but chuckle. She felt much more at ease. Dotia seemed kind and wonderfully interesting.

Dotia smiled knowingly at Emily, "Come inside and let's have some tea."

The pair proceeded along the stone path towards the cottage entrance. Emily was so busy glancing around at the variety of shrubbery and flowers that she almost tripped over her own feet. She caught her balance and hoped Ms. Hazell had not noticed her clumsiness.

"Ms. Hazell, where did you get all these plants? I've never seen such an amazing landscape."

Dotia smiled pleased with the girl's interest in her collection. "Wait till you see the backyard. And, please call me Dotia."

Emily followed Dotia through the front door, into the quaint living room.

Dotia explained, "Here are a few of my feline friends. The solid black female with golden eyes is Kitty. On the couch is Felix, on the pillow is Princes, and over on the marble shelf is Mr. Grumpy! Everyone, this is Emily."

Like a trained choir, meows resounded. Emily's eyes widened. "Oh my!"

Dotia reassured, "They are saying Hello."

Surprising herself, Emily blurted "Hello, everyone. I'm sure I'll learn your names very soon. Thank you for the warm greeting!" She was not sure if she had lost her mind or not. Talking cats?

Dotia took Emily's hand, "Now Dear, let's get that tea. There will be time to get more acquainted with everyone later. Let's see, you'll probably like rose hips with a touch of honey." Dotia led Emily into the kitchen and over to a chair.

"Just relax here and I'll heat us some water in the microwave. I love these modern appliances."

Emily looked around, "Ms. Hazell, what are in all the colorful bottles?"

"Emily dear, please call me Dotia. The bottles contain herbs that I gather or buy. I have something good for whatever ails you. So, tell me about your project." Dotia went about gathering the tea cups, filling them with water, and putting them in the microwave.

"Well Dotia," Emily began, "I have to keep a weekly journal about our time together. Then, at the end of the semester, I must turn in a 15 page written report about what I learned. So, I guess, I want to know everything about you and your life so far."

Emily's nervousness was fading now. Dotia had such a calming presence about her. Emily felt like she could talk to her about anything.

The microwave timer rang. Dotia brought the cups over to the table. Bustling around, she gathered some colorful jars, two tea leaf strainers, honey, and spoons. She carefully scooped tea out of the containers into each of the tiny strainers and placed the strainers into the teacups. She placed a spoon on Emily's tea plate and motioned for Emily to help herself to some honey. Emily scooped some honey out of the old-fashioned jar and plopped it into her cup. She slowly stirred the mixture. The sweet aroma filled the kitchen.

"I guess with you having to learn so much about me it's a good thing I'm not shy," Dotia chuckled. "But, there's not much to tell. I'm afraid you may be very bored having to spend so much time with me. How about you? Do you have a suitor? I wouldn't want to take time away from any boyfriend."

Emily blushed, "I'm afraid I don't have any of those. Maybe in the future I'll meet Mr. Right. I'm not into Mr. Right-Now like some college girls." Emily couldn't believe she had just exposed her inner thoughts like that. She never told people very much about herself. She lifted the spoon, blew and sipped. It was delicious.

"Good for you!" Dotia chimed. "One wonderful day with the right person is better than years with the wrong one." Dotia now knew she had made the right choice.

Suddenly, a man's voice boomed, "Dotia, what am I going to do with you? The front door was unlocked again! That crazy murderer is still out there you know!" A young man in a policeman's uniform appeared in the kitchen archway.

Emily dropped her spoon. She tried not to stare at him, but something about him was so very attractive to her. Her heart fluttered. The room felt a little too warm. She struggled to regain her composure.

"Why Grant! I'm so glad you stopped by," Dotia crooned. "Grant this is Emily, the lovely young lady from the university working on that class project I told you about."

Dotia was out of her chair and standing next to Grant in seconds. She swung her arms affectionately out towards him, "Emily, this is my God son, Grant. Isn't he handsome?" Dotia paused and gave Emily a sad, loving gaze. "Emily dear could you do me a huge favor please? You see there is an annual Police Officer's Ball next week. Grant had asked me to go with him, but I really do not like all that modern music. Would you please go in my stead? I would be so grateful."

Grant interjected in a scolding tone, "Dotia, Shame on you. You set this up. To ambush ..."

Dotia interrupted turning her charming sad gaze towards Grant, "Why Grant, how could you think that?

Am I not but a sweet little old lady minding her own lot in life? However, I can sense that Emily would be a much better dance partner than me. Heaven knows you could use the help, Mr. Two Left Feet." Grant was thrown off guard. Dotia was much more strategic than he could ever be. Emily too sat silently, unable to react to the scene unfolding before her.

"Fantastic!" Dotia continued, "It's settled. Emily, Grant will pick you up here next Friday at 6pm. What fun you both will have!" Dotia clapped her hands softly like a small child seeing Disney for the first time.

Grant's words rushed out, "Emily, I must apologize for my adorable Godmother. If you already have plans, I'll understand." Grant hoped she would not. "But, if you can go..." He looked down at his feet afraid to see her reaction.

Enchanted, Emily stared at Grant; her voice trembled, "Yes, I mean, No, I don't have any plans, so I can go if you are sure...,"

Dotia chirped in, "See it will be wonderful! Grant can you stay for tea?"

"I've really got to get back on my beat," Grant replied.

"Okay, but don't be late next week to pick Emily up." Dotia gave Grant a big hug and then turned him around, ushering him out of the door. "I wouldn't want you to lose your job. Out you go. Love you!" She patted him on the back as he exited the doorway.

Grant called back, "Okay, I get the hint. Oh, I'll lock the door on my way out!"

Dotia returned to the table and situated herself across from Emily. "Now, for a second cup of tea."

Before Emily could respond, Jacque jumped into Emily's lap. Startled, Emily jumped slightly.

Dotia cooed, "It's okay. He really likes you. Don't be afraid."

Emily reached her hand out and brushed it across the cat. Loud purrs erupted. Emily laughed delighted.

"My, My," Dotia remarked, "Jacque has never taken to someone this much." Dotia's brows narrowed in thought. "You know, it may do Jacque good to get extra attention for awhile. I have so many companions here that sometimes they don't each receive enough attention from me. Being that you don't have any pets, could you take Jacque with you for a little while? Could he stay with you at your place?"

Emily beamed, "Can I? Really! I've always wanted a cat! I mean I know he is your cat, but I'd love to have him visit for awhile."

"Good! I have a cat cage, food, a pan, ... I'll pack you everything you need. It's settled. Jacque can be your temporal companion."

Jacque meowed. His brilliant emerald eyes blinked up at Emily several times. Affectionately, he licked Emily's hand. Emily giggled.

Chapter 13

What's That?

Emily walked up the stairs to her and Ria's apartment. She carried the cat cage and a large bag with her. The gigantic rosebush again caught her gaze. She paused staring over to it. An animal's howl snapped her from the trance. She continued towards the door. She was so happy. A cat! Her hand turned the knob while pushing the door in a solid motion.

"Hi Emily," Ria's cheerful voice rang out. "Brad and I are watching the new vampire movie. It is sooo scary!" The pair were side by side on the couch with the TV blaring.

Emily's voice rushed out, "Where are you at in it? Can you rewind? I want to see it to! I heard it was too phenomenal!"

Brad smiled, "You girls are so funny. I guess since we've only seen 15 minutes or so, if Ria doesn't mind, I'm okay with it ⸱⸱"

Ria gushed, "Brad, you are too wonderful. What sweetness...where have you been all my life?" She reached over and firmly hugged him. Then, Ria turned and smiled up at Emily, "I'll make some popcorn while you catch upon the movie." The energetic girl bounced off the couch and made her way into the kitchen.

Following Ria into the kitchen, Emily dragged her bag of stuff and the cat cage into the kitchen. "First though, you gotta see what I have." She dropped the bag of stuff and gently sat the carrier down. Emily knelt down beside it, opened the cage door, and tenderly lifted Jacque out.

"His name is Jacque. He's from my senior friend Dotia. Oh, Ria I hope you do not mind. I know I should've asked, but he is... He is so beautiful! She said I could borrow him for a short while."

Ria stared. "Wow! He is huge! What does he eat?"

"I know, he is big. Is it okay?" Emily begged with her eyes.

Ria could see how much it meant to Emily. "I guess so... But please make sure he doesn't make any messes. Are you sure he's not part panther?"

Beaming with joy about her new housemate, Emily giggled.

Jacque lazily stretched around in Emily's arms. Emily nuzzled his forehead and then set him on the floor. Jacque strolled around unconcerned about his new surroundings. He sauntered into the living room and effortlessly leaped into a chair. He circled once and then curled up into a ball tucking his tail beneath him.

Emily followed him into the living room. She patted him lovingly. "I hope you like it here. I set some water and food up the kitchen for you. And, your kitty box." Settling into the chair next to Jacque, Emily situated a small pillow on her lap.

Brad queried, "You really don't think that cat understood you?"

"Wait till you get to know him. He's amazing. He does understand what I say," Emily confided.

Brad commented, "I'll take your word for it. We better start the movie now so we can finish it before midnight. After all, I have to go to work tomorrow."

Ria passed out the popcorn bowls and resumed her cuddling spot on the couch next to Brad.

"Okay, but give me just a second 'cause I got to know, Emily how was your old person?" Ria begged.

"Not much to tell yet. She is a sweet, tiny, kinda of odd, elderly lady with tons of cats. We had tea and ...."

Ria interrupted, "Witches have tons of cats... and seem really sweet at first till they pounce, taking young virgins for their blood to stay youthful forever...like a vampire..."

"Ria, you watch way too many movies!" Emily cut-in. "Anyways, she introduced me to a guy, a policeman, her Godson. I think she set us up on a date next Friday."

"Is he cute? What's his name? Do you have a date or not?" Ria would have continued, but Brad began clearing his throat in a most annoying manner.

The suddenly chatterless girls stared at him.

"Now that I have your attention, can we watch the movie? Not to be rude or insensitive, but we can hear all about the escapades of Emily, dear friend to Ria, my love, after the movie because I have to get up early in the morning." Brad smiled trying to be most charming.

Emily blushed, "Brad, so sorry. Yes, let's watch the movie."

Brad hit the play button and increased the volume.

Soon, the trio sat mesmerized by the movie. Emily clutched a pillow tightly against her chest. Jacque slept calmly by her side, despite her erratic twitches every so often when a real scary part ensued.

The movie ended with the prominent male vampire disappearing into the night after telling the leading lady he would come back for her one day. She cried out as he vanished into the mist. It was hard to tell if she was afraid or heartbroken, since in the movie she had wrestled between falling in love with him and being repulsed by the idea of having to live off blood.

"Wow," Ria sighed, "How scary, yet somehow romantic."

"It'll definitely be hard for me to sleep now," Emily added.

Brad rose up from the couch and kissed Ria on the top of her head. "Well ladies, on that note, I better get headed home. Tomorrow starts early for me."

Ria grunted, "Don't remind me. I have an early class tomorrow. I hate summer classes." Then her voice changed to sweetness. "Brad, do you really have to go now? You could sleep on the couch."

He lifted her up by her open arms and pulled her softly towards the door. Gently, his lips touched hers for a fleeting moment. Then, he looked firmly into Ria's eyes and shook his head no. "Ria you know that's not a good idea. I might sleepwalk. Who would defend your honor?"

Emily, not wanting to invade on their privacy, lifted Jacque in her arms and headed towards her bedroom. "Goodnight, guys, sweet dreams if you dare to dream at all. Ha ha ha ha," she laughed employing her most sinister effort."

Ria flinched at Emily's evil rendition, "Emily, please don't do that! See what I have to put up with? Brad, you should marry me and take me away! Save me!!"

Evil laughter floated down the hallway.

"You girls need to be part of the drama club." Brad kissed Ria once more. "See you tomorrow, my love. Gotta go." He slipped through the doorway. As he closed the door, he cautioned, "Lock the door behind me!"

Ria's fingers turned the latch, locking the door. She pressed her cheek against the cold wood and sighed.

After a second, she moved towards the living room and tidied up. The kitchen was next. But, there was not much of a mess to clean up. After a few minutes, her hand hit the light switch off, and she headed down the hallway to her bedroom. Shadows, from the outside lights filtering through the windows, danced on the wall. Ria jumped. "Oh man, I should have left the lights on."

She opened her bedroom door slowly and hit the light. The tidy bedroom seemed too quiet, but she pulled the door closed behind her anyway. Her white bedcovers looked so inviting. She carefully pulled the covers down and then went over to her dresser and picked out her nightgown.

Once changed, she reopened the bedroom door. As soon as her hand left the door knob, she scurried across the room and jumped into bed.

The wind outside howled. Shadows threatenly shifted around the room. Ria grabbed her spare pillow and pulled it over her head. "Oh, I'll never get to sleep with all of this going on." Ria tossed and turned.

Emily lay snuggled under her thin blanket with Jacque curled up next to her. His emerald eyes were wide open. Emily smiled happily as she closed her eyes. A cat. Finally a cat. She fell into a deep sleep comforted by the presence of her new companion.

As the time passed, Ria slowly drifted into sleep. The night advanced. Still at his post, Jacque raised his head as though he heard something. He moved silently across the bed and landed on the floor. Without making a sound, he trotted out of the room.

In the dark, the brindled cat was invisible, but his shadow made its way into Ria's room. An eerie screech erupted. Jacque's hisses sounded, through the blackness, more deadly than a viper.

He growled and spat. More screeches emanated.

Within seconds, all noise ceased. It was quiet.

Jacque's shadow flickered on the wall as he returned down the hallway back into Emily's room. He leaped onto the bed and settled back in next to Emily. It was surprising that neither girl had awoke during the commotion. Jacque decided not to wake them. After all, what good would it have done?

The morning light flickered across her room. Ria rubbed her eyes. She restlessly swung her arms out and propped up on her bed. Something gooey hit her left hand. As she lifted her hand, she looked over to inspect the strange wet substance. It looked like blue watery ooze. Grossed out, she instinctively wiped off her hand on the bedspread and shot out of the bed away from the disgusting fluid. "Yuck!" She screamed.

From her more distance position, Ria looked around. Everything else seemed normal. The only thing strange was that blotch of blue gunk on the white bedspread.

Emily popped her head in the doorway while brushing her teeth, "What's wrong?"

Ria pointed to the blue goo. Emily asked, "What is it?"

"I have no idea! Maybe your cat peed on my bed," Ria growled.

"You sure are grouchy. Who ever heard of blue pee? I'm sure it wasn't Jacque," Emily announced. She disappeared, off to finish brushing her teeth.

Ria gathered up the bedspread and put them in a clothes basket. Hollering loudly she informed, "Guess, I'll keep my door closed from now on so there's no more blue cat pee on my bed."

Ria sat down in front of the mirror to begin her morning ritual of beauty. Grabbing the comb from the vanity top, she swiftly combed in repeated down stokes through her short styled hair. Having a shorter hairstyle was much better than a long or curly one. It saved so much time and it hadn't deterred her from gaining a boyfriend. A smug smile came over her face.

Something black fell out of her hair onto the dresser. The movement caught her eye. The black thing was thin and narrow. Leaning down to have a closer look, Ria thought it looked like a cat's toenail or maybe it was a weird roach leg. Yes, a weird roach leg.

Picking it up with a tissue, she paraded her find into the kitchen. Opening the cabinet doors, she began her search for a small baggy, in which to place the grotesque item.

The toaster popped. Emily grabbed the heated bagel and plopped it onto a plate. As she spread cream cheese on the bagel, she watched Ria out of the corner of her eye.

"What cha doing?" she asked in a sweet voice. Emily was curious, but didn't want Ria to become even grouchier. Maybe Ria was in a better mood.

"Oh, I found this ucky piece of bug part or something in my room. I figured I'd give to the landlord and ask him to spray. I thought it may be a cat toenail for a second, but it has little hairs on it. The nauseating thing was it fell out of my hair as I was brushing this morning," Ria explained giving a little shiver reliving the event. "I'll put it over here on the counter top for now. Don't accidently throw it away."

"Can I see it?" Emily asked walking over to the bagged specimen. Ria dumped the thing out on a paper towel.

"See," she said. "It's disgusting."

Emily peered intently at it. "I think we should give it to the lab at school to identify. I can drop it off later this week. Then we would know what to tell the landlord what to spray for."

Ria nodded in agreement.

Chapter 14

The Date

Friday felt as though it would never arrive. At the same time, Emily had dreaded its entrance. At the apartment, the girls were preoccupied with getting Emily ready. She even had her nails and hair done at the local beauty shop, which was a first. What if he didn't like the dress she had painstakingly found and altered? It had Ria's absolute approval, so maybe she was over worrying.

The clock struck five. It was time to go over to Dotia's. Ria grabbed Emily's hand and tugged her towards the door.

"Come on! You'll be late," Ria commanded. "I wish he was coming here to pick you up so I could see what he looks like. The first time you get a date and I don't even know what he looks like!"

"It's not really my first date," Emily retorted slightly embarrassed. "I have been to school parties and such." Emily pulled her hand loose from Ria's and reached over to Jacque in the living room chair. She stroked his ears lovingly. "I'll be back soon. Behave yourself and don't annoy Ria," she cooed.

The pair excitedly closed the door, locked it and ventured down the stairway.

"You should grab a few roses to put in your hair," Ria suggested.

"What if they clash with the corsage that Grant gives

me, if he gives me one? Do they do that kind of thing at a Police Ball?" Emily's nervousness and hesitation resurfaced.

"They probably do, but don't be disappointed if they don't," Ria paused contemplating the matter. "I know, you can grab some roses and give them to Dotia. If he doesn't have a corsage, maybe Dotia will offer one of the roses for your dress or hair... I would like it better in your hair."

Ria raced ahead to the car. She dove into the passenger's door and emerged back out waving a pair of scissors. Emily had walked over to the rosebush to select the most perfect blooms. The flowers were enchanting, deep ruby red. With a few snips, Ria secured a small bounty and wrapped them in a piece of newspaper she had also retrieved from the car. Handing the choice blossoms to Emily, she ordered, "Let's get a move on my queen!"

The pair hastened to the car with the acquired prize in hand.

******

Grant uneasily straightened his tie in the mirror. He was glad that Dotia had arranged this because it would have taken him a long time to get the courage up to ask Emily out. Her vibrant green eyes lingered in his mind. He was extremely surprised with himself. He didn't even know this girl. What if she were a flake? His muscles tensed; there was something very alluring about her. The allure had haunted him all week. At work he had been distracted to the point that he had even forgotten to sign out. On the way home, he missed his turn twice. This wasn't like him, which made him even more wary.

The light blue truck pulled up alongside the street at the end of Dotia's pathway. Grant jumped out, his black shoes hitting the pavement rather hard. The jolt helped him clear his head.

Reaching back into the front seat, he retrieved the corsage he had purchased at the florist. Dotia had suggested a light rose or pinkish white. Hopefully this combination of both would be perfect. He studied the arrangement curiously for a second.

He had heard that girls could get rather upset and hurt by these tiny details. Surely Emily wouldn't be one of those types of girls. Grant couldn't imagine her acting so childish and immature. If so, there definitely wouldn't be date two!

With the corsage in hand, he forced himself steadily up the path and knocked at the door. Why did he knock? It was Dotia house. He had always just stridden right in. he turned the handle. Surprisingly, it was locked. "Oh, so she decides to lock it now, at a time like this!" His uneasiness returned.

The door cracked opened about an inch. Dotia peered through the gap. "I guess I'll let you in... no wait.... Did you remember?"

To the narrow opening, Grant offered up the corsage for Dotia's approval. "That's perfect! So lovely...," Dotia cooed as the door opened wide.

Grant gathered his courage and stepped over the threshold. He couldn't believe that he felt this shy. He was used to being in charge. From the moment he had graduated the academy and donned his dark blue uniform, he had been forced to assume responsibility and command of any given situation. At that second, he realized how much he had grown and changed over the last few years. He wasn't a kid anymore. He had become a young man. A surge of pride swelled up inside of him; His shoulders broadened and his eyes focused straight ahead alighting on the dazzling image in the center of the room.

Like a princess out of a children's tale, there stood Emily, in a velvety crimson gown. A shimmering veil wrapped loosely around her shoulders. Her long dark hair was loosely gathered at her temples, sweeping back, highlighting her silky completion. The rest of her brown locks elegantly cascaded down her shoulders like the mane on a magical creature.

Memorized by her image, Grant stumbled, but managed to regain his balance. As though not noticing the misstep, Emily smiled, her eyes meeting his, and she extended her hand unconsciously. Grant felt his arm reach forward; they were hand in hand. Her hand was so delicate, soft, warm....

"Now then, move over Grant," Dotia commanded breaking the trance. "I need to put the corsage on Emily. This really is a perfect corsage Grant. You've outdone yourself." Dotia nudged Grant over and gently pinned the flower on Emily's dress. The coloring was perfect. Dotia beamed. It was like seeing her own son and his future wife go on their very first date. This was perfect! Tears misted her eyes. Her heart filled with happiness. It was just what she had wished and prayed for.

Then another thought crossed her mind and her countenance regained its former more dignified manner. Hopefully, the two of them would realize and not mess it up as children had habits of doing.

She patted Grant on the arm and placed his hand back in Emily's. "Off you two go now. Grant, I know you'll drop Emily off at her apartment at a reasonable hour."

"Yes, mam," he grinned like a school boy getting to stay up late for the very first time. "I'll mind my manners, Dotia." Grant moved towards the door with Emily on his arm.

He turned slightly back towards Dotia just before stepping through the doorway, "Make sure you lock up and don't be out in that garden in the middle of the night! You think I didn't know?" Grant scolded.

Dotia feigned innocence with her gestures. Emily laughed delighted at the display of the warm familial affection between the two.

******

At the dance, Grant handed Emily a cup of punch. She sipped the white frothy nectar, while glancing around. Blue, white, and gold streamers and balloons floated everywhere lending a soft elegance to the community center's average-looking banquet room. Decorations on the walls and tables also carried the blue, white, and gold color scheme, which represented the local police colors.

The small police force only consisted of thirteen policemen, two supervisors, one chief, and three administrative personal. This was one reason why the whole town was always invited to the police ball. A ball needed more than 19 people and their guests. Plus, it gave all the locals a chance to catch up on friendly town gossip.

A middle aged woman approached Grant and Emily. "Hi Grant. Glad to see you," she purred. Cheri's fingers toyed like a spider up his forearm, but Grant politely dislodged her hand.

"Hi Cheri. I'd like you to meet Emily, my date." Grant placed his arm around Emily and pulled her close.

"Well, Grant... it's a shame all the good ones are taken... Is it your first time at the Ball dear? I don't think I've seen you before." Cheri was curious about this new interference in her plans to one day hook Grant.

"It's very nice to meet you Cheri. Yes, this is my first time at the Ball." Emily felt a little embarrassed by the lady's obvious infatuation with Grant.

"Well, dear, let me tell you all about it." Cheri knew

she couldn't win over Grant's affections with such a cute girl beside him, so the least she could do was play nice for now.

"The Ball's entertainment activities are highly praised every year. I always help with the planning. It's important to stand behind our handsome police force." She batted her eyes at Grant and then turned her attention back to Emily.

"This year, a dance-off is scheduled and a name-that-tune game. Plus, awards for various categories such as youngest and oldest attendees are going to be presented. Awards are a ribbon of some sort and a small gift, like a toaster. The gifts were donated by local businesses. Sometimes there are gag gifts. Can't remember last years, do you Grant?" Cheri purred his name.

"Nope, Cheri, afraid not. You finish telling Emily about the Ball, I'll be right back." Grant didn't wait for a reply but headed off towards two guys standing by side wall.

"Don't worry honey. I'll take care of you. Let's see, where were we... Oh entertainment... the favorite is the biggest yarn contest, where best-told, most outlandish tale-tall wins. Another custom is to pin a number on each couple as they enter the dance for a chance to win by vote "Couple of the year" award. It's a romantic dinner for two at a local resort. Oh you are number twenty-four. Not a lucky number.... Single party-goers are pinned with letters, men with vowels and ladies with consonants. Then later on two letters will randomly selected from each tub. Those lucky or unlucky individuals are given a shared gift of a dinner for two. In the past, this often has comedic effects. Last year an 86 year old lady and a 23 man had won together. Can you picture it?" Cheri let out a shrill laugh.

Emily was interested in the Ball and wanted to be

polite, but this lady hadn't stopped to breathe. And, she was still going on.

"The food selection is a party enticement too. Every year hamburgers, hotdogs, and a variety of small sandwiches, including vegetarian, are served along with cake, ice cream, punch, tea, soda and water. The yearly Ball has grown into of the town's most important social gathering traditions."

Before Cheri could continue, Grant grabbed Cheri's hand and placed it in the palm of a robust fellow who had walked over with him. "Cheri, Paul needs a dance partner. Can you do a handsome police fellow a favor? Knew you could...off you go." He gently shoved her in the direction of the dance floor.

Taken off guard, Cheri could not figure out a way out of her dilemma without embarrassing herself. The robust fellow, Paul winked at Grant as he spun the talkative lady off into the dancing crowd.

"Sorry about that, Emily. She's really a nice lady, but she could drive a deaf mule insane. Paul owed me a favor, so I'm collecting. She'll be occupied for awhile now." Grant chuckled.

Not sure what to say, Emily nodded. She hated to say it, but she was glad that the non-stop voice was gone.

"There are a lot of people here this year," Grant commented. "I'll try to keep you away from the crazy ones from now on." His eyes sparkled and his smile drew her lips into a smile too. She knew he was jesting about the crazy people.

Surveying the room, Emily thought it must have been so wonderful to grow up here with these friendly, happy people. The party-goers were immensely enjoying themselves, smiling and laughing. Her hometown had never developed this kind of a sense of community. Maybe it was because her hometown was a poor rural area with people moving in and out all the time. It had lacked job opportunities and social networks for the residents, not at all like here. Here, the atmosphere was almost like an extended family.

Hal waved from across the room as he bustled over to see his favorite young person.

"Grant, glad to see you. Where's Dotia?" Hal asked, looking around searching for her.

"She asked me to bring Emily instead of her this year." He gestured towards the girl standing next to him, providing insight as to who, was Emily. Then, to be clear he followed, "Hal, this is Emily my new friend, Emily this is Hal, one of my dearest long-time friends."

"I'm glad you didn't say oldest! I'm pleased to meet you young lady." Hal chuckled. He extended his hand in friendship towards Emily.

"It is wonderful to meet you as well," Emily stated as she accepted his extended hand.

Hal gently lifted her hand up as he bowed slightly and bestowed a light kiss upon it.

"Yes, a pleasure. Where did you arrest her at?" Hal taunted.

"You should have asked what she was arrested for," Grant bantered back. "I think her record stated... her crime was running her car over a hand-kissing pet store owner. Of course, she got off light because he survived." He grinned wide, knowing that he'd got one on Hal.

Hal, acting as though he was not the subject of the taunt, inquired, "Emily would you like to dance since Grant has effectively robbed me of Dotia tonight? That is if Grant will spare you for at least a few minutes. He seems to be awfully taken with you." Hal liked his last sentence since he knew it not only would embarrass Grant, but was true. He had seen the way Grant looked at Emily. There was definitely something special between these two even if they didn't know it yet.

"Only if I can have her back within the half-hour," Grant instructed. "I know you'll try to monopolize her all night." Usually when Grant came with Dotia, Hal and Dotia spent hours together. He couldn't figure out why Hal hadn't just broke down and asked Dotia out.

Hal, pleased with his conquest, tugged gently at Emily's hand. "Come on, it will be fun," he chuckled.

"I'm not very good, but if you don't mind, I'll give it honest effort," Emily offered.

Almost an hour passed as Hal and Emily danced. Grant strolled up and tapped Hal on the shoulder. "Hal you don't mind if I cut in now? You're past your allotment."

Emily felt Grant's hand on her shoulder. "Emily, would you give me the honor?" He slid his hand down her arm and smoothly stole her hand out of Hal's. Then, he cleverly twirled her into his arms.

"Thank you Hal for the dances," she called back as Grant swept her away.

He warned as he pulled her closer, "I'm not as good at dancing as I noticed you are, and frankly I would not want to dance with myself, but I can't face the disapproving look Dotia will give me if we don't dance most of the night together. Plus, someone had to rescue you from Hal. I think he has a thing for Dotia, but for some reason those two have never gotten together."

Emily nodded glad that Grant wasn't being too quiet. It always made her nervous when someone was real quiet.

"Maybe you should set them up," Emily suggested.

"Naw, that's not something I want to step in. I'll leave that to someone else." He looked down into her eyes as he grinned hinting to her that she could be that 'someone else' matchmaker.

Grant had the most beautiful dark blue eyes she had ever seen. She really hoped this would not be their only date. It was so hard to find a great guy; one who was real, possibly even wanting a friendship or relationship, not just a fly-by-nighter. So many guys had abusive control issues or other hang ups.

Could she dare to trust her feelings? There couldn't be any truth to love at first sight or the thing that Mary always said about you'll know the one for you when you meet him. But something was there; she couldn't deny it as hard as she tried to push it from her mind. Anyways, she told herself, "It is will be okay, cause such a wonderful person, like Dotia wouldn't steer me wrong. So, it will be okay, even if my mind's playing tricks on me."

Her mind continued to race, "Grant had practically been raised by that kindly old woman. Hopefully, he really is this great and it was not just a show." "But," she worried, "there must be something wrong with him if he wasn't taken or married by now." Arguing against herself, she thought, "Of course cops don't make much money, so maybe that's it..."

Her mind quieted as the dancing began to distract her. The night was flying by. Emily was having so much fun. This was amazing. For so long all she had done was study. She hoped Grant was having as much fun, too.

"Attention!" a voice over the loud speaker called, as the music faded to a hush. "Hate to call it a night, but the midnight clock is about to strike. It's time to announce this year's couple of the dance before we end."

Everyone drew closer to the make shift stage where the announcer stood. "This year's tally has selected couple number 13 as Dance Royalty."

"We're 13! We're 13!" a very cute elderly lady gleefully

squealed.

Everyone turned to view the lady who was ecstatically waving her arms up in the air. She was standing very close to an elderly man with a 13 on his shirt. He just smiled contently. The crowd cheered her exhilaration.

The aged couple slowly made their way up towards the front of the stage to accept the gift. Then, the letters were drawn. "AA and D are this year's single match," called the announcer.

A tall skinny man and a short plump female approached to collect the prize. The two looked at each other with surprise. Although the crowd gayfully applauded, it didn't appear like this year's random choice would end in a love connection.

As the music restarted, the clock struck midnight. Confetti exploded into the air and the announcer cut in once more, "Well folks, midnight is here and time for all the Prince Charmings and Cinderellas to say farewell till next year... wishing you all a good night and God Bless."

At that, everyone, including Grant and Emily headed out.

Chapter 15

Lively or not?

The drive to Emily's apartment was quick and quiet. The apartment was only a few blocks from the Community Center. Emily wasn't sure what to say, so she decided to let Grant initiate any conversation. Emily didn't want to talk just to break the silence filling the truck. After all, it is often said that women generally talk too much, so guys just tune them out or get annoyed. The silence was actually very peaceful. She was content just to be with Grant.

The truck pulled up to the front of the apartment. Grant opened his door and walked around to Emily's side. Emily was already sliding out by the time he arrived. He gently grabbed her arm with one hand and her waist with the other bringing her close to him. Without thinking, he was drawn forward, his lips towards hers. Emily's heart pounded, all thought diminished. The warmth of Grant next to her, his scent,....

A car horn sounded. Balammmm Balammmm. The entangled couple flinched before the kiss could connect. "Okay, you two break it up," a man's voice commanded.

Grant and Emily turned to see Brad coming around the side of the truck where they were standing.

Emily confused questioned, "Brad, what are you doing here so late? I thought you had to work tomorrow?"

"Well, I couldn't get Ria on the phone, so I thought I'd

better see what was up," He continued. "We always catch up after I get off work."

Squinting her eyes as she wondered why Ria had not answered her phone, Emily volunteered, "Maybe, her cell is dead again and she can't find it." Then realizing that Brad didn't know Grant she added, "Oh, Brad, so sorry, this is Grant, my date. Grant this is Brad my roommate Ria's boyfriend. Well, let's check on Ria."

Emily was glad to have the company of two guys to walk her into her apartment. With that serial killer still at large, it was discomforting to be out alone, especially at night.

The three walked up the stairs and entered the apartment. The TV was on, but there was no sign of Ria. Jacque ran up and rubbed forcefully against Emily's legs. "Meoooow," he cried. Emily scooped him up in her arms.

"Ria, I'm home and I have company," Emily called out as loud as she could. There was no answer. "Ria, Ria, are you awake?" she shouted with so much force that her voice echoed in through the apartment. Ria was not that deep of a sleeper. Emily sat Jacque down on the chair and proceeded back towards Ria's bedroom. Jacque jumped out of the chair and ran down the hallway. "Meoow," he called.

The hallway was dark. No light crept out from the cracks around either door jam. The bedroom lights must be off, Emily thought as she tried to focus her eyes in the blackness.

Grant put his hand on Emily's shoulder and pulled her back. He held a finger up to his lips signaling for her not to make any noise. He motioned for Brad to stay put in the living room. Emily leaned forward and whispered in his ear that Ria's room was the left door.

Out of a concealed holster strapped to his calf, Grant retrieved his gun. Gun in hand, Grant cautiously inched down the hall. Emily was surprised about the gun. "Did he always carry a gun?" she wondered. Regardless, she was glad he had one now.

Reaching Ria's door, Grant slowly turned the handle. It was unlocked. With swift motion, he pushed the door open, flipped on the light switch, and spun back into the hallway out of view from any possible intruder lurking in Ria's room. No noise emitted from the room. It was eerily silent. Jacque ran past Grant and across the room jumping up on the bed. He sniffed Ria still body, then meowed.

Strategically, Grant peered around the door jamb into the room. Ria was sprawled across the bed. Faint chest movements indicated she was breathing. She was alive, but either deep in sleep or unconscious. With his instincts heightened, Grant investigated the room. First, the closet and then under the bed. No one. Everything looked in place. No signs of a struggle, either. Jacque had settled down at Ria's feet as though he was waiting for the people to do something.

"Emily, it's okay. You can come in." Grant beckoned to her. Grant put his fingertips on Ria's wrist checking her pulse. It was weak and slightly erratic. The coloration of her lips looked normal, as did her fingers tips. He checked her arms. No signs of drug use.

Upon entering the room, Emily broke into a run, racing over to her friend. "Ria!" Emily cried. "Grant what's wrong with her? Why is she so still?" Emily clutched Ria's hand.

Brad rounded the doorway and stood frozen. He wasn't sure what to do. Had it been a total stranger lying there, his mind would be able to work. But, it was Ria!

Grant shook his head as he dialed 911. "I'm not sure what's wrong. Ria isn't diabetic, is she? Or, on any medications. Has she ever taken any drugs in the past?"

Emily interrupted, "She would never do drugs! She's never sick either!" Her disconcerted tone didn't unnerve Grant as she continued, "Her mom was a drug addict, Ria pledged to never do drugs."

"Emily, I'm just doing my job. I'm not implying anything, just trying to gather facts." He knew he wouldn't get much out of the sobbing girl. Tears streamed down her patchy red face. Grant glanced around for tissue paper. A box of them sat on the dresser. He snatched a few up and handed them to Emily.

Emily wiped her face and blew her nose. She was angry with Grant for asking such a horrible question. It didn't matter if that was what cops normally did. He should know that *her* best friend wouldn't do those types of things.

"Brad, when did you last see Ria?" Before Brad could answer, Grant put his hand up signaling him to wait a second before replying. Speaking into his cell Grant stated, "Yes, this is Officer Grant Rawlins. I need an ambulance at New Haven apartments 2901 Rose Way, Apt 613. I have a Caucasian female, approximate age 23 years old, found unconscious in her bedroom. No apparent signs of drug use or history of drug use. No history of medical problems. She's likely been unconscious for several hours. Heartbeat is faint and breathing is shallow. Skin color slightly pale."

Emily had regained control of her emotions. She reached over and soothingly stroked Ria's hair. "Ria."

Glancing down, Emily noticed something reddish-brown on Ria's neck. She delicately turned Ria's neck to get a better look at the area. It looked like dried blood on Ria's neck. Had Ria hurt herself?

"Grant, Ria has something on her neck," Emily continued, "I'm going to grab a disinfectant wipe."

As she started out of the room, Grant called to her, "it

would be better to use a clean paper towel and then put it is a plastic bag. You never know what lab results can find if we are careful with any findings."

"I wouldn't have thought of that. Okay, I'll grab some." She ran out of the room and returned with the supplies within seconds.

Upon entering back into the room, she rebuked herself for being so selfish. She had only thought of this as her and Ria's tragedy. But seeing Brad sitting on the bed at Ria's side, gently holding her hand, staring at her motionless face, made Emily realize that she wasn't the only special person in Ria's life.

Emily handed the paper towels to Grant. Grant swiped the spot firmly and then dropped the evidence into the plastic baggy Emily was holding open. After sealing the baggy, she handed him the disinfectant wipes. He took a wipe and gently cleaned the area. Thin blood oozed out of two evenly placed marks on her carotid artery. It looked like puncture marks.

"How did Ria hurt herself way up there? Why are the marks oozing at the slightest touch?" Grant commented.

The trio stared at the odd revelation.

"Looks like something bit her. But, those marks are far too wide for a bug or spider. Couldn't be a snake, could it? I hate snakes," Brad remarked.

"This is too weird," Emily shivered. "But, wouldn't a snake have bit her on the hand or foot... not the neck."

Brad glanced nervously under the bed and then around the room. "Hey, what are those scratch marks on the door?" He pointed to the hall side of Ria's door. The door was clawed up as though something had been trying to get in.

Grant picked up Jacque's front paw. There were white wooden splinters stuck to matted bloody fur. It looked like Jacque had scratched so hard to get in that his claws had bled.

"I'm not sure what happened here. I wish Jacque could tell us." Grant said patting the furry creature affectionately.

"You don't think that cat bit her?" Brad looked maliciously at Jacque. "Could Ria gotten sick from a cat bite? Maybe he has some kind of disease."

"No, this isn't a cat bite. Plus, I've never heard of someone having this kind of reaction to a cat bite. Whatever happened, Jacque is not the cause," Grant reassured. He ran his fingers through the cat's fur. "I don't see any bite marks on him. If it was a snake, he would have gone after it and probably caught it. If it had been a rat, he would have definitely caught it. He's one of Dotia's best hunters." Grant patted Jacque again on his head before walking over to examine the door.

"Looks more like the door was shut tight and for some reason Jacque was trying to get in. Maybe he sensed something was wrong." Grant looked at the cat wishing he could read Jacque's mind.

A knock sounded on the front door. Grant rushed to greet paramedics. He quickly led them into Ria's room. The EMT's worked quickly moving Ria into a gurney and then carried her off with Brad, Emily and Grant following. After Ria was loaded into the ambulance, the trio watched as the red flashing lights headed out of the parking lot.

"Emily, there's nothing more you can do tonight. Do you have someone you can call to come stay with you, or somewhere you want to go?" Grant questioned.

"No, I'll be fine staying here by myself." She didn't want to let on that she didn't have anywhere to go and no one to turn to.

"Are you sure?" Grant asked.

"Yes. But, could you please help me recheck the apartment? I got to admit, I'm still a bit shaken," Emily confessed.

"Sure, I'll walk you up to the apartment and check it out again. I'd like to get a look at the windows and dust for prints. I have a kit in my truck," Grant reassured.

Grant glanced over to Brad. Brad's overly calm demeanor worried Grant. Sometimes things like this could make a person go into shock. "Brad, how are you holding up? Emily, do you have some hot tea or coffee that Brad and I could get a cup of?" He figured it would be wise to keep an eye on Brad for a few more minutes.

"Sure, we have regular or herbal tea, plus regular Columbian Coffee," Emily caught herself before she blurted out 'pick your poison'. "Wow," she thought. Then her knees went weak. She felt the embrace of warm muscular arms, as her mind lost all awareness.

Grant had caught Emily's swooning body just in time. He swung her up in his arms and headed towards the apartment. "Well, guess you and I will have to make our own coffee."

Brad laughed. At least, for a second, humor had stolen the sting of tragedy away.

Grant laid Emily on the couch. He grabbed a blanket from her bedroom closet and spread it over her.

"Brad, if you put the brew on, I'll grab my stuff from the truck," Grant volunteered.

"Sure." Brad made his way to the kitchen.

When Grant returned, Brad was in the kitchen pouring two cups of coffee. "There's cream and sugar in here."

"Thanks. I'll grab it as soon as I take some pictures of the room and dust for prints. I don't see anything that would lead me to believe anyone was in here, but its best to gather what you can in any situation," Grant explained causally. He tried not to think about how he would feel if that had been Emily.

He walked over to the sleeping beauty and felt her pulse. "She's still okay. Her pulse is good. I think we should let her rest."

Brad nodded. He settled into the oversized living room chair with his coffee as Grant began his investigation.

After a few seconds, Brad glanced at his watch. "Guess I'd better stay here tonight, since it's so late. I live about sixty miles away. It's a bad drive... when I'm not tired," Brad called out to Grant. He sat his cup down and pulled out his cell phone to set the clock alarm.

"Good idea. It'll be good for Emily to have someone here," Grant called out.

A few minutes later when Grant appeared back in the living room, he found two sound asleep bodies. Jacque had curled up protectively on Emily's abdomen. Grant silently finished his investigation. Then, he rinsed out his and Brad's coffee cups. Heading towards to door to leave, he altered his course and returned to Emily's side. He leaned down and kissed her forehead.

"I know, you're a good cat, boy. I'm counting on you to keep an eye on her," Grant whispered as he gently patted the cat's enormous head.

Grant strolled over to the door. As he stepped outside, he double checked to make sure the knob was locked behind him. As he descended the stairway, something caught his eye.

"The rose bush," he murmured. He headed down the stairs and disappeared into the night.

******

When Emily awoke, she was flat on the couch with Jacque on her stomach. Everything was a bit fuzzy. Detecting someone over in the chair, she flinched. It was only Brad sitting up, asleep. The clock on the wall displayed the little hand at three and the big hand around the five. 3:24 am.

The last thing she remembered was standing in the parking lot talking to Grant and Brad. She must have fainted. That had never happened to her before. *How embarrassing.*

But she was glad to see Brad over in the chair and Jacque sitting on her. Waking up alone would have been alarming. Jacque purred as Emily subconsciously petted his back. The feline humming was so soothing. Her weary eyes closed again and once more Emily's mind was void of thought.

Chapter 16

Are You Mad?

Brad awoke. His neck was cramped from sleeping upright all night in the chair. Trying to ease the pain, he stretched his neck around. Emily wasn't on the couch. Hearing the shower water running, he figured that's where she was. He hoped she was okay, 'cause he didn't want to have to go in there. That would be awkward, he thought. He wished Ria was here.

Images of Ria's still body flashed in to his mind. He clasped his cell phone attached to his belt. It wouldn't do him any good to call the hospital again. He had called last night, but since he wasn't family they wouldn't tell him anything.

It was a good thing that Grant had called to check on Emily. Or, Brad wouldn't have had any news of how Ria was doing. He guessed being a police officer had more perks than he had considered.

At least Ria was stable. But, the doctors weren't sure what was wrong. A coma-like state... she had always been healthy. Brad couldn't figure out what happened. Earlier that day, Ria had been fine. She and Emily had gotten Emily ready and off to the dance. Then, Ria called and told him she was going to work on some homework. Everything sounded fine. Had he missed something in her voice?

So busy in thought, he hadn't noticed that the shower water had stopped. Emily bounced into the room shrouded in a thick bathrobe, her long hair wrapped in a swami turban.

"Brad, I made coffee before I jumped in the shower. I'll get you a cup. How do you take it?" Emily offered, heading into the kitchen.

"One sugar and two creams. Glad to see you're feeling better," Brad replied. He glanced at his watch; it was almost 11:00 am.

Emily interjected, "Yes, I feel much better. I am so embarrassed though about fainting."

"Don't be. After what happened.... That's a natural reaction," he offered trying to make her feel better.

"Speaking of Ria, I checked my cell when I woke up. Grant left a message that she's still stable, but in a deep sleep of some kind. He said something about ... he dusted in her room for prints, but nothing panned out. It's like there is no explanation of what happened. The doctor said the marks on her neck were probably a bug bite and nothing to worry about. They said it wasn't connected."

"Thanks. I called the hospital last night, but they wouldn't tell anything. Boyfriends aren't family. Good thing Grant is a police officer, he was able to at least tell me she was stable," Brad reported.

Emily traipsed into the living room with a cup of coffee in each hand. She handed Brad the one made for him. "Here ya go."

Balancing her filled cup, she sat down on the couch. The aroma of the coffee was relaxing, but energizing. Sipping the creamy ambrosia, she wondered about Ria's comatose mind? Would it be like sleeping? Or, would it be like having a nightmare that you couldn't wake up from?

Her eyes watered up. She fought hard to keep the tears back. Crying wouldn't help right now. She had to get to her 2:00 pm class and then visit Dotia later. Why did, when something wonderful happen, tragedy always follow? Last night with Grant had been magically, until... She downed the rest of her coffee trying to chase away the overwhelming sadness.

"Brad, thanks for staying. It was very comforting to wake up and see you over in the chair. Sorry again." she confessed.

"It's okay. Just promise to keep me updated on Ria."

"Will do. Well, I've got to get dressed and make it to my 2 o'clock class. Then, I've got to visit Dotia," Emily said as she rose from the couch. "You are welcome to stay here." Emily took her cup into the kitchen and placed it in the sink.

"I've got to get home and get ready for work," he replied. "But if you need anything, let me know. I can come back over." Brad took his cup into the kitchen also.

"Thanks. I'll be okay though," Emily gave him a quick hug and then headed down the hall to her room. She didn't want to admit how afraid she really was. It was best to just stay busy and not think. She heard the front door open.

"Bye Emily. I'll lock the door behind me. Remember, I'm only a phone call away," he called out.

The door thudded shut. Emily felt very alone. Something warm and soft brushed against her leg. "Oh Jacque, I'm so glad you're here with me. I'm scared for Ria," she admitted.

"Meoow," Jacque responded.

She felt his soft purring as he pushed into her calf again. Emily bent down and picked him up. Gently squeezing him, she rubbed her face into his soft coat.

"You're so sweet." She kissed his head and sat him on

her bed. "Gotta go, though, so you be good. I'll be home later."

Locking the apartment door behind her, she glanced around at the revealing daylight. Everything was strangely silent, Emily noticed. It set her a little on edge. She paused on the stairway outside the apartment and listened more intently. That's what was off. No chirping birds. Maybe it was the warm air, she thought. Glancing around, her attention was drawn to the Blood rose bush. It was more captivating than ever.

A car horn sounded startling Emily. Her feet resumed down the stairs. Loud arguing voices drifted up from the parking lot. Instinctively, Emily reached in her purse and clutched her cell. Every since Pontiac Guy, caution took precedence.

"Get the hell out of my way!" roared a male voice. "What the hell are you trying to do? Creep!"

Emily rounded the building's corner. Two men were grappling in the parking lot. The taller man was pushing away the second man. It looked like the second man was trying to bite the taller man. The biter's eyes held a dazed look and he was laughing oddly. His hair was uncombed; his clothes dirty and disheveled.

The biter knocked the taller man to the ground. Taller man pounded Biter with his fists. The hard smacks didn't seem to have any effect. Biter continued trying to sink his teeth into the Taller man.

Frighten, Emily tapped her cell to call Grant.

"Yes Grant, I'm outside my apartment and two men are fist fighting. I think one may be stoned on some kind of drugs. He's acting really weird. He's trying to bite the other man." She paused to listen to him.

"I just walked down the stairs and they were out here in the parking lot shoving each other ..... Yes, I'm staying back away from them.... Okay, I'll wait here out of the way till you get here. Thanks Grant."

As Emily click off the phone, she felt strange calling him because she needed a police officer. He was going to think trouble was always finding her. "First Ria, and now this. If he hears about Pontiac Guy, he'll think I have a black shadow. Always bad luck," she murmured.

Taller man raced past her. She had been so deep in thought that she had forgot to keep an eye on the brawling pair. Instinctively, she ducked behind one of the cars. If crazy biter caught sight of her, he might decide she was an easier target. Grant's police car pulled up.

She glanced over the car's roof. Biter was still on the ground thrashing around like a demon-possessed actor in a movie. "Good thing he's still here or Grant might have thought I was crazy.. making stuff up, or something," she breathed.

She sprinted over to the police car. As Grant got out of the car, she felt her cheeks grow warm. Her heart fluttered. "He's too handsome! That dark blue uniform really looks good on him," her mind whispered. Then she thought, "Please don't let me faint again!" She tried not to stare at him. "Act natural," she told herself.

Grant strode towards her. She tried not to smile, but she couldn't help it. Inconspicuously, she reached down and pinched herself hard to counteract her irrepressible smile. She wanted to at least look disinterested if she couldn't muster solemn. Trying to sound official, she stated, "The guy rolling around on the grass was trying to bite the other guy. The other guy took off." She pointed over to the left at the mad hatter.

"Back up should arrive in a moment. Stay put. I'll go check it out," Grant ordered. When he was on duty, his demeanor was always professional and he always maintained a level head. After all, if he wasn't careful, a perp could get away or worse someone could get hurt or die.

Staying by the police car, Emily watched him stride over to the biter man. Grant held her attention so intently, that she didn't notice that Biter was foaming at the mouth.

Grant clicked his radio "Need an ambulance at New Haven apartments 2901 Rose Way outside on the front lawn. We have a Caucasian male, approximate age mid-thirties, lying unconscious in fetal position, foaming at the mouth. Eye-witness stated the man was acting extremely aggressive and bizarre few moments ago. I'm going to try to take vitals. I'll radio back in a sec. Over and Out." He placed his radio bank in its holder and took a deep breath.

Cautiously, he reached down, placed his fingers on the guy's wrist to check the pulse rate. It was racing wildly. "Can you hear me? I'm here to help. I'm Officer Rawlins."

Biter didn't respond.

"Could be some kind of shock or maybe drug use," Grant said out loud. Having completed a Drug Evaluation program, Grant had been trained in drug use recognition. He lifted one of the guy's eyelids. The eyeballs were jerking radically and the pupils were constricted to tiny black pinpoints. Biter's short-sleeved shirt made it easy for Grant to inspect for needle marks. None. But there were puncture wounds on his hand, slightly down from the thumb on the soft side of the palm. He'd never hear of anyone using intravenous drugs in that location. Maybe, an animal bite? He'd have to remember to show it to the paramedics.

While Grant was occupied checking Biter's vitals, his backup, Bill and Dan arrived. Dan sat in the car fumbling with some papers. Bill, favoring his back, crawled out his open door. The prior night's dance had been a little too much exuberance for him.

"Not as young as I used to be. Next time remind me not to dance so much," Bill told Dan.

"Next time don't drink so much. All it takes is a fewwww drinks and everybody thinks they're super human. Next day, ya wake up and realize while you were superhuman.... you're muscles weren't!" Dan lectured.

Each of Bill's muscles screamed in resentment as he moved. Hobbling over to the eyewitness, Bill gestured a salute-hello to Grant.

She looked very familiar. Then, it dawned on him. "Say... weren't you the girl at the dance with Grant?" Bill asked.

"Yes," Emily blushed. "I live here. I was on my way to school, when I saw two men arguing. I called Grant, cause I wasn't sure what to do."

"Well, you did right. No telling about situations now days. So, what did you see?" Bill investigated.

"I was coming down the stairs and heard loud arguing. One man was telling the other to get away. The guy, over there on the grass, was attacking a taller man... the one who was saying 'get away'..." Emily continued her story to Bill as he wrote it down.

An ambulance pulled up. The ambulance ETs jumped out, gathered a gurney and proceeded over to Biter. While strapping Biter into the gurney, one of the ETs griped to Grant, "This is the third time today we've had to come out here. Peculiar things are going on. Early this morning, it was a hysterical woman. She was rambling on about monsters and demons. A few hours later, apartment security called. One of the tenants hadn't paid rent last month and hadn't responded to the landlord's phone calls. Security unlocked his door... found the poor sap dead with hundreds of small puncture wounds all over his body. The guy didn't have any blood left. Don't know what's going on... could be a viral epidemic or maybe some weird chemical in the drinking water, or ....? Anyways, don't drink the water and in case it's contagious take precautions not to catch whatever it is."

Grant nodded. "Definitely odd."

Carrying Biter on the gurney, the ET's trotted back to the ambulance. Grant retreated back over to Emily, Bill, and Dan. Since everything seemed under control, Dan had decided it was safe to get out and join in the conversation between Emily and Bill.

"Not, sure what's going on, but the ET said he was out here twice before this. One was a hysterical woman seeing monsters and demons. Another was a dead guy found in his apartment. Emily you need to stay somewhere else till this is figured out," Grant instructed.

Bill rubbed his head puzzled, "Well it isn't just here, Grant. Got a call while driving here. All over town people have been getting sick, acting weird.... The hospital almost to capacity. Going have to start sending people over to Taylorsville if this keeps up."

Emily's eyes got wide. This was like something out of a movie, not real life. Considering the circumstances, Bill and Grant seemed usually calm. But, Dan shifted around nervously like a child who had done something wrong.

Grant stated, "These occurrences must be related somehow." Then remembering what the ET had said he asked, "Do you think it's something in the water? Better only drink bottled water till we know what's the cause."

Everybody nodded. At least drinking bottled water was something they could do. Not knowing what they were up against gave each of them an unsettled feeling.

"Well, I've missed my class, so I guess I'll head off to Dotia's for a few hours," Emily said.

"Oh you know Dotia too?" Bill asked. Now I get it, he thought. He had wondered how Grant had scored a date with this lovely young lady. He wasn't one to pry, but curiosity got the better of him.

"Yes, I met her as a result of a class project I'm doing. She's a wonderful lady and so fascinating."

Bill mumbled under his breath, "You don't know the half of it."

"What? I'm sorry I didn't hear what you said," Emily politely stated.

"Oh, just said, yes, you are very fortunate. Dotia is a rare bird... very special, magical in her way." Bill smiled trying to convey that he meant no disrespect; he truly admired the old gal. It was just that people needed to be cautious around her. He was convinced there was magic around her, but he would never say such a crazy thing out loud.

"Best be off. Come on Dan. Nice to meet you Emily. Be careful about dating this boy here. He's a good boy on the outside, but on the inside a red blooded male animal..." Bill winked at Emily then added, "See you later, Grant."

Dan sniggered. He walked over to the police car. Right before he got in, he shouted to Emily, "If Grant doesn't treat you right, you just call me. I'll take you out on a real date."

"Dan, it's not a real date having a lady over to clean your house," Grant chided loudly.

Emily giggled.

"Do you want a ride to Dotia's?" Grant asked. "I'm headed that way. I usually check on her about this time of day."

"Well, I have the car Ria and I share...."

"It's settled then," he said ignoring her excuse, "I'll take you over and check on Dotia. Then, I'll run home, change, and be back over to Dotia's to pick you up to take you back here later." A satisfied grin spread across face as he pulled gently on her arm, leading her to his car.

"Okay, but only if it's not too much bother." Secretly, she was thrilled to be going over with Grant. Being shy, she wasn't sure how to flirt or capture a man's heart. Good thing she did have to resort to any feminine charms 'cause she wasn't sure how it was done.

Chapter 17

Visiting

Sitting in Dotia's kitchen, Emily sipped her herbal tea. Across the room, Dotia was taking cookies out of the oven.

"All done," she chuckled stacking them on a platter.

"They smell delicious." Emily's mouth watered. It had only taken a few minutes for Dotia and her to mix up the batch of Dotia's family recipe, oatmeal chocolate chips. This was so nice, warm and comforting, making cookies with a .... *Mom.* That was it, Dotia made Emily feel like her daughter. For just a second, there was a pang of sadness. She had never made cookies with her mom.

Dotia brought a plate of the warm cookies over to the table. She motioned for Emily to take some. Emily picked up two and placed them on her plate.

"What really goes good with these is milk.... Emily, how about a cool glass of milk?"

"That sounds wonderful!" To Emily, milk was a creamy white nectar. She loved dairy foods. Ice cream, cheese, cream cheese, sour cream.. yes, sour cream was a favorite food. She smiled remembering Mary once said that sour cream was not a food, but a condiment.

Dotia stepped out of the room in a brisk fashion. Emily wondered if something was wrong. Emily didn't have to wonder for long. The bustling little woman flew back into the room carrying something enclosed in her right hand.

"I've grown tremendously fond of you. And so, I have something for you. It's been in my family for years. I'd like you to wear it for good luck," Dotia smiled lovingly. She held her palm out to reveal a delicate gold chain necklace with an amulet on it.

"Oh, it is gorgeous. But I couldn't accept such a precious keepsake. I mean what would happen if I broke it or something. I would feel terrible."

"I insist. With all this commotion, it would make me feel better." She laid it down on the table in front of Emily.

Emily gingerly lifted it up. Admiringly, she examined it.

"You're not allergic to gold are you? Both the chain and the amulet are 14 karat gold. Let me show you how it opens." Dotia held her hand open.

"Okay," Emily laid it in Dotia's palm.

"Lift this tiny latch and then press this button," Dotia demonstrated. The tiny door swung opened. Inside was a strange mat of what looked like dried mashed up tea leaves.

"It's not hard to open once you learn how. The herbs inside ward off evil. They smell good too."

"This amulet looks awfully familiar," Emily absently stated.

"Oh, it's probably because Grant has one around his neck. But his is on a leather strand. He's not one to wear jewelry. Leather was the only way I could get him to wear it." Dotia laughed with delight. "Over the years, looking after Grant has been too much fun. I'm fortunate he's been in my life. Everyone needs the energy and excitement of youth around to keep things fresh."

******

By the time Grant arrived, Dotia and Emily were preparing dinner. Dotia had pinned Emily's braided hair up to keep it from becoming part of the meal. The amulet, latched securely around Emily's neck flashed brightly as she busied about the tasks Dotia had laid out for her.

"Oh, she got you too...," Grant congenially mocked pointing towards Emily's trinket. "Did she tell you it will cure anything wrong with you, destroy demons, and perform miracles?"

To see the amulet on Emily's neck gave him of feeling of relief. That meant Dotia really liked her. He liked her too, maybe too much. It had been hard for him to concentrate at work. Tasks had to be redone because of simple mistakes. Her scent, her scent lingered in his mind. He had never thought about any girl this much before.

Dotia's voice broke into his thoughts, "Grant, instead of distracting my excellent help, please grab some dishes and help set the table. Everything's almost ready," She knew he was pleased to see the amulet on Emily.

Grant grabbed some silverware, plates, and glasses, and began setting the table while watching Emily out of the corner of his eye. He couldn't help it. They way her waist angled in and ...... he chided himself for not being a gentleman. A hand towel swatted him lightly on the shoulder. "Pay attention to where you're setting those," Dotia nagged warmheartedly.

He looked down. Each glass was on top of the corresponding plate, instead of beside it, and the silverware was all over the place. Quickly, Grant reset the table. Trying to save grace he off-handedly mentioned, "Guess I need more practice, eating alone a lot makes you forget proper things."

Dotia set the potholders on the tabletop, followed by Grant placing a pot from the stove onto each. Emily slid warm dinner rolls off a thin oven sheet into a bread basket laced with cloth. She centered her bounty on the table. Surrounding it were green beans, mashed potatoes, roast beef and a large pitcher of tea.

"Dotia, is there anything else I should get?" Emily asked.

"Let's see, drinks, food, bread, butter, salt, pepper... oh...could you grab a few napkins from over in that cupboard?" She pointed to a tall thin upright cabinet in the corner. "I think we're ready." Happiness beamed through her spontaneous smile.

"Dotia, after grace can I turn the news on for a sec while we eat.... After all, it's not healthy to talk and chew food at the same time." Grant figured Dotia might concede if he offered rationale with his request. He wanted to get an update as to what was going on around town. The town was small, but it had its own news channel. With all the strange occurrences, he needed to know what was being said.

"Okay Grant, I'll concede this once... but only since strange things are going on." Dotia had heard the stories on the afternoon news. She too was curious about the latest development.

The trio folded hands and bowed heads. Dotia chanted a Prayer.

"Miro gulo Devel, savo hal oté ando Cheros,
te avel swuntunos tiro nav;
te avel catari tiro tem;
te keren saro so cames oppo puv,
sar ando Cheros.
Dé man sekhonus miro diveskoe manro,
ta ierta mangue saro so na he plaskerava tuke,
sar me ierstavava wafo manuschengue saro so na
plaskerelen mangue.
Ma muk te petrow ando chungalo camoben;

tama lel man abri saro doschdar.
Weika tiro sin o tem,
tiri yi potea,
tiri yi proslava akana ta sekovar."

"Okay, now, we can eat," Dotia declared.

Emily raised her head and unfolded her hands. She noticed that Grant was already up and moving towards the small TV over on the counter.

Emily commented, "Those were beautiful sounding words. What do they mean?"

"It's the Lord's Prayer in my father's tongue. In English it translates roughly to:

My sweet God, who art there in Heaven,
may thy name come hallowed;
may thy kingdom come hither;
may they do all that thou wishest upon earth, as in
Heaven.
Give me to-day my daily bread,
and forgive me all that I cannot pay thee,
as I shall forgive other men all that they do not pay
me.
Do not let me fall into evil desire;
but take me out from all wickedness.
For thine is the kingdom, thine the power,
thine the glory now and ever.

Grant turned the TV channel to the local news station. "Is that okay or too loud?" Grant asked raising the volume.

"It's good," Dotia smiled.

Emily nodded. She was more interested in not spilling her food. It was always embarrassing to spill something. Maybe people should just go around and spill things all the time, then it would never be embarrassing. The thought made her giggle inside. Life was too full of worry... worry about what people think about what you wear, worry about what people think about what you say or do... worry about having enough money, worry about health, worry about accidents, worry about crime...

Fortunately before she depressed herself further, the news announcer's deep male voice interrupted, "The update on the strange wave of afflictions to recently hit our quaint town does not offer much in solutions. So far, about 25 people have exhibited bizarre behavior or fallen ill to an unknown culprit. Three unrelated people have been found dead in different locations; the police have not disclosed much information on those deaths. They cite the investigation is ongoing and that they will release information when it is conclusive. However, sources revealed to us, that in each case, the deceased individuals were found with multiple small puncture wounds, and the bodies' blood level was minimal. Ginger what do you think about this?"

The second announcer, a manicured very nice-looking lady turned and stated, "Well, Bob since you asked... Bloodless? It sounds like vampires have invaded our little paradise. Let's see what Dale has to say. He's on location, where a group of 'Believers' have gathered, at the site where once stood the infamous Windel mansion. Dale?"

"That's right, Ginger and Bob. I'm here on location of the former Windel Mansion site, where two of the victims who died were residing, and 12 individuals were found either ill or exhibiting bizarre behavior. As you can see behind me, a group of people calling themselves 'Believers' have gathered. Let's go see what they have to say."

Dale strode over to some of the group who were standing up holding signs. One sign read, "The Dark Lord is here! Join Him and Live Forever!" Another sign stated, "Vampires are not a Myth. Believe or Die!" A

third sign, "Windel Vindication! They have returned!"
Another only had in large letters, "Choose me!"

The majority of the Believers were appareled in Goth
fashion, dark make-up, black clothing. Black, red, purple,
blue, or a mixture of those shades dominated the
unnatural hair styles of the members. Several flaunted
elaborate tattoos featuring sculls, demons, and vampires.

"I'm here from News Channel 5 to get your opinion on
what's happening," Dale stuck the microphone next to one
of the men's mouth.

The man was only too ecstatic to have a moment of
stardom. He began to elucidate, "Hi I'm Trendor. The
dark ones have been around forever, living among us.
Most of the time, we don't notice. But, I'd say tearing
down the Windel mansion, their resting place, forced
them into action. They had no choice."

Dale briskly moved the mic back to himself, "Are you
saying the Windels were vampires and the old house was
where they were resting? How come we didn't know
about them before?"

Trendor snatched the mic away from Dale. Dale was
startled and somewhat frightened by Trendor's sudden
aggressive actions. Being the ham that he was, Dale
reached forward to regain his treasure. His hand received
a harsh, stinging pop from Trendor, which led Dale to
decide that it might be wiser to let Trendor hold it for a
few seconds till he could think of an alternate plan. Dale
had never been very brave.

Pleased with his triumph over the fancy dressed man,
Trendor's lips curved up in a perverted manner. "Resting
vampires only feed a little now and then. Usually there
are enough women who give themselves over willingly, so
no one dies. Women throw themselves at Vampires and
fletchings, like me. I mean, look at me, who wouldn't
want this?"

Trendor was so busy exalting himself that he didn't notice a guy walk up and hand Dale a second microphone. With the backup mic, securely in his grasp, Dale made a cut signal towards the Van. Trendor's mic fell silent. Unaware that his voice was not being heard, he kept talking and talking.

The camera's view phased from Trendor to Dale. It followed Dale as he moved towards the far left side of the Goth group. A few women were perched on a blanket, spread over the grass.

"Well, that was exciting," Dale raised his eyebrows high on his forward in a slightly exaggerated mock surprise. "But now, let's hear from the ladies."

"Hi Ladies. Would you mind commenting on the current state of affairs here?" Dale leaned forward placing the mic about a foot from one of them. This time he was not going to take a chance on losing his lead. There wasn't a third mic in the van, and the first mic was still in the clutches of Trendor. Dale hoped the van driver would wrestle Trendor and retrieve the mic after they wrapped up the segment. After all, a reporter couldn't be seen scuffing with a weirdo.

The girl in front of the mic, puckered her lips and answered in a soft babyish drawling voice, "I'm no lady, and I don't know anything about state affairs." It may have sounded cute if she hadn't been covered in piercings, Goth attire, and brash, thick, dark-black eyeliner. The ragged lines on her face suggested she was a few years over thirty.

The scene in front of him distracted Dale. He didn't notice the vehicle entourage besieging the parking area far behind him. Newcomers popped out from various autos; cars, trucks, vans, and motorcycles.

In one group, each was dressed in a silky white robe, with a golden braided rope for a belt, and no shoes. A few of the guys had shaven heads. Strange multi-colored symbols and figures occupied the hairless area. From their vehicles, the white robed people pulled out cardboard signs on tall poles. Signs in hand, they headed towards the front of the apartment building, chanting unintelligible as they sauntered. The signs referenced aliens and doomsday.

A different faction was composed of a team of guys and gals dressed in military fatigues, armed with shotguns, canteens, flashlights, and walkie-talkies. One of the guys, probably a leader signaled hand signs to the others. Teams rapidly formed and began spreading out into multiple locations.

Out of the corner of his eye, Dale saw the white gown group making headway towards the building's front center. He spun around to investigate more fully. Only then did he become aware of the events unfolding.

"Well, Ginger and Bob, maybe this young lady... uhhmm, woman doesn't know the state of current affairs, because it changes minute by minute. Look around me as the camera spans the area. We have several new interesting additions to our populace." Dale paused as the camera panned out and presented the developments in real time. Then, the camera shot back into focus on Dale.

"The people in the white gowns over there are carrying signs that make it clear they believe aliens have something to do with our crisis." He pointed over to the white gown group's direction.

Then, gesturing towards one of the military units, he calmly stated, "I'm not sure about the people in military garbs. Those look like real guns, so I'd say it's time for me to get the heck out of here and let the police take over. Back to you." Dale smiled broadly into the camera and waited for its red light to signal he was off air. As soon as it lit, he shouted to his crew, "Wrap it up. Let's get the hell out of here. These people are loonies. Those are guns! Real Guns!"

Dale raced over to the van. Climbing in he asked one of the crew, who was busy packing up equipment, "Did someone grabbed the other mic from vampire nut? If not, the station can to take it out of my pay. It's not worth risking my life over. I have suits worth more than that mic anyway." Perspiration beaded on his thin lips as he waited for the rest of the van's crew to wrap things up.

******

Back on the TV screen, the station viewers had missed Dale's brave retreat. Instead, the screen had flipped back to Ginger and Bob. Ginger, delighted to be back in view batted her eyes as she crooned, "What will we do now, aliens, vampires, and vigilantes? We can always try locking our doors and windows to protect against vigilantes. And, I heard a few shops in town have stocked up on garlic and vampire repellants, but how do we defend against aliens?"

"Yes, Ginger that may prove difficult. It looks like the prompter is alerting us that an accident has just taken place on Highway 29. A semi ran out of control and crashed into several cars. The semi driver was found unconscious, maybe suffering from the same mysterious ailment of so many others here. A few drivers and passengers were hospitalized with minor injuries. Fortunately, no deaths have been reported."

"Thank you Bob for that update. It's the end of our broadcast for this evening, but catch us first thing in the morning for your update on what's happening now. Goodnight." Beaming at her viewing audience, Ginger's lips seeming proportionately larger than the rest of her face. Bob yielded a goodbye nod with a reserved grin, while Ginger tried to appear important by picking up a thin stack of papers in front of her. Holding the stack vertically, she tapped them on the desktop as if straightening important documents. When the camera's red light lit, she threw them down on the desk. "God, I didn't think Dale was ever going to shut up. What a ham."

Bob nodded, "I'm off to the bar to grab my evening nightcap. See you tomorrow."

******

Emily's eyes were wide. "I think that was my apartment complex, isn't it?" She looked with a perplexed expression at Grant.

"Yes." He finished his tea and poured himself more. He avoided eye contact lest his eyes confirmed he had other knowledge, darker knowledge of the place.

"So, that was where the Windel Mansion was at? I heard stories, but never went by it. At least, I don't think. What did it look like? What really happened there?" The intrigue sounded in Emily's voice. Remembering her manners, she turned slightly towards Dotia and sympathetically smiled smoothing her tone. "I'm so sorry; I didn't mean to ask too many questions. It's okay not to answer. I know things like this can be hard for people to talk about."

"Nonsense child," Dotia's gentle voice alleviated Emily's apprehension that she had offended her host. "Let me show you a few pictures I have. Let's pick up in here and we will move to the living room to reminisce."

All three arose from the table and began cleaning chores.

Gathering the plates and utensils, Grant quickly cleared the dishes from the table to the sink. "We'll have to take a rain check on reminiscing Dotia." He didn't want to scare Emily away. Dotia's pictures would reveal too much. Emily might not be ready to know the truth. "On the way to taking Emily home, I gotta stop by the hospital and check on some things."

"I see," Dotia relented as she placed some food storage containers on the table. "Maybe next time."

Selecting a reasonably sized container, Emily carefully scrapped the mashed potatoes into it and snapped its lid shut. "Definitely, we'll have to do it next time." She smiled. "It was nice sharing this evening like a family. Wish Ria could have been here too."

Thinking of Ria, she had an idea. "Grant, do you think I could sneak in to see Ria."

Grant smiled, "Got one better. I'll escort you to see her. Being an officer in a small town does have some privileges."

Chapter 18

As Some Will Have It

At the hospital the pair popped into Ria's room. Ria was unconscious, but stable. Emily hastened over and grasped Ria's hand. "Ria, I hope you hear me. I'm right here beside you. You've got to wake up soon. I miss you so much."

Grant felt like an intruder. "I'll leave you here for a few minutes and go check on a few things, okay?" He thought it might be better to give Emily some privacy with Ria.

"Yes, I'm sorry Grant. Yes, please, I mean, I don't want to hold you up from work. I'll be here when you get ready to leave. Thanks again for bringing me."

"Speaking of leaving, are you sure you want to stay at your apartment? Dotia has an extra room, if you'd like. After all, there are a lot of strange people hanging around there right now." Grant coaxed.

"I'll be fine. After all, since you are dropping me off, you could check out the apartment with me and make sure no one's inside." Emily blushed. It was slightly embarrassing to ask. But, she would feel much better entering the apartment with Grant by her side. She tried not to think too much about it. It *was* going to be hard to spend the night there alone without Ria since all these weird things were happening, but she couldn't to impose on Dotia. She looked up at Grant. It was clear he worked out. His shirt clung snug to his defined muscular arms.

At six foot tall with a medium build, he definitely wasn't a wimp. She felt much safer with him nearby.

"No problem. I'll be glad to check out the apartment and make sure it's all clear. Actually, I'd feel better about leaving you there if I checked it out first." Grant confided. He tried not to let the uneasiness show in his voice. There were some real crazy people showing up around the apartments, not to mention that no one had yet uncovered why all these people were sick or why two people had died. He knew it could be dangerous for Emily to be there alone.

"Thanks." Emily's face felt hot. It was terribly warm all of a sudden. Had she been staring at him? She diverted her eyes and pretending to be looking at something on the small table stand next to Ria's bed.

"Are you feeling okay? You're cheeks are pretty flushed." Grant moved over close to her and put his hand up to her forehead. Without thinking he lifted her up towards him, his embrace tightened, his lips neared hers. Emily wrapped her arms around him.

A loud thud erupted. "Don't mind me. I'm just checking on the patient. None of my business as to what else is going on." A burly nurse briskly moved over to Ria's bedside. She checked the fluids in the hanging IV bag.

Grant forced himself to release Emily before their lips touched. He moved away slightly and returned his hand to her forehead.

"Yep, you're forehead's a little warm. Maybe you're coming down with a cold," Grant grinned staring into her eyes. He knew she had just been blushing, but it was a little fun teasing her.

"I'm... I'm fine; it's just real warm in here," Emily stammered. "Guess you'd better go check on your work." She pushed him slightly and returned to Ria's side.

The nurse made some coughing noises to conceal her chuckling.

Grant exited, grinning.

The nurses' station was where all the gossip was known. That's where Grant intended to find the latest on who was admitted and what the doctors thought so far. Grant made his way down the hall..

"Grant!" a familiar voice called out. "Grant, tell them I've got to go home. I don't want to stay here. I'm fine!" A few feet away, Hal sporting a hospital gown was scolding a nurse. A large cast engulfed his right arm from his fingers to his shoulder.

"Mr. Littonal, you have a serious concussion. You cannot go home tonight. Someone has to keep an eye on you." The nurse seemed about out of patience.

"Young lady, I'm old enough to know what is best for me. Grant, tell her. Now, you go get me my clothes before I walk out of here showing my hinny to the whole world!" Hal flopped his gown around threateningly.

"Hal, give me a minute and I'll get you out of here." Grant paused, "And, stop giving Sally a hard time. She's only trying to do her job. If you go back to your room, I promise I'll come get you in a few minutes," Grant pleaded.

"Okay, I'll do it, since you promised," Hal grumbled as he marched defiantly off towards his hospital room.

"Thanks Grant." The nurse batted her eyes at him and then in her best Mae West impression she purred, "You're a welcomed sight for sore eyes. Where've been lately?"

"Been working. Sorry about him Sally. What's he in for and how did it happen?" Grant quizzed matter-of-factly.

"Oh, he was in that accident, the one with the semi. Got hit pretty hard on the head, has a few cracked ribs, and his arm is broke in several places. Other than that, ornery as ever. We gotta keep an eye on him at least overnight. He can probably go home tomorrow, but that cast is going to be on for weeks. Too bad it wasn't a broke jaw. He complains more than a cat in heat." The nurse giggled at her own choice of words.

"Okay, let me see what I can do about him. Give me a few minutes to make a call." As he reached into his pocket and grabbed his cell phone, Grant strolled down to a small waiting area at the end of the hall. This area would provide a bit of privacy ensuring his conversation wouldn't be the next string of nurse fodder. He hit a few buttons and began talking.

Nurse Sally studied him as she tended to her charts. Whenever he turned towards her direction, as he talked on the phone, she would smile and wink. Each time, he acted as though he hadn't seen the wink. He knew not to encourage her. Sally was a few years older than him and a lot more wild. She had dated every policeman, fireman, and available man in the county under thirty, except for Grant.

A few minutes later, he ended his call. His plan was going to work out fine. He brushed past the nurse's station, down to Hal's hospital room, only sending Sally a causal wave as he passed. Later, he would find one of the other nurses to give him the news scope, avoiding Sally's insatiable flirtations. That was the wisest strategy. As he entered Hal's room, Grant had to force back the laughter that was trying to explode from his mouth. Sitting in the guest chair naked with his hospital gown folded across his lap, Hal's face was twisted in a half-pout, half frown like a little kid who had just been told it was time to leave the carnival.

"Hal, I can get you out of here, but you can't go home. I found someone you can stay with. You'd only have to stay for a few days, till your doctor says you can stay by yourself."

"I don't need a nanny," Hal snarled. "I'm not going stay at anyone's house or at some facility! You can't..."

Grant interrupted, "This place is like heaven. It's at Dotia's. I told her about your concussion and broken arm. How you were being forced to stay at the hospital because you needed some help with things for a few days. I mean with a concussion and broken arm, how can you cook and clean? Let me tell you, she volunteered the moment I told her that you were very upset about having to stay at the hospital and would rather die in your own home than be subject to hospital food." Grant noticed Hal nodding in agreement as he thought about it. Grant pushed the idea a little harder.

"I don't know about you, but, I'd jump on it. Dotia's a great cook and no one's a better nurse. I'd offer my place, but I have to pull overtime till things settle down. Too many weird things going on."

Hal looked deep in thought. Then he looked directly at Grant, "Well, if you think it'd be okay. I mean two unmarried people sleeping under the same roof. You don't think people would jump to the wrong conclusion do you?" Hal asked.

Secretly, Hal was thrilled about to spending this much time alone with Dotia, but nervous too. Maybe she wouldn't like him as much after spending day and night together, 24/7. Maybe, he wouldn't like her. Naaa, he would always be soft for her. For years now, he had longed to spend time with Dotia and maybe even ask her out. But being old and bashful, he had convinced himself that it would be just be silly to ask Dotia out on a date. After all, old people like him and her dating like two kids in love?

Grant's reassuring voice invaded Hal's thoughts. "Of course it'll be okay. Anyways, people won't have time to think about what you two are up to with all the crazy stuff happening around town. Plus, you do have one broken arm, so Dotia could easily fend you away."

Hal chuckled. "I'm quite the gentleman, I'll have you know."

"I won't argue that. Oh, we have to take my friend Emily home first. She's here visiting her roommate, Ria. Ria fell ill with whatever is affecting people."

"Emily's the one from the dance, right?" Hal sympathized. "Poor girl having to go through her friend being ill."

"Yeah. Also, I'll need to check out her apartment to make sure it's safe, but you can stay in the truck if you want. May not be good for you to climb a flight of steps in your condition," Grant remarked as he headed towards the door. "I'll let the nurse know to bring your clothes. I'll be around to retrieve you after I check on a few more things. So, behave and don't flash the nurses again!"

"Thanks Grant. You always were such a nice and thoughtful boy. Glad to see some things don't change!" Hal beamed. Grant disappeared through the doorway leaving Hal to await the arrival of his clothes.

******

Grant's truck pulled up into the apartment complex with Grant, Emily, and Hal lined across the seat. The trio stared in disbelief for a few minutes.

A sea of oddities lined up and down the street. The area had taken a bizarre Mardi Gra appearance. Some people were dressed in outfits resembling dark-themed Halloween costumes (vampires, goblins, & demons), others wore alien-type, several dawned plain white gowns, and a few were in gypsy garb.

A hundred feet away, in a small clearing off to one side of the entrance road, a scattering of canvases created make-shift shelters. There were also about ten RV's and some pop-up campers dotting the tiny acreage. The parcel's owner had figured it was a good way to make some quick money. Let people camp there temporarily and rake in the cash. How often did an attraction like this fall into one's lap? The city had objected and tried to force the parcel's owner to vacate the intrusive residents. But, that parcel was in county zoning and there wasn't a county ordinance prohibiting it. The only resolve for the city was to ask the local sheriff to contribute a few watchful deputies to the area and the city would likewise supply a few patrolling policemen.

"Wow, what a circus," Grant commented. Grant jumped out and offered his hand to Emily. She scooted over, grasped his hand, and slid out. The truck's side door creaked opened and Hal carefully stepped down onto the parking lot. Emily and Grant rounded past the front of the truck and met up with Hal.

"Well, at least there are lots of eye witnesses around if anything like an alien abduction does happen," Hal snickered.

"Looks like I'll be on overtime till this mess clears up," Grant complained. "I really wanted to take Emily fishing this weekend."

Emily grinned, "How do you know I like fishing?"

Thrown off, Grant stammered, "Well, I ..."

"It's okay, actually I do like fishing, but don't have any fishing poles. I'm probably not very good at it, but I can bait a hook." She had successfully returned the teasing Grant had inflicted on her at the hospital.

The trio climbed the stairway and entered Emily's apartment. Jacque yowled.

"Oh, you poor thing. It must have been lonely here for you. I'm home now." Emily scooped in him up in her arms.

"Isn't that one of Dotia's cats?" Hal asked.

"Yes, he's on borrow. She was kind enough to let him come stay with me for awhile. Isn't he is wonderful?" Emily nuzzled the large tomcat on his forehead. Jacque's purr sounded like a small lawn mower.

"Okay, let's check the place out." Grant moved into the kitchen and quickly searched areas large enough to hold even a small person. "All clear in here. I'll check the bathroom and bedrooms. You guys stay up here. If you see anything, let me know," Grant instructed.

Room by room he investigated as Emily, Jacque, and Hal stood guarding the only passage way out. Returning towards them, Grant informed, "All clear. But, make sure you lock your door and keep your cell phone charged and next to you."

Emily nodded. She didn't like the idea of being alone with all the horrible events that had been happening, but she was determined to be brave.

"Guess I'd better get Hal over Dotia's so he can begin recuperating," Grant mischievous expression made Emily giggle.

"What's so funny?" Hal whined. "I didn't have any choice. It's that damned hospital's fault... poking its nose into other people's business."

"I'm sorry; I was just tickled by the thought of seeing Dotia scurrying around playing nurse maid. I know she will be very happy to have someone to look after," Emily lied. She wasn't going to divulge her suspicions about Grant's matchmaking attempt. And, as an afterthought the image of Dotia trying to heal Hal was funny. Anyway, she didn't want to hurt Hal's feelings or embarrass him either.

"Sometimes, she'll look after you a bit too much. Be

careful of her herbal concoctions. She'll swear they're for your own good. One time she fed me some worming herbs, I was sick for days. But, on the other hand, if you ever get a wart, she's your lady." Grant knew Dotia's cures usually worked. He had learned a lot from her over the years. But, people normally didn't take too well to Dotia's type of medicine, much less her other practices. It was a wonder that someone hadn't tried to burn her at the stake for witchcraft. Grant silently chuckled at the thought of someone trying to take her on. She was a fierce opponent and would have the better of most in seconds.

"That rub she makes is fantastic. She should commercialize it." Hal hazily reminisced over the deep warm and ease of pain, the ointment instilled.

Grant motioned to the door. "We'd better get going. Emily, call me if you need anything. Anything at all." Grant's eyes locked on hers. He longed to spend more time with her.

"I'll be fine. Don't worry. I'll make sure to lock the door, check the cell charge, and keep it handy... Anyways, I have Jacque here to protect me. He's almost as big as a mountain lion." In truth, Emily was comforted by the enormous cat's presence. She gently sat him down on the living room chair. Jacque curled up into a ball taking up most of the cushion.

The men opened door and stepped outside. Following them, Emily stopped on the threshold, and clasped the door ready to secure it closed. "Thanks again for everything Grant. ··· And Hal, it was great to see you again. I hope you mend fast."

Grant called back to her as he headed down the stairs, "I'll call you tomorrow afternoon. Tuesday I'll take you to lunch." He didn't wait for her answer but kept his pace transcending the stairs. He hated goodbyes.

Emily shut and locked the door. Grant's comment about lunch sent a quiver over her. She wasn't sure why she liked him so much and why would he truly like her?

Jacque bumped up against Emily's leg as she stood daydreaming.

"Hi sweetie. You like me, so I can't be all bad, right?" She patted him on the head.

"Okay, time for a quick shower. I really smell bad," she grumbled as she lifted her shirt out and smelled downwards. "I'm afraid to even check my underarms. My chest is fragrant enough."

She picked him up and sat him on the living room chair.

"I gotta confess, Jacque, it gives me the creeps taking a shower after all that's been going on... me alone in the shower... isn't that when the victim always gets attacked?" Emily moved towards her bedroom. Jacque jumped off the chair and followed her down the hall.

Cautiously she entered her bedroom. "I know they checked in here, but I still got the hibbie jebbies. I don't think I'll get any sleep tonight, with or without a shower."

Emily grabbed her bathrobe. As she headed out towards the bathroom, she flipped the light off and closed the door behind her.

Jacque padded along behind her.

She paused at the bathroom door and looked pleadingly at him, "You keep watch. Don't let any weirdoes in. I can't take any more excitement tonight."

"Meow." His bold green eyes stared into hers giving Emily the ounce of courage she needed.

She reached over and flipped the shower on then closed the door. Like a sentinel, Jacque sat outside the door.

Chapter 19

Here To Stay

The knock came at the door as Dotia had just finished meticulously preparing her spare bedroom for Hal. Quickly she placed the last pillow in just the right spot before dashing off to welcome her guest. She could hear the front door opening.

"Dotia, again the door's not locked! I could have been a robber," Grant shouted out. It annoyed him how lightly she took his warnings.

"If you were a robber, you'd be in big trouble," Dotia cautioned as she pulled out a small hand gun from the fold in her skirt. Hal flinched.

"I don't like guns, they make me nervous. Are you supposed to have that?' Hal turned and looked at Grant for confirmation of Dotia's competency to possess such a weapon.

Grant shrugged hopelessly, "She has a concealed weapons permit? What can I do?"

"I'm very talented," Dotia smirked.

"I'd say! Is that freshly baked cookies I smell?" Grant chuckled as he rushed for the kitchen.

"You leave some for our guest. It's Hal's favorite, chocolate chip oatmeal cookies," Dotia warned.

Then kindly to Hal she offered, "After we get you settled, I thought a nice glass of milk and cookies would do you good." Her face glowed with happiness.

"You remembered my favorite cookie?" Hal gushed.

"Of course. Now, let me show you to your room. You can stay as long as you need." Dotia strolled across the living room and down a small hallway with Hal in tow.

A few minutes later, Dotia and Hal joined Grant in the kitchen. Grant had nearly finished a tall glass of milk. A plate sat in front of him with only two cookies, but it was covered in crumbs.

"Shadars! How many did you eat Grant? Did you make supper out of them?" Dotia exclaimed.

Grant snickered. In fact, he hadn't eaten any supper. The cookies hit the spot. It would hold him over for a few hours. "I'm still a growing boy; I eat a lot." Grant defended himself.

Shaking her head at Grant's behavior, Dotia moved about setting up a plate and glass for her and Hal. Hal, meanwhile, settled in a chair next to Grant. He felt right at home. Why he hadn't figure out a way to spend more time over here at Dotia's before now, eluded him.

Hal picked up a large cookie from the plate in front of him. Biting into it, he was overcome with joy. Absolutely remarkably delicious. Crisp on the outside, soft inside with creamy bits of chocolate.

"So Hal, what do you make of the recent turmoil here in town?" Grant asked. Over the years, Grant had discovered that Hal possessed an uncanny ability to analyze things. He was fantastic at puzzles, politics, science, and animals. People were Hal's shortcoming. Hal tended to shy away from people and most people just thought Hal was too eccentric for their taste.

"First, tell me what you know Grant, cause I haven't heard much except that something's making people sick, some died, some just act crazy. Grab a pencil and paper and write it down as you go," Hal demanded. He took another bite of cookie and then a gulp of milk.

Dotia sat unpretentiously across from Hal slowly eating a small cookie. Inside she was ecstatic that he was devouring the cookies with so much enthusiasm. It was going to be fun hosting Hal at her house. She had always liked him even if she didn't know a lot about him. But what she did know was that he had been a true friend to Grant over the years.

Pencil and paper in hand, Grant began, "Let's see. Fact one, to date 27 people have fallen ill, but symptoms vary. These people were found in multiple locations."

"Stop there and go get a map. I think it may be important to chart the locations," Hal ordered.

As Grant jumped up to retrieve a local map, Hal turned his thoughts to more important matters. "Dotia, these are the best cookies ever. What else do you make? I'll buy all the groceries if you'll do the cooking! I'm so tremendously glad that you are allowing me to stay here."

"It will be my pleasure to have someone to do for. As for cooking, name your poison and I'll see what I can do," Dotia affirmed. Cooking was one of her favorite things to do.

Grant appeared back in the room with a large map and a handful of papers. He scooted over the center piece on the table and plopped the map down. Waving the papers he commented, "I got the police reports so we can be more accurate."

"Good thinking Boy," Hal affectionately stated.

On the map, Grant drew with a colored marker, a small dot where each ill person was picked up. Then he drew a small square where the three dead people were located.

"What about where each of these people live or where they stayed within the last 24 hours. Can we note any differences on the map as well?" Hal queried.

Grant studied the reports one by one, marking any variances as he processed through the files. "Okay, that will do it."

"Dotia, do you have some yarn laying around?" Hal glanced around as though expecting to see some setting on a countertop or strewn on the floor somewhere.

"With this many cats? Of course, how much do you need and what colors?" She sprung up from her chair and was at the kitchen doorway before he could reply.

"Oh, at least four colors, about two foot long each..." Then he remembered his manners, "Please."

Grant snickered. Hal shot a grimaced look at him daring Grant to even try to tease about it. "You want my help, Boy, or not?" Hal threatened.

"Alright, I'll keep it to myself," Grant promised. It was going to be a hard night on Grant having to hold in all his teasing. He couldn't help but notice the way Hal lit up around Dotia.

Dotia popped back in carrying several colored strands of yarn. She laid them on the table for Hal to inspect. Hal picked up one and strung it along the map connecting the dots. Then he grabbed each in turn connecting the dots in a different sequence each time. "Any of these patterns look familiar to either of you?" Hal knew there was a very odd connection.

Grant shook his head no. But Dotia sat motionless, discreetly, as though she knew something, but was not willing to reveal her knowledge.

"Years ago I studied the geology around here. Simply fascinating." Hal paused and took another bite from a cookie.

"What does that have to do with anything? Are you

saying there's something in the soil causing this?" Grant remarked impatiently.

Hal took his time, finishing his bit of cookie and chasing it with a gulp of milk.

"Oh yea of little knowledge. If I get this right, then you have to promise to go back and finish your college degree. Can't have you dumber than me." It was Hal's turn to snicker.

"I'll think about it. Now, stop playing around and tell me. People are getting sick and dying out there. This is serious business," Grant argued.

"Education, my Boy is also serious business, so promise," Hal relentlessly demanded.

"I give, you stubborn old Coot," Grant blurted. He was beginning to get frustrated with Hal. Hal knew something and Grant needed to know it too.

"Do you see the lilac thread?" Hal pointed to it and ran his finger along its path.

Grant nodded. Dotia trying to feign a lack of interest set about getting three glasses of water for them.

"Okay, you two have to promise to keep something a secret. Do you swear?"

Grant nodded again.

"Dotia, I need you to swear as well," Hal stated in a serious tone holding a steady gaze at the woman while she bustle around the kitchen.

She placed one glass of water in front of Grant, another in front of Hal.

"Okay," she agreed. She gathered her water glass and resumed her seat at the table.

"Years ago, many, many years ago, I was unloading some pets at the store through the back door. A cage of iguanas came open and the sneaky little band of lizards took off running into that pasture behind the store. Back then, there wasn't any fencing. Long story short, one of the little guys ran under some rocks. When I moved the rocks and a few planks of wood, I found a cave... right about here." Hal pointed to a location on the map underneath the lilac thread.

He sipped his drink and then continued. "Indiscreetly, so no one would learn of my ... uhmmm ... trespassing, or about the cave, I searched for information about the cave. It wasn't on any registers or government radars." He paused again a little embarrassed about what he would have to reveal next.

"I know it was private land, but I couldn't resist." – his eyes twinkled and his lips curled impishly remembering those early days" – "My hobby for many years after that was exploring what turned out to be an incredible underground labyrinth. An underground natural cavern runs for miles along this lilac thread."

He waited for his investigative brilliance to be congratulated by his audience. Instead, Dotia sat silent, her head slightly down, acting as though she hadn't heard a word. Whereas, Grant was staring at Dotia with a shocked expression. Puzzled by this unexpected reaction, Hal decided he needed to explain his genius by putting it all together for them.

"Thus, whatever is affecting the people is using that tunnel. Okay, now let's go over the rest of the information. Grant, resume your factual listing, please." Hal instructed.

Grant, boring his deep blue eyes into Dotia, burst out, "I never knew about any tunnels! Dotia, did you know?"

Trying very hard to keep a neutral expression, Dotia leaned over towards the map pretending this was news to her. Not knowing what to think, Hal leaned back in his chair. He glanced back and forth from Grant to Dotia trying to figure out what was going on.

Grant struck his fist on the table. "Damn, you did know, I can tell by your face. How come you never told me?" He shook his head in disbelief.

The scene bewildered Hal. He was speechless. What was Grant talking about?

Realizing the secret was out, Dotia reached over and placed her hand on Grant's. Sorrowfully, she cast her radiant blue eyes up at him, asking for understanding and forgiveness.

"Cause I knew you could have never resisted exploring them. That was a danger I didn't want you to take. The caverns were... are a heavily guarded secret. I can't believe someone found out about them and is using them to hurt people... I'm sure I would have sensed if it was someone... maybe it is something, not someone..." as she confessed Dotia's voice grew faint. Grant didn't want to push the issue at the moment. She looked too frail in this light.

"You and I are going to talk about this later. I can't believe you sometimes. What else don't I know?" He shot a concerned hurt look at her.

"Not sure what's going on between you two, but enough of the squabbling, do you want to solve the mystery of not?" Hal interjected figuring now was not the time to unravel Grant and Dotia's story. People had died and many were sick.

Grant picked up the paper and pencil from the table. "Fact one was, the sick people and each one's location. Fact two was, dead people and each one's location. Three, sick people displayed various symptoms. Four, dead had numerous small puncture wounds and little blood left in the bodies. Five ··· "

Hal cut Grant off again, "How about the sick people. *Any* wounds on any of them? Maybe not a puncture but any marks, bruising, discoloration anywhere on the skin, etc..."

"I'll call the hospital and see what I can get from Maria. What do you think so far? Could someone be using the tunnels?" Grant needed to see where Hal was heading on his theory.

"It's too soon to make any projections. I need more information. Instead of calling, could you run down to the hospital and get copies of all the patients' charts."

"I guess if that is what you need," Grant surrendered knowing he'd have to wait for Hal's real answer. "I'll be right back. Do you want me to pick up anything from the store while I'm out? I got to make a quick trip because I have to start my shift in a little over an hour."

Dotia smiled. Grant was so thoughtful. "I'm fine. Do you need anything, Hal?"

"I'm good," Hal continued staring at the map as though in a trance, ideas running through his mind.

Grant skillfully bobbed over kissing Dotia on the top of her head. "I forgive you. BUT, we still need to talk." He could never stay mad at her long. She had always looked out for him.

On his way towards the door, Grant patted the old guy on his back, "Behave while I'm gone."

As soon as Grant was out of ear shot, Hal broke the silence. "Okay, so how did you know about the tunnels?"

"Well, I guess I should tell you. Better yet maybe I should show you and if you don't want to stay here after that, I'll understand." Dotia rose up slowly from the table.

"As long as you're not going to turn into something that

will hurt me or scare the hell out of me!" Hal didn't like the way Dotia had said that. And, more so, he didn't like surprises.

Dotia laughed. The somewhat frightened look on Hal's face surprised her. "Of course not. I'm only a *good* witch." Her eyes twinkled as she slurred the word good. "I'm just going to show you a book of mine. I'll be right back."

Dotia left the kitchen and returned a moment later with a huge black book and a smaller satchel containing documents and maps.

"Here." She waited a second for Hal to move his plate and glass. Then, she set the large monstrosity down in front of him and the satchel beside it. "It's my family's history and in the satchel there's a complete map of the caverns as well. My ancestors had it mapped out. I knew about you toying around down there, but ordered that you be left alone. I knew you'd never tell."

Hal stared up at her in silent reverence. Dotia smiled weakly and shrugged her shoulders. What else didn't he know about her? After an uncomfortable second or two, he situated himself and began digesting the revelation before him.

Dotia fixed herself a cup of herbal tea while Hal skimmed through the volume. There were several sections. The first was on the family history. The second on trees, shrubs, flowers, vegetables, and herbs. Another for animals and animal husbandry. But the one most astonishing was the section on charms, potions, and spells. Each section contained pictures and elaborate hand sketches.

By the time she returned to her chair opposite of him, he had quickly covered most of the first section. He raised sorrowful eyes, "I... I don't know what to say. It must have been very difficult on your ancestors to have to flee like that after investing so much into living here. What a burden, keeping the Windels' secrets all these years."

"Well, now you know what happened and where the Windels went. So you can share my burdensome secret. Good thing my mother, Oana and her sister had prepared a plan with the Gypsy tribe; else I wouldn't be here today. Those natural caves were a God send. They lived in there for months." She stirred her tea and took another sip.

"What a clever idea, as well, to use the tunnels to reclaim most of what was in the house without being seen, using the townsfolk's superstitions against them. Can't believe they thought the lanterns were spirits and marked it up to being haunted." He chuckled.

"I wish more of the family would have stayed to live with the Gypsy tribe and not returned to Transylvania. Sometimes, my mother was extremely sad about being separated from her family by miles of sea and land. However, I had quite a fantastic life with my Gypsy family. Every day was a magical adventure." The gaze in her eyes told him she was reliving wonderful memories.

"How come you didn't stay with the Gypsy tribe after your husband died?" In front of him, the book lay open to a picture of Dotia and her Gypsy husband. Above that was a picture of when she was very young, with her mother and father.

"Things change. With the Matron, my Mother and Father all passed on, I felt it was time for a change, so I came back here. Plus, my Windel family needed someone to manage all of their investments. There's a lot of profit in leasing land and/or buildings. Altogether, they own most of the county. They even own the land under the hospital as well as all of the land above the caverns. That cave system is unique and holds valuable resources. Besides that it holds sentimental value because of the role it served in saving my family's life."

"I didn't realize you were such an accomplished

business woman. This is truly amazing..." Hal glanced down at the book unable to put it all in words.

"Well, one does what can, especially after the tragedy of losing the love of your life. Even though I was only married a few years, it was hard to go on without him. He was a wonderful kind-hearted man." Brimming with tears, Dotia's deep blue eyes shimmered like crystals. A single tear streaked down her cheek, which she caught with a daub of her napkin.

Hal knew how she felt. He had suffered a similar loss. "I lost my wife after only five years of marriage. It broke my heart. I withdrew only allowing myself to get close to my pets and finally to the boy. Grant had a way of piercing my armored heart."

Hal chuckled shaking his head as he reminisced at some of the things Grant had done over the years. "When he first started helping out at the store, I left him alone for about two hours. When I came back all the rabbits were together in one large cage. He thought they were lonely having to all live in separate cages. Can't tell you how many customers weren't happy that they ended up buying a two-for-one special that year."

Dotia couldn't help herself and laughed heartily.

Chapter 20

Feeling Better

The shower had been just what Emily needed. To her relief, no horrors had attacked her while she was bathing. Wrapped in her bathrobe, she sat on the couch reading a book. Jacque nestled beside her. She reached forward, took another sip of tea, and then returned the cup to the small table. The necklace hanging fast around her neck slipped out from under her robe with the movement. Unconsciously she tucked it back under the cloth. Its presence comforted her. She turned another page, reaching the end of the chapter. It was time to set the book down and attend other matters.

"Well Jacque, I think I'll sleep fully dressed out here on the couch with you. After the way things have been going, I'd rather be found fully dressed than half-naked." The cat looked up at her with his large emerald eyes.

Emily sat her book aside. With a quick bounce, she was off the couch and headed towards the bedroom. Jacque leaped off the couch and followed her.

"The apartment is eerily quiet without Ria here," she remarked to him.

The closed door to Ria's bedroom sent a chill through Emily. She slowly turned the knob to her own room and pushed the door open. Steadying her nerves, she reached over to the light switch. It came on with a click. Everything looked normal but it didn't help calm her nerves. Emily grabbed a pair of jeans, some under clothes and a shirt. Quickly she dropped the robe and dawned the selected clothing.

Having her attire in order she reached into her closet.

"I know there's a sheet in here somewhere." Tugging at a folded cloth, it dislodged. She held in cradled in her arm and with her other hand, snatched the pillow off the bed.

"Let's go," she called to Jacque. The cat trotted out behind her, his large padded feet barely making any noise on the carpet. She turned, flicked the light off, and closed the door. Once back in the living room, she spread the sheet out of the couch and placed the pillow at one end. Approving of her arrangement, she crawled inside the folded sheet and adjusted her head. Jacque took his usual spot upon her stomach. "I'm not sure what I'd do without you," she confessed stoking his soft fur. His purring soothed her anxieties. With the hypnotic purring, it wasn't long before she was sound asleep.

Emily tossed around forcing Jacque to jump over to the chair for safety. A loud sound disturbed her slumber. Her eyes flicked open.

"What's that noise?" She said out loud.

Even her own voice seemed out of place in the otherwise still apartment. Emily sat up, shaking the disorientation away. It sounded like a metallic rock band playing right outside her door.

"How rude! Don't people realize that other people are trying to sleep?" She looked at Jacque for confirmation. "I'll never get back to sleep with that racket."

Emily crawled off the couch and went over to the door. As though it might help, she unlocked the door and peered out. The refreshing night air did little to dampen the loud intrusive noise. She stepped out on the stairway and gazed down to where the invaders had set up. She shut the door behind her so Jacque wouldn't get out. At least there were lots of people around even if half of them seemed crazy.

As her eyes adjusted to the dim night light, she scanned the area. Where was the abominable noise coming from? Maybe the police would soon demand they shut it off. What a strange picture, all of these strangers cast, she poetically thought.

Suddenly, Emily's knees felt weak. It couldn't be. There it was, a car just like the one that had chased Ria and her. It was. It was the Pontiac. It was him....sitting on the hood.

Nausea took over... Had he seen her? He was facing her way. She abruptly retreated into the apartment, securely locking the door behind her. Terrified, her mind tried to figure out whether he had seen her or not. She knew he had been facing her direction, but had he seen her?

"Calm down and think!" Emily ordered herself. "If he did see me, then he might come up here. Okay, what should I do?"

It was too late to think about it more, there was a knock on the door. She didn't have to guess who it was because the next thing she heard was a man's voice.

"I'm so glad we get this chance to see each other again. Hope you're in there all alone and waiting just for me." A garish evil laugh erupted behind the thin wooden barrier.

The door knob twisted. Pounding ensued on the wooden structure. It would only be a few minutes before it gave way. Emily would be face to face with her attacker.

As she ran into the bathroom, she thought maybe she could hide in there. No, if he could get through the front door, he could easily get through the bathroom door.

Hastily she sped out bathroom locking the door closed behind her. She ran down the hall, opened Ria's door, hit the lock button and closed it. Then, she did the same for hers.

Grabbing Jacque, she dashed towards the kitchen. She sat him done for a second and patted him on the head. "Stay, Jacque."

The pounding on the door continued. If it wasn't for all the loud music outside, someone would be able to hear all the noise her soon to-be-attacker was making. There wasn't any chance of someone coming to her rescue.

Hastily, she opened the bottom cabinet door next to the sink. She lifted the few pans out and placed them inside the unlit oven. "That should be enough room," she told herself confidently as she scoped the awaiting cat back into her arms.

With Jacque secure in her arms, she climbed under the kitchen sink and closed the cabinet doors behind her. Hopefully, Jacque would not give them away. She held him snug and gently patted him, more to reassure herself than him.

She looked around at her hiding spot. The big gaping hole a few feet away on the backside of the cabinet gave her the shivers. Something scurried by in the darkness of the hole. Or, least she could swear she saw something scurry by.

Jacque squirmed. Trying to settle him down, she readjusted her hold. His paw caught in her necklace. A grey-brownish dust burst out of the sprung amulet. Her arm burned and itched. She wondered if she was allergic to whatever had been in the necklace chamber.

Emily held back a sneeze as she heard the front door thud, striking hard up against the interior wall. It was open. She held her breath and concentrated on keeping Jacque quiet and still. It would only be a moment now.

"I know you're in here," the sinister male voice called out. "Where are you my little pretty? Are you waiting for me in the bedroom like a good little girl?" He cackled.

Footsteps echoed across the kitchen floor as the heavy boots pounded the tile, coming closer to Emily in her hiding spot. The boots hitting the floor stopped.

Emily knew he was only a few feet away from her. Her body froze in fear. Jacque licked her hand as if to give the petrified girl courage. The footstep sound moved away from her, back into the living room. The soft thud on the carpet let her know he was headed down the hall.

The stinging on her arm was more intense now. She glanced over at the aching area. A rash had erupted. She fought the urge to scratch and her need to sneeze. Emily knew her life depended on her being perfectly still.

"That's not nice to lock me out. You're slowing down all my fun." The angry excitement in his tone scared her. It was all she could do to keep herself from screaming. She heard pounding on a door down the hall. She couldn't figure out which door he was trying to bust in. Suddenly, a tune rang out in the distance. It was her cell phone. She had left it in her room.

The pounding increased and she heard a loud snap. That was her cue. Without making a sound, she rolled out of the cabinet, Jacque tight in her arms. Guardedly, she sped across the kitchen, across the living room, out the front door, and down the stairs. Her intruder had been too involved, searching for his victim, in the newly conquered room, to hear her escape.

Once down the stairs, Emily bolted over to one of the local sheriff cars. Where were they? She scoured the parking lot. A few yards away she spotted a man in beige uniform. She took off running, Jacque held firmly captive in her arms. The beige suit turned towards her as she barreled in like a wild woman. "A man,... rapist, ... in

613." Being frightened and winded, her jumbled words spilled out; she wasn't making sense to the deputy.

"Okay, I need you to calm down. Catch your breath. Then, try again slower so I can make sense of what you are saying," he said slowly. The deputy figured it was another drugged up partier, but he would go through the motions.

Emily took a deep breath and then started again, "Just now I was up in my apartment, 613, and a man forcefully broke in. I managed to run out the door as he was searching my bedroom. He thought I was hiding in there. I think he's that rapist that hurt that girl a few weeks back."

"Mam, have you been drinking or maybe indulging in any other substance. There *is* a lot of partying going on around here. You can trust me. You won't be in any trouble. So trust me and just relax. I won't let anyone hurt you. *Things* can appear very confusing sometimes, but I want you to know, it's okay. You're okay."

Emily was appalled. He didn't believe her. The stinging on her arm was irritating enough, but now this idiot was testing her nerves. She calmly but firmly stated, "No disrespect sir, but I was almost attacked. I could be laying dead right now in apartment 613. I am not drunk. I do not and have not consumed any drugs. Since I had to run off and leave my cell phone, I need you to *please* call a friend of mine, Officer Grant Rawlins. He's a policeman with the city. If you can't call him, let me know and I'll find someone else to."

"Okay young lady; let me see what I can do. Let's walk over to my car, so I give him a call." He instructed, motioning towards the Sherriff's vehicle a short distance away.

The deputy lifted his radio to his mouth. "Harry, do you copy? I have a lady here. Says there is a predator in apartment 613. Can you assist? Over."

A male voice returned, "Be there in a second. Over."

Arriving at the car, the deputy opened the car's back door. "You sit in here with your... cat? I'll check out the apartment. Deputy Daniels will be here in a second."

Emily was certain from watching movies that police and sheriff cars had back doors that you couldn't open from the inside, once locked in. She wasn't about to be locked in like a criminal. "I'd better stand here. My cat might have to potty." She improvised. It sounded logical to her. The deputy looked at the cat and decided not to push the issue.

The street light was brighter at the car. Emily maneuvered Jacque and glanced at the throbbing skin on her forearm. It was forming small bubbles and looked like some kind of science fiction plague. She wasn't sure whether it burned more than it itched or itched more than it burned. She'd have to get something on it pretty soon. The bright red rash caught the eye of the deputy.

"What did you get into? Is it some kind of *drug* reaction?" The deputy sniped.

"No, I think I bumped into some kind of bush... maybe poison ivy." Emily hated to embellish the truth, but this guy was a jerk.

"Maybe if girls like you covered up a bit more, wore proper clothes, and acted a more decent, you wouldn't get such rashes," he mocked, believing it probably was some drug reaction, and that she was one those girls that had just gotten what was coming to her.

"Reap what yea so," he mumbled.

"Officer, I don't know what you are alluding to... but if that killer gets away.." her voice quaked with anger. How could this idiot be a servant of community?

"Which way is the apartment?" he asked.

"613's around that side of the building... see the bottom of the stairway barely sticking out at the corner of the building?" She pointed as she continued, "Up the stairs, at the very top is 613. The doors are well-numbered. Plus, he busted in the door." Emily shuttered.

"Stay here, I'll be right back," he commanded as he began walking away.

"Could you call Officer Grant before you leave please?" Emily gently requested. She didn't want to make the reluctant deputy mad at her, but she needed a friend right now. She had nowhere to go and a crazy man was after her. Plus, she was still holding tight to Jacque. What if he got loose and ran off. Dotia would never forgive her.... She would never forgive herself.

He stopped and gave her a squinty glare. "Mam, I can handle this. I *am* a trained law enforcement officer," he remarked snidely. Disgruntled, he turned his back to her and trudged slowly off in the appointed direction.

A few seconds later Deputy Daniels appeared at the car. "Are you the alleged victim?" Deputy Daniels grumbled.

She could still see the other deputy moving like a snail across the parking lot. He hadn't even made it to the stairs yet. At this rate Pontiac guy would definitely be gone before the slow deputy reached the apartment.

She replied softly, trying to invoke his sympathy so maybe he would treat her nicer than the other deputy, "Yes, I was the intended victim. Fortunately I got away."

She paused wondering whether to waste time asking him and then decided to. Trying to muster a helpless damsel in distress look, she purred, "I'm surprised someone would be so crazy to try such a thing with a big strong officer like you around." She'd heard Ria do it a thousand times. It had always worked for her. Emily didn't have anything to lose but a few seconds.

The deputy grinned soaking in the exaggerated praise. "Well, I do work out a little." His posture straightened and his shoulders squared.

"Ohhh, I can tell! You're so fit and healthy looking. You're wife is a *lucky* woman." She cooed. She waited for her complements to soak in. His ear to ear smile and slight facial reddening signaled the time was right.

"Would you, could you grant me a tincey wincey favor?" Emily's voice sounded foreign to her as she did her best babydoll imitation. Ria would be proud of her. "I had to leave my cell upstairs in order to get away, but I promised to call my boyfriend, Officer Grant and tell him goodnight. He won't be happy with me. Is there any way you'd let me use yours? I'd *only* be a second. I'd really *appreciate you* for lending it to me... so I don't get in *trouble.*"

The deputy was captivated. Emily's emerald eyes sparkled with angelic innocence. He felt an overwhelming desire to protect this vulnerable auburn beauty. Without even being conscious of it, he reached for his cell and handed it to her. "I wouldn't want anyone mad at you."

"Oh, you're sooo kind and such a gentleman." She continued the façade as she took the cell. She adjusted Jacque in her arms so she could dial. Good thing she remembered Grant's number. "I'd better step over here a little. I don't want you to over hear any incriminating evidence." She winked at the deputy and then casually sashayed a few feet away.

Chapter 21
Everyone Wants a Hero

Holding the borrowed cell, Emily whispered into the phone, "Oh hi, Grant? It's Emily. I don't want to bother you, but I have a slight situation and was wondering if there was any way you could help me. A man broke in my apartment..." she paused as Grant interrupted her.

"Yes, I'm okay. I ran out of the apartment while he was searching in my bedroom. I grabbed Jacque and ran out the door. So, now I'm in the parking lot holding Jacque." The voice interrupted her again.

Grant couldn't believe his ears. This girl sure seemed to have misfortunes follow her. It was a good thing he was patrolling close by.

"I'll be right there. Can you go to the apartment offices or to somewhere safe? How about the officers patrolling in the area? Do you see them?" Grant turned his red lights on and sped down the road, leaving the sirens off. The loud screaming noise would draw too much attention.

A rush of relief waved over Emily. Fighting back unexpected tears swelling up in her eyes, her quivering voice answered, "I'm standing near one of the deputies. He let me use his cell, so I have to be quick. My door's busted in, so I can't go back into my apartment and the offices are closed. I'll wait next to the sheriff's car till you get here. Okay goodbye."

As she ended the call, Jacque meowed and began

purring. Emily realized that he was trying to comfort her. She laid the side of her face on his soft fur in a half snuggle and then kissed him on his forehead.

"Thank you," she murmured looking into his big green eyes. She felt much calmer.

Emily regained her composure and sashayed back over to return the cell. "Thank you, Officer," she cooed in her made-up persona. "You've been too kind."

BAMB! BAMB! Gun shots rang out from the stairway area. Deputy Daniels ducked down by the car forgetting to act brave. He had never been in a shoot out. He felt embarrassed when he realized he had left Emily standing there. "Get down, Miss, before you get shot!" he screamed.

Emily ducked around the back side of the sheriff's car and peered over, staring towards the stairway. Pointing, she, forgetting the babydoll accent, told him "That's where your partner, the other deputy went. Do you think he's okay?"

Loud thuds preempted the presence of the missing deputy tumbling into sight near the stairway vicinity. "I see him. He must have fallen down the stairs. Wait! There's the guy. He jumped over him and is running behind the building!" Her play-by-play reminded Deputy Daniels of a sports announcer.

Deputy Daniels jumped up and ran over to the fallen deputy. Emily could see him talking into his phone, but she was too far away to hear him. Cautiously, she scanned the area for her assailant. After reassuring herself, she trotted over to the two deputies.

"Can I help?" Emily asked.

"No, unless you're a doctor. I think he knocked himself out falling down the stairs. I called an ambulance." Deputy Daniels seemed pretty shook up.

Red flashing lights distracted Emily. It was Grant! "I'll be right back," she promised.

Emily ran over to Grant, who had just emerged from his car.

"Let me take him," he coaxed as he lifted Jacque from her arms and placed him in the back of the police car. "What's going on? He nodded towards the two deputies.

"The one on the ground went to check out my apartment. I don't think he believed me. I'm not sure if he was pushed or if he fell down the stairs. The other one called an ambulance. The guy, who broke into my apartment ran away behind the building," Emily briefly recounted.

"How long ago did the guy escape?" Grant quizzed.

"A few minutes, maybe four," she estimated.

"What's wrong with your arm?" The inflamed patch stood out like a scourge. Grant gently grabbed her wrist and inspected the blistering stretch of flesh.

"I must be breaking out from something. My amulet came open and it went all over me. But, the only place I have this is on my arm. So, it must be some kind of reaction to a chemical I came in contact with under the sink. That's where I hid right before the guy broke in. I ran out when he was in the bedroom searching for me." Emily didn't like thinking about her narrow escape, in her own apartment, where she should have been safe.

"We'll get something for it soon." Grant let go of her arm. It didn't look good, but there were other things he had to attend to at the moment.

"Just sit in my car with the doors locked. I'll be right back." Grant opened the front passenger side door. Emily complied, settling into the patrol car. He closed the door and then rushed off to check on the deputies.

A few minutes later, Grant returned to the car and grabbed something out of the trunk. Passing by Emily's window on his way back towards the building, he gave her a small wink. In seconds he had disappeared up the stairs.

Emily shuttered again. She didn't like waiting helpless in the car. She scanned the area again for Pontiac guy. Once she was satisfied that he was nowhere around, she hopped out of the car, locking the doors behind her. Now, she had no way back in. Jacque would be okay for a minute by himself. The night air was cool, so he wouldn't get too hot in there.

She bounced across the lawn. The ambulance had arrived and the EMT's were loading up the hurt deputy. Emily sped by them and up the stairs after Grant.

The door looked bad. The front had been kicked in, the door jam ripped at the lock site, and the hinges hung twisted. There was white powder all over the place. Grant must have dusted for prints she thought. It was too quiet though. She couldn't hear anything. What if something had happened to him? "Grant," she called out standing in the doorway. "Grant?"

Without making a sound, Grant appeared from the hallway. "Emily... thought you were going to wait in the car?" The half-grin reassured her that he wasn't angry about her noncompliance. Grant figured she wouldn't wait very long in the car. To him, Emily seemed full of curiosity and impatience.

"I got worried. Plus, thought I could help. And I need to get a few things for Jacque, too." Emily rationalized her actions.

"What do you need? I'll get it for you. Stand right in the middle of the kitchen. Don't touch anything," Grant admonished.

His tone left her feeling like an incapable irresponsible

child. "For Jacque, kitty litter box and litter, cat bowl, and food; for me, pants, shirt, my purse, cell phone, *underwear, bra...*" She slurred the last two items figuring to get back at him.

Grant didn't flinch. He disappeared silently back into hall. Emily waited, fidgeting. The cabinet doors, behind which she had hidden, leered at her. The sounds from the crowds outside drifted in making it uncomfortably quiet in the kitchen. All of a sudden, she realized she had to pee. This was awkward.

Emily left her appointed spot and tiptoed down the hall. Abruptly, someone emerged from her bedroom. Emily jumped, then she recognized it was only Grant.

"What are you doing in the hall? Thought you were waiting in the kitchen. You don't know how to stay put, do you?" He admonished. Then winked at her to let her know she hadn't really made him angry.

She blushed as she whispered, "I have to use the lady's room."

"I glanced in there earlier and don't think any evidence will be destroyed if you just use the toilet. But, don't touch anything else. I'll stand out here... holding your bag." He folded his arms across his chest. Clasped in his hand, the bag containing items gathered from Emily's room dangled from his side.

"Well, I don't need a babysitter. Please do whatever it is that you need to do. I'll be quick and promptly return to my spot in the kitchen. Promise." She didn't want him waiting right outside the door for her. It would make her too nervous. She did dumb things when she got nervous.

"Not sure there's anything else left. The place has been dusted and checked. I'll check underneath the kitchen cabinet. That's where you think you encountered whatever it was that gave you the rash?" Determining the cause of her affliction intrigued him.

"Okay," she smiled being relieved that something else would occupy his time.

Grant trodded off towards the kitchen. It was hard to believe that someone could fit underneath the sink area. He was proud of Emily for coming up with that kind of escape plan and relieved that it had worked. Laying the bag down on the floor, his rough hand opened the cabinet door. Bending down he inspected the unusual hiding spot. There were no dividers in place. The whole cabinet area was one long continual storage space. Grant noticed the huge holes in the wall area around the piping.

"Ready when you are. Good thing I wasn't the bad guy. You didn't even hear me sneaking up!" Emily taunted.

He turned and smiled up at her, "Soft feminine footsteps of someone about 5'5 and 120lbs couldn't be the bad guy. And, if it was, I'm certain I could take him."

"Sure, I'm not convinced," she replied.

"About what?"

"Either! That you heard me, or could take a bad guy whose 5'5 and 120. What if he was an expert or had a gun?" She laughed feeling exceedingly clever.

"Okay, I'll concede to the gun..." Grant straightened up. "Were those holes in the wall always there?"

"Yes. Gross huh. Talk about throwing together buildings cheap. When I was hiding in there, I thought I heard a mouse or something scurrying around back there. Good thing I had Jacque on my lap." Emily didn't like thinking about and was glad it was over.

"Well, let's go. I'll take you to Dotia's to get that arm looked at." He snatched the bag off the floor and held it out towards Emily. "Here are your necessities."

"Thanks." She took the bag slowly. She hadn't thought about it till now, but where would she stay?

As though he had read her mind, Grant said, "After Dotia fixes your arm, you can stay at her house or my apartment. I work nights this week, so it's no big deal. I'll be gone; you can sleep in my bed. Of course, if you hang out during the day, you'll have to be quiet so I can sleep." Grant commented nonchalantly moving towards the front door.

Overwhelmed by his perception and kindness, she fought to hold back the tears brimming in her eyes. Helplessly, she followed him. "Do you read minds too?" she whispered.

"What'd you say?" he pretended not to hear. She was becoming easier to read by the second. Hal and Dotia were always saying Grant had a keen sixth sense. Maybe, it was true.

As the duo cleared the last step, Emily noticed the Pontiac was still there. She tugged on Grant's arm and pulled him close. In a soft voice she said, "I'm sure that's the guy's car... that yellow Pontiac. Don't draw attention to it. He could be standing and watching us." Emily had watched many detective shows.

"Are you sure?" Grant realized that Emily hadn't told him the whole story. How did she know what kind of car a random stranger drove?

As the couple resumed walking to Grant's car, Emily tried to explain. "Yes, it's a long story. He followed Ria and me the other day when we went for a walk, but we lost him. Earlier tonight, right before he broke in, I stepped out on the stairs to look at the crowd. I couldn't sleep. The car just happened to be there with him on the hood. Immediately, I ran back inside. After that, he broke in. He must have seen me."

"Did you tell the sheriff?" Grant asked.

"I didn't get a chance." She tried to hold her voice steady, but it trembled slightly.

Grant opened the car door for Emily. She was visibly shaking. He closed his arms around her and pulled her tight against him. "It's okay now Emily. I'm here. I'm not going to let anything happen to you." He soothingly whispered into her ear. Then, he kissed her on top of her head.

Emily's body felt so tired. She felt like she could sink into his arms, and stay there resting forever.

"Okay, Emily, I need you to trust me." Grant's voice was firmer now. "Get in the car and this time stay put. Do *not* get out or I'll have to arrest you for disobeying a direct order of an officer." His voice had grown much sterner.

Changing his grip, he firmly pushed her into the seat and slammed the door shut. He hit the lock button on his key clicker and strode off towards the mob of partying people near the woods.

Emily's emerald eyes fixated on him as he crossed the lot and approached one of the groups. After a few seconds, Emily lost sight of Grant as he drifted into the crowd. What was he doing? She didn't like losing visual contact with him. Taking a deep breath, Emily was determined to be brave. Her arm throbbed. Blisters covered her arm and the reddening was darker.

Jacque meowed in the back of the car, breaking Emily's thoughts. That poor sweet cat, stuck in the back seat. She felt comforted by his presence; although she wasn't sure what help a cat would be against a crazy killer. At least neither of them was alone.

"Jacque, I'm so sorry it's taking so long," she cooed. "We are going to Dotia's, soon." Emily wished she could get him out of the back seat and hold him. The metal wire barrier in between the front and back area was in the way.

A few minutes after sitting in silence, she glanced

around to see if she could see Grant anywhere. "Okay Jacque, let's hope it doesn't work out like in the horror shows. Girl sits alone in car, guy gets killed, then girl gets brutally killed as well."

She tugged on the door handle. No use. Locked in. It must be one of those child safety locks, she thought. She scooted over to the driver's seat, hit the master unlock button and tried the handle. The door released. Just as she spun her legs out, a man's hand slapped her leg hard clutching it firmly.

Startled, Emily jumped and shrieked. Instinctively, her legs kicked and her arms flew at her assailant.

"Whoa, easy girl," Grant called to her. "It's me."

Forcing herself to stop fighting, she stared at him. "Don't scare me like that!" she cried.

"Don't be trying to sneak out again. Do you want to go to jail? I wasn't kidding about telling you to sit still. Get back over in your seat!" Grant scoldingly demanded.

As Emily slid back over, Grant opened the back door, lifted Jacque up, and closed the back door. "Here," he gently thrust Jacque over to her. "Jacque can keep an eye on you on the ride home." Grant had to bite his lip to keep from smiling at her. She certainly was a handful. He hoped she never completely grow up.

Chapter 22

Tattered and Torn

Dotia opened the entrance door. "Oh you poor dear!" She exclaimed. "Come into the kitchen, so I can see your arm. I'll fix it right up." Dotia gently ushered Emily into the kitchen as she continued. "I couldn't believe what Grant was telling me when he called. Don't you worry about a thing.... I have plenty of room here, so you can stay if you want. We can have fun! Maybe even make cookies tomorrow!"

Grant shut the door with his free hand. The other he had full with Jacque. Jacque squirmed free and leaped from Grant's grasp. "Impatient aren't you," Grant scolded the cat.

Before trailing behind the nurse and her unwitting patient, Grant locked the door.

Emily's voice echoed from the kitchen. "I don't want to be a burden." Emily felt guilty for imposing but sensed Dotia was being sincere.

"No burden at all," she coaxed. Dotia's kind smile and hypnotic blue eyes vanquished Emily's qualms. She felt very sleepy and relaxed now.

Dotia motioned to a chair right beside Hal. Emily felt her body glide into the chair without a thought. Hal nodded and smiled at the helpless child.

"Strange things happen now and then," Hal commented. "That's quite a rash," he blurted out as

Emily extended her arm for Dotia to mend.

In Dotia hand was a small blue jar. She opened the lid revealing a creamy white substance. "It's an old family remedy. This may burn just a little. Okay, maybe a lot, but then the pain will subside," Dotia confessed.

Gingerly, Dotia patted the substance on it. Black specks dotted the surface of the applied ointment. Dotia peered down.

"Grant, come here for a second, please... and bring the lamp for a little extra light," she instructed.

Obediently, he secured the lamp from across the kitchen, sat it down near Emily's' arm, and strung the plug across to the outlet above the counter. "Good thing it has a long cord," Grant remarked.

Staring at the black flecks, Dotia had a confused expression. "Emily, have you been near any cactus plants?"

Emily shook her head no.

"Hal, look at this. What do you make of it?" Dotia positioned the light at a conducive angle for Hal's inspection.

Hal leaned over. "Do you have a magnifier? These old eyes aren't what they used to be."

Dotia reached over to a drawer, shuffled a few things in it and pulled out a magnifier. "Will this do?' She handed it to Hal.

He nodded in acceptance as he clasped it in his hand. Holding it over the Emily's arm, he studied the area.

While Hal's expert eyes reviewed the enigma, Dotia fixed Emily a special blend of tea.

"Looks like miniature quills from a micro porcupine, if you ask me. Wonder if there are porcupines that small..."

Hal amused himself with the thought.

"Emily did you rub up against any bushes or animals?" Grant asked as he leaned in peering over Hal's shoulder viewing the magnified area.

Emily shook her head no. It hurt. She just wanted it to stop hurting; she didn't care what it was now. The pain seared up her arm.

"Here you go dear, drink this." Dotia placed a large cup of brew in front of Emily. The aroma was strong, but pleasing. Emily picked up the cup with her free arm careful not to move the other still being scrutinized by the investigators.

The strange tea was warm and soothing. Within seconds, she had reflexively downed the nectar leaving the cup empty. Dotia swiftly seized the cup and within seconds had it back in front of Emily, full to the brim again. Within seconds, Emily polished it off as well.

A warm sleepy feeling rose up over Emily. Her eyelids felt heavy, as she blinked hers eyes to focus on Hal, curious as to what his prognosis would be. He had leaned back in his chair with a perplexed appearance. This allowed Grant a closer look at the injury.

"Looks like cacti spines to me," Grant added. "I'll get the tweezers."

"No, not tweezers, Grant. We need wax," Dotia corrected.

Grant didn't mind the instruction from Dotia. Although he was proud, he was wise enough not to let pride interfere with learning or relearning.

With a serious grimace, Dotia gathered the required paraphernalia, an unusual pot, ladle, and blocks of wax from the cupboard.

"I'll heat this gummy wax up and pull them out that

way. We'd do a sugaring technique if there were time, but wax will have to suffice." She procured a flatter rectangular pan out from the lower cabinet and laid it next to Emily's injured arm.

"Meanwhile let's soak the area in some warm Epson salts. The ointment will have done its job for now. I'll reapply it after the stingers are out."

As she prepared the water, Grant brought the Epson salts over and sprinkled some in Emily's rectangular pan. Dotia was not long behind with the hot water.

"Okay Emily, place your arm in there till we're ready with the wax." Dotia's smile warmed Emily's heart. It was incredible to have someone care this much. Emily felt overwhelmed, like she was going to cry.

Thankfully, Hal's chuckle deflated the urge, rising up in Emily's chest, to burst out sobbing.

Hal's eyes twinkled with admiration. "I'm impressed. Dotia, is there anything you don't know?"

Dotia blushed. "I'm just happy to be of help in someone's time of need."

"Well, since this is all under control, I need to go out and patrol a bit. I'll come back later and check in. But, if you need anything, call," Grant insisted.

"Yes, you go now. It's all going to be okay," Dotia affirmed. "Emily, I'll get you a snack and more tea while your arm soaks. Then, we will start on removal."

At the mention of food, a loud rumbling sound emanated from Grant's stomach, reminding him that he hadn't ate in a while.

"Dotia do you have any pecans I could snack on. I missed supper in all of the commotion tonight."

"Grant... pecans are not a meal." She turned to Emily. "One of Grant's favorite foods is pecans. He'd eat them all the time if he could. They're only in season a short time. Out-of season, there are too expensive. Plus, they're fatting. While he can afford those calories now, one day, that metabolism will slow down."

Emily nodded, but her mind was starting to drift. The room was cozy, warm, with pleasing scents. It was nice here.

Dotia soothing voice continued but had turned its direction towards Grant. "I'll give you a bag of pecans to take with you, if you fix yourself a sandwich. You can fix Emily one too while you're at it. I'll get Emily's sleeping quarters ready." Happy with her scheme, she hustled off to fix Emily's room.

"Alright. Emily is peanut butter and fruit good or do you want chicken sandwich?" Grant asked. "I could get a glass of milk too."

"Peanut butter is good. Yes, milk, please. What is fruit?" Emily felt strange, but at home with these people, new to her. Everyone's interaction was like a soothing rhythm creating an unseen harmony even with the world's chaos lurking outside. Here inside, all was calm, peaceful, heartfelt.

"Fruit is blueberry spread. It's real fruit that Dotia canned up." Grant's was thinking he'd make at least two for himself and maybe snatch some leftovers from the frig as well. He had spied some leftover banana pudding.

"Okay." Emily voice sounded light. Her eyelids were heavy. Sleep sounded good, too she thought. A little while longer and she could rest. The day's events, no the week's events were taking toll, her mind strolling through it all.

"Here ya go." Grant placed the sandwich and glass of milk down beside her where she could secure it with her non-soaking arm.

******

Before Emily and Grant had finished their sandwiches, Dotia had reappeared. Diligently, Dotia patted Emily's arm dry and began the process of removing the black specks with wax strips. Emily braced herself for pain, but between the effects of the ointment and soaking, her arm felt much better. She didn't even flinch when Dotia yanked the first strip off.

"Does it hurt?" Grant grimaced at the sight of the wax being yanked away.

"Surprisingly, no. The pain's gone. It just feels warm now," she confessed. A yawn escaped her lips.

Knowing the poor girl was exhausted, Dotia comforted her, "This will be done in a second and you can scoot off to sleep. I've fixed up the spare room next to mine. Though, I hope you don't mind, Jacque has decided that he wants to sleep in there with you. He's curled up at the foot of the bed sleeping soundly. I didn't have the heart to move him. He's very, very old, so I guess I have a tendency to let him have his way." Her crystal deep blue eyes revealed the tenderness in her heart that rivaled her steadfast discipline.

Emily laughed. "I'm actually glad. I've gotten used to him keeping me company at night. He curls up on my stomach almost every night."

Pushing back his chair, Grant cleared his and Emily's plates. Reluctantly he snatched up the bag of pecans that Dotia had laid on the counter for him. "Okay, I really have to go and cruise the streets. Hal, I'd say you're in charge, but..." He pointed teasingly over Dotia's head. Dotia swatted at him with her free hand.

Hal chuckled as Grant scampered out the door. He stood up and smiled, "Well, ladies, I must retreat to my sleeping chambers, if there is nothing further that I can assist with. I'd wash the dishes, but.." Hal lifted the casted arm and stood silently waiting for Dotia to dismiss him as a measure of respect.

"Guess we're almost done here. I usually have breakfast about eight; if that's not too early, please join me," Dotia told him.

"I'd be delighted. Oh, Dotia, save some of those black specks. I know a lab we can send them to. Fare thee well and good night." He bowed low and stylishly departed.

"He such a nice man. How long have you known him?" Emily questioned.

"Grant met him as a young boy, so I guess since then. He's always been wonderful towards Grant." Dotia sighed thinking about the length of time passed since Grant was born. She glanced over at her family history book, left on the counter after her and Hal's earlier review. So much history, pain, suffering, love and joy... the book held it all. What would the future hold?

Noticing Dotia's intense gaze towards the other direction, Emily followed the line of sight. An enormous book rested like a forbidden ancient relic beckoning to be rediscovered.

"What's that book over there?" Emily tried to sound nonchalant. She didn't want to intrude on her host's privacy.

"That?" Dotia pointed to the thick writings. Should she enlighten the dear child after all the recent trauma? Dotia pulled the last cloth strip pressed into the wax and rechecked Emily's arm.

"Yes. It has such a beautiful covering on it. I guess I didn't notice it before with my arm hurting so much. But my arm feels better now." Emily examined the patch with its small red raised dots.

"I believe I have gotten them all. Let's put more ointment on and wrap it up for the night." She was still contemplating how to answer regarding the book. Dotia reasoned now was not emotionally the right time for a family introduction. "As for the book, it's my family history. Tomorrow holds many hours for us to invoke ghosts of the past. For tonight, sleep summons. Come, I'll wrap your arm once you're still upon your bed."

The gentle leading voice, kind smile, and deep blue eyes transfixed Emily from further inquiries. Her weary eyes closed for a moment. As Dotia hand clasped hers, Emily hazily peered through sleepy eyes. It took all of her strength to follow Dotia to the guest room. The soft warm bed enveloped her as she drifted off, barely sensing Dotia treating her arm with a fresh lather of cream, or Jacque resituating himself on her stomach. The bandaging that ensued didn't register with Emily's oblivious conscious. The tea had completed its purpose.

Chapter 23

Morning Coffee's the Best

The morning light streaming through the curtains woke her. It took a moment for her dreams to release their hold and for Emily to remember where she was. Jacque stretched lazily next to her feet.

"Still here. Good morning," she whispered to him. It was too hard to tell what time it was. There was no clock. The house was silent. The soft sunlight was the only indication that morning had arrived.

The room was small, but quaint. Her small overnight bag sat in a plush ornate antique chair a few feet away. Yes, she remembered, her toothbrush had been packed in there.

Lifting up the window curtain, she peered outside to get a better idea of the time. The many bushes and trees dominating the landscape obscured direct sighting of the sun. Letting the curtain back down, the white bandages on her arm caught her attention and reminded her of last night's drama. At least her arm felt better. All the pain was gone.

Emily crept around the room, gathered her toothbrush, and tiptoed down the hall to find the bathroom. Her teeth really needed brushing.

In the kitchen, Dotia and Hal had been up for a few hours. First cups of coffee had been shared on the outside patio under the morning dew. Now the pair sat at the kitchen table, each reading a section of the newspaper.

Emily wandered into the kitchen. Her silky brown hair swept around her like a gentle mane.

"Good morning sleepy head," Hal greeted her as he folded his paper and placed it on the table.

"Good morning," Emily shyly replied, her green eyes lacking confidence to meet his or Dotia's. Last night seemed like a distance dream. They must think she was odd to have all this happen to her.

Dotia sensed the girl's uneasiness. "Come on in and have some coffee and breakfast. How do you like your coffee, or would you rather have orange juice, milk, water...? How's your arm feel?"

"Coffee would be wonderful. My arm is completely cured. I'm so sorry to be burdening you like this. I can't tell you how much I appreciate you letting me impose like this..."Emily began but Dotia stepped in.

"Emily, you are not burdening me and I am truly overjoyed to have you visiting. Although, it's a shame you've had to suffer through so much lately...." Dotia shook her head disagreeing with all the trouble that had been laid on this undeserving child.

She continued, " Anyways, I don't want to hear another apology out of you. You are to consider yourself family whenever you're here. But that also means you'll have to pick up after yourself and wash your own dishes," she chuckled. "Make yourself at home, truly!" she added.

"Yes, mam," Emily stuttered. "Where are the coffee cups?"

"And Dotia will do just fine, not mam. Don't be getting formal on me. The day is too young and I'm too old. Sit and I'll get that cup of coffee. Can't have you undoing all my hard work on that arm."

The warmth in Dotia's eyes filled Emily's heart. Emily felt the tears wetting her cheeks before she realized she was crying. No one had ever treated Emily with this much motherly love and acceptance. She tried to turn away to hide the tears, but it was too late.

"Here child." Dotia handed her a few napkins and leaned over giving her a gentle comforting hug. "You've been through a lot over the last few days. No need to fret. It will be okay. You can stay here as long as you want or need."

Hal had sat by silent, knowing better than to say anything at all. It was best to let a woman handle woman stuff. He tried to pretend he wasn't present.

Wiping her tears away, Emily fought back the rising emotional storm within her spirit. "I'm sorry. I'm not usually so emotional like this."

"What did we say about apologies?" Dotia reminded her as she poured a cup of coffee for Emily. "Cream? Sugar?"

"Two creams and two sugars please." Emily regained control.

Dotia rose from her chair, secured a cup, and poured the fresh hot liquid into it. After placing the cup before Emily, she continued her task by adding a sugar bowl, creamer cup, and a spoon next to Emily's cup. "I'll let you add them, 'cause Grant usually says my spoonful is more like a-half.

"Thank you." Emily glimpsed around the kitchen trying to take in as much of the blissful moment as she could, and make it a memory to never forget.

Figuring Emily was emotionally balanced now, Hal decided he could stop pretending he wasn't there. "Emily, I sent off some of the black specks to a friend of mind at the lab. He should have something for us by tonight or tomorrow."

"That's smart thinking. I wouldn't have thought of that," Emily quipped.

Hal beamed from ear to ear.

She would have normally thought of it, but she was in no shape last night to think of anything but rest. Most of all, she wanted someone else to be as happy as she was at this moment. At the moment, she felt like complementing everyone in the world.

"Dotia, this is the cutest kitchen. I love all your things, like the different color bottles and the antique dishes." Emily pointed to an old teapot on the counter.

Past the teapot, on the counter, the voluminous book, she saw last night, again captured her focus, beckoning to be retrieved from the counter.

Hal caught the stare. "That's Dotia's family book. Contains amazing things, it does," he volunteered not considering that Dotia might not want the information shared.

Then, realizing that he may have overstepped, he added, "Of course, Dotia may have secrets too secretive to share with us. Don't think I want Dotia to kill me." His hand held up an imaginary noose, choking the breath from his neck, lolled over to the opposite side of his hanging noose.

"And how would I do that?" Dotia taunted seeing his feeble attempt at humor. "A wicked potion, poisoned desert, perhaps a dark spell?" She sat her coffee cup down.

"Maybe a dart to my heart," Hal grinned patting his chest. He wished he had the nerve to tell her she had already struck him. He adored her even more now.

Emily didn't know what to think about the strange

banter between the two. At least it sounded friendly.

Dotia saw the confusion "Emily, don't mind Hal. He's being silly. What about some breakfast? Do you like oatmeal? I have some ready to heat up. I also have brown sugar and cream to put in it, if you'd like."

"That would be lovely. Thank you." She did like oatmeal. The conversation had momentarily distracted her from the book, but out of the corner of her eye, it intruded. She wasn't going to ask. That would be rude, prying about someone's precious heritage. She would be patient.

Dotia sat the warmed bowl of oatmeal in front of Emily complete with brown sugar and creamer.

"Okay, you can brave the book while you eat your oatmeal. Hal can go watch TV in the living room unless he promises not to interrupt." Her lips pursed sternly at him.

"I promise to be good. I didn't get to read it all yesterday. So, may I stay? Can I peek over Emily's shoulder?" In truth he liked being around Dotia more than he liked watching TV.

Dotia laid the large bound holder of her secrets on the table between Hal and Emily. "Just try not to spill any oatmeal on it. One side is in my native language and the inserted pages are in English."

The cover had strange script and intricate drawings. They reminded Emily of something she had once seen, but it eluded her memory.

"Ohhh, wow Romanian Royalty, Transylvanian. This is incredible!" she gasped after skimming a few pages. Hal scooted closer to read along with her. The stories were just too fascinating.

"I'm out to gather some herbs from the garden. I'll be right back." Dotia felt uncomfortable exposing her secrets while sitting idly by. Without waiting for a reply, the agile older lady was through the door, out of sight to the captivated readers.

Picking her basket up from the porch, Dotia began methodically selecting cuttings for her remedies and teas from the dazzling hodgepodge of vegetation thriving in her backyard paradise.

******

Grant rolled over throwing the sheet from his shirtless body. He had only been out for a few hours. The clock said twelve pm. His 16-hour shift had ended at seven am. And he'd have to pull another long one today too. Swinging his feet over to the floor, he leaped up, grabbed a pair of jeans and a police shirt from his dresser top, and headed to the bathroom, flipping the TV switch on his way.

The news show with Ginger, Bob and Dale blared from the TV as he got ready to begin his day.

"Yes, Bob we have the latest tips on keeping your home vampire free," Ginger purred. "Here to help us with that, is Vampire expert, Reynard Louis."

The camera panned out capturing Ginger and Reynard in the expanded view. Ginger was turned intently focusing on a middle-aged overweight man wearing thick, bi-focal glasses and unstylish clothes.

"Thank you Ginger. Yes, there are many things one should know to deter a vampire attack," the odd Vampire expert nervously started.

Any audience member, unfamiliar with the news show, may have been led to believe the coverage was nothing more than a hoax. But, this news show interweaved entertaining segments along with real news to boost its ratings. Most viewers wouldn't watch real news. Everything had to be over the top, inflated, or odd to catch their attention.

On the display table before him, Reynard had several helpful arrangements of items. "Here, you have a garlic necklace. Everyone knows the power of garlic to ward off the biters. But also, a garlic rub will do." He pointed to the second item before him.

"But Reynard, aren't there items that are less smelly, or more fashionable, for us sensible girls?" Ginger's rehearsed laugh made the nervous man feel he was the butt of a joke.

"Well, Ginger... you could hire a witch or warlock, natural enemies of vampires." He felt like adding that no legitimate one would protect the fake likes of her, but he held in his quickly acquired distaste for the overly primped woman. "However, that could be very expensive and dangerous depending on the crafter. Plus locating one is always difficult." His fat lips curled knowing she hadn't expected him to go off script.

"Yes, Reynard, I can see how putting out an advertisement for a witch or warlock might not be successful!" A fake laugh once again completed her sentence.

Bob popped into the picture's frame next to Reynard. "What's this?" he asked pointing to the next item on the table about the size of a man's palm.

"This is a silver cross." Reynard picked up the work of art. Holding it between his thumb and forefinger he turned it slowly allowing the audience to view it fully.

"And this?" Bob had been in the business awhile and knew you had to keep it moving.

******

Grant hit the TV switch, turning it off. "People will believe about anything," he mumbled. He had overheard the discussion while he was getting ready.

People amazed him sometime, or at least what they would say or do, did. He definitely didn't have time for such nonsense today. With his teeth brushed, hair groomed, and clothes on, Grant was out the door on his way to see Emily, and solve a mystery.

Out in the back garden, Dotia's keen ears heard Grant's truck pull up. She cut over through the side pathway and bounced out to the front.

"Grant, do you want some lunch? I have a stew in the crock pot that should be ready now." She knew he'd be over as soon as he woke up. Young love's attraction.

"I barely pulled up. How'd you get around here so fast?" Grant marveled. "Stew sounds great! Is Emily up? How's her arm?"

Dotia laughed. She could see the narrow focus in his eyes. "Why Grant, I think you're hooked on Emily," she lovingly teased. "Can I start planning the wedding now before she tries to run away? I could throw a potion in her tea, if you'd like, just be on the safe side mind you."

"Okay, just get smart..." he tried to sound gruff but he couldn't contain the smile engulfing his face at the thought of seeing Emily again.

He followed his tormentor around the entrance to the backside garden. Essences from the garden filled his nostrils. The afternoon sun coaxed the flowery shrubs and greeneries into releasing their perfumes. As Dotia entered the kitchen, the garden fragrances flooded in, filling the room with powerful scents.

"Wow, I have to see your garden. Those scents are incredible!" Emily exclaimed as she closed her eyes letting the aroma fill her mind.

"That's me," Grant remarked trying his smoothest approach as he strolled in behind Dotia.

Hal couldn't resist. "Boy, that's not the scent she was

referring to... she said incredibly delightful. But maybe you'll luck out and she'll tolerate you anyways."

"It's a wonder she can smell anything after sitting next you all morning," Grant picked back kiddingly. "But at least you couldn't cover up the smell of that tantalizing stew Dotia fixed for me," he bragged.

"You're in for a surprise, cause I helped with the stew! And Dotia fixed it for me, not you!" Hal's broad smile eliminated Grant from teasing further.

"Still smells good....And, you can't eat it all, so I'll have to help," was all Grant felt he should add. The older man's jubilance needed to be left unscathed. Small things in life often bring the most joy.

"Only if you help with dishes," Dotia reminded. "Do you want some coffee?' She glided over to cupboard and selected Grant's favorite mug. Within seconds she had it poured and waiting for him at the table next to Emily.

Grant pulled back the chair to take a seat. The open Family Book glared at him from its spot in front of Emily. Quickly he shot a look of concern over to Dotia. He hoped she knew what she was doing. Dotia returned his concern with a knowing smile.

"Emily, now that you've read the stories, what do you think?" Dotia took her chair on the other side of Grant, across from Emily.

"It's fascinating... so tragic in places, but still what a story." Emily had so many questions bouncing around in her head.

"It's so hard to grasp that people were murdered simply from being different. I can almost understand superstition and how the town acted back then, but your husband murdered by that group of men just for being a gypsy? I can't imagine being a young widow, all alone. Why didn't you return to Romania to your relatives there?" The words had just blurted out before Emily realized she was saying them. Her face reddened embarrassed by her inability to control her curiosity. To avoid eye contact, she pretended to look at the open pages in front of her.

Dotia was not shaken or upset at all by Emily's questions. She had considered those same things herself. It was good to sweep out the cobwebs once in a while.

"I've only been once to my ancestral homeland. That was to collect my God-daughter and niece, Grant's mom after her parents died in a plane crash. Maybe we should have stayed, but it was all too unfamiliar to me. There I would have been forced to live under my family's reign."

She sighed thinking back to the past, "More than likely, I'd be coerced to remarry a man of family's choosing. Plus, America is where I was born and raised. So, I guess to me America's home."

Dotia had enjoyed living independently away from controlling family ties. "Maybe I'll return to visit in the future. You could come with me Emily!" Dotia eyes twinkled.

"It sounds like a wonderful adventure! But, I have to graduate first." Emily knew she had a long struggle ahead of her getting through college, especially with no family support, emotionally or financially.

Dotia gracefully sprung up from the table. "Enough of reminiscing for now," she stated closing the large book. "We can continue with the stories later." She placed the encyclopedia-sized treasure back over on the counter.

"I was hoping you and Grant would to run a few errands for Hal and me. Someone needs to stop by and check on Hal's store. And we need some butter and whatever else you guys want from the store."

It would have been hard to resist appeasing Dotia's

deep blue eyes, so both Grant and Emily nodded accepting the challenge.

"No problem. I can head over there in a few minutes," Grant offered.

Emily nodded in agreement.

Chapter 24

Helping Out and Traveling About

The pair trampled through the pet store, filling up water bottles and feed trays. The colorful store for some reason reminded Emily of a carnival. Cage after cage lined the shelved walls. Aquariums of various sizes hosted the space between the last shelf and floor. The center rows held multiple types of pet items from food to toys. Any spot not home to an animal or commercial item displayed an information poster of some kind.

"This is much more work than I imagined!" Emily exclaimed.

"Yeah. It's looks easy, but managing a pet store is a lot of work. I used to come by almost every day and help Hal out. He's really a neat guy. I guess he's like a father to me in some ways."

"I read about your father's death in the book. That was bizarre and horrific." Emily confessed. Once again, she hadn't thought about what she was going to say before saying it.

"Well, I was young at the time. I only remember the funeral, everyone standing around in black, his body lying in the casket like he was in a deep sleep. I remember thinking I could reach in, shake him, and he'd wake up." Grant's casual tone made it seem like typical conversation about the weather, not something as life-changing as death.

As she scoped up some feed and filled a rabbit dish, Emily peeked over at him trying to catch his facial expressions. Did he really not feel any pain over it, or was he just holding it in? She couldn't read his stoic façade.

"Okay, that's the last one." Grant closed the lid. "While we're here, there's something I'd like to check a few yards behind the store. It won't take but a minute."

"Okay. What is it?" With her arm healed, Emily was feeling adventurous.

"I'll have to show you." He waved her to follow him as he headed out towards the back door. After Emily cleared the back threshold, Grant closed the door and locked its two deadbolts.

The back area of the connected stores contained a paved area for trucks to circle around to make deliveries or pickups. Behind the pavement's ending, lay a vast field. Interrupting the sea of wild grasses and flowers were thick patches of trees and boulders jetting from the grassy earth sharply in discrete areas.

Surrounding the uninhabited land, a barrier, inhibiting wandering souls from entering into the field, an eight foot tall chained-link fence stood. It was plastered with several metal 'No trespassing' signs.

Grant climbed over the fence and set off through the grass, not waiting to see if Emily was behind him or not. He knew her uncontrollable curiosity would have the better of her. Behind him, the chain fence clanged as Emily followed his lead in violating its warnings.

The grass rustled under her feet as she rushed to catch up to him. Her shorter legs, being no match for his long strides, forced her to break into a jog. Meeting his side, Emily continued the brisk trot. She hoped whatever he wanted to show her wasn't far.

Grant advanced towards a large patch of trees, leering over huge thick boulders randomly jetting out of the earth. The trees and rocks slowed his pace allowing Emily to regain her breath.

The winding unmarked path Grant was forging sloped gently downward. Before long, Emily realized that they had ventured into a gigantic dip in the Earth. It was deep enough for a large house to disappear into. Emily couldn't see anything but the brim of the grassy field and some trees. The nearby stores had all disappeared.

"Here we are," Grant stated halting in front of several large rocks and huge boulders. He lifted one of the large rocks, set it to the side and grabbed another. Emily had no idea what he was doing. She stood silent and perplexed a few feet behind him watching rock after rock being relocated.

A loud scraping noise sounded. Grant appeared to be wrestling with something. Emily moved closer and peered over. There was a huge metal grate about four foot high and three foot wide bolted at the top of the boulder. Grant had thick padlock clasped in one hand and a knife in the other scrapping caked on debris from the keyhole. Behind the grate, a black expanse piqued her curiosity. Emily could feel the cool air seeping out. The air smelled earthy, moist like clean dirt.

Once the keyhole was readied, Grant slid a key from his pocket into it. The key turned, but the u-shaped bolt did not spring loose. Grant pounded the iron fastener against the side of the grate. Reluctantly it slowly popped open, freeing the grate from the closed metal hoop bolted deep into the boulder. Grant removed the lock and dangled it on the grate. Pushing the lock's loop in, he latched it to the grate.

"Let's go!" He lifted the grate high enough for Emily to pass under.

"Do you think it's safe? Where does it go?" Emily paused at the opening, not sure if she had the courage to follow her curiosity this time.

"It'll be okay. This is an entrance to a cavern that winds underground, below the whole town." Grant's blue eyes burned with excitement and a sly smile formed on his lips.

Emily took a deep breath and ducked under Grant's arms as he held the metal grate up. Once she was through, he agilely twisted underneath the grate and then released it behind him. The metal clanked as it slammed down against the opening's rock face.

"Oh... Don't tell Dotia we did this. She gets funny about some things," he warned Emily as they proceeded into the cave.

"Oh, so now I hold a secret over you, huh?" she giggled, her emerald eyes mischievously sparkling.

"Be good, or I won't let you come," Grant warned.

As they moved deeper into the cave, all the guiding daylight from the cave's entrance was fading. Emily could only see a foot in front of her. Grant took a small flashlight from his back pocket and turned it on. The tunnel engulfed the small ray of light only allowing them to see a few feet ahead. "Guess I should have brought a flood light," Grant mumbled.

"Wait, you've never been down here before?" Emily surmised that if he had been here before, he would have known what size light to bring.

"You got me." He grinned broadly. "But, that's the fun.... first adventures!"

Emily had to admit, she too loved adventure. The hair on her arms tinkled as they progressed deeper and deeper into the cool brisk darkness. With Grant at her side, Emily wasn't afraid. In her mind, his broad shoulders and muscular arms could wrestle a bear.

Grant on the other hand was too intrigued to be concerned with danger. He knew to watch his footing, to test each step, before committing all his weight to keep from falling into a lower chamber. Plus, he only had a visual of about four feet in front of him. Like a panther, he stalked his path with precision.

Their footsteps echoed softly through the silent black space. The tunnel was barely four feet wide at most areas, but in some places, the passage swelled forty or fifty feet in width.

The pair had been walking for a few minutes sticking to the largest route. Grant figured it was wisest not to veer down any of the smaller side paths. The secret cavity seemed to stretch on and on, endlessly.

"Grant, how deep do you think we are now? It's gotten much colder and feels damper." Emily ran her hands rapidly up and down her arms to bring a little warmth into her exposed flesh. Good thing she had the bandage on. It offered a little extra coverage.

"Not sure. But you're right, it's cooler here and the ground's different." He flashed the light around the area. The rock walls had changed composition. Earlier the sides were mixed hues of browns and grays. Here, black expanses were streaked with glittering veins that looked like some kind of metal ore. The black floor held small pools of scattered water.

"Too bad I didn't take any geology courses at school," Emily reflected. "I think different levels have different compositions and minerals."

Time slowed for the adventurers. Too engrossed in this extraordinary hidden world, neither talked or made any sounds other than soft footsteps. The soundless air was laden with moisture and every exhale frosted in mid-air. Grant observed the beam coming from the flashlight. It was still strong, showing no signs of dimming.

No wonder Dotia hadn't told him about this place. How many miles did it run? Maybe it was time to turn back for now. They could return later, fully prepared for an exploration.

The path felt as though it was inclining beneath his feet. Were they traveling up? The air grew lighter, fresher, warmer, but still carried the heaviness of dew on an early predawn morning.

A slight humming captured Grant's attention. The new sound broke, what had become unnerving silence and Grant's hesitation of continuing forward. Whispering for an unknown reason, he asked Emily, "Do you hear that?"

Instead of verbally replying, uncomfortable with disturbing the seemingly sleeping world, she nodded.

The next few strides brought renewed passion as the humming transformed into the soft rushing of water. With every step the sounds became louder. Abruptly a few feet ahead, the ray of light no longer bounced off narrow walls. The central corridor opened up into a much larger space.

Grant held his hand up. "We should move very cautiously. I've heard that around large expansions in caves there are sometimes weak spots. I don't want either of us to fall into a bottomless pit. Plus, I didn't pack a rope."

Carefully, they ventured nearer to the edge of the huge opening. Dim light emitted shadows on the walls and ceiling.

"Where's that light coming from?" Emily asked.

"I'm not sure. Where're too deep for sunlight. Maybe someone ran artificial light or it could be some kind of chemical or mineral reaction," Grant theorized.

The passage below their feet became a steep cliff. The ceiling and walls stretched up and out, forming an underground gorge. An unknown source of light was being reflected from crystals and minerals embedded in mountainous thrusts of earth before them.

Leaning cautiously forward, Grant moved his flashlight's diminutive ray down at the sharp drop-off a few feet in front of him. He aimed the light around, sweeping the drop-off. The flashlight's small beam set off a cascade of reflections from thousands of crystals. The majestic beauty left the pair spellbound.

The enormous magnificent cavern was further graced with a sparkling waterfall jetting out of a crevice near the chamber's ceiling. Although the falling water was hundreds of feet further in, its echo surrounded Emily and Grant. The splashing water was joined by lesser streams forming a lake to the right side of where they stood.

"Wow!" Emily gushed breaking the trance. "Absolutely breathtaking! I'm in a *Tom Sawyer* meets *Lost Underworld* episode. Have you been here before?"

"No, I never knew this was here. Wherever here is ... Incredible." Grant was too captured by the stunning scenery before him to notice the beam of his flashlight was weaker.

"Should we venture down? How much time do you think it would take for us to cross this?" Emily was too intrigued to know fear.

"Time." Grant turned his wrist and shined the flashlight at his watch. The weakening ray sent a chill up his spine. It was time to leave before they were stuck in the dark. "Speaking of time, my shift starts soon. We're going to have to race out of here for me to get back on time."

Grant didn't want to let on about the failing flashlight

and his stupidity. He had led them here unprepared, placing them both in possible mortal danger. Would Emily panic if she knew their reality?

"Okay, but can we come back again?" She sensed something was wrong. His voice had been too stern.

"Sure, but now... we have to get back fast. Keep hold of my hand, tight!" Grant grabbed her hand and pulled her into an accelerated gait.

The swift pace continued back through the icy cold section. It was hard to tell how long they had traveled or how far they had returned. Her feet and legs ached trying to keep up with Grant's strides, but at least the movement was keeping her warm.

Each smaller tunnel, veering off, looked like the next. A few times, tunnels of almost equal size appeared and Grant had to pause, struggling to remember which passage would yield true. On the way in, he had selected the largest opening from the left, but sometimes that was the center one and sometimes it was the one falling most left. What if they accidently took the wrong branch, Grant wondered. His confidence was failing with the fainting of the light.

The weakening pale beam caught Emily's attention. That was why Grant wanted to hurry. Realizing the deadly consequences of losing the beacon, an adrenaline surge coursed through her veins.

The light faded, then died. Surrounded by absolute darkness, Grant paused and shook the tool. Nothing. He smacked the thing lightly against the wall. A flicker gave way to a weak, but steady glow. They resumed speeding through the passage, only able to view the few feet in front of them at each step.

Without a sound, the glow died again. Pausing, he repeated the earlier succession of shaking and smacking. It was dead.

"Okay, we shouldn't be far. Don't panic." Grant attempted to sound smooth and confident even though he felt a twinge of anguish in his chest.

He continued, in a lower masculine tone, "Let's keep one hand locked with each other. Spread across the tunnel's width, and place your other hand on the wall, as high as you can reach. That way we should be able to figure out what is the main passage and what is a side branch. The main one was the tallest all the way in. Plus, there shouldn't be too many side branches this far towards the entrance." Or, at least he hoped not.

"Okay. Good thing I'm not scared of the dark. But I warn you if something hairy crawls across me, I'm going to scream and throw punches." The situation may be grave, but humor gave Emily a way to deal with it. Whenever things got tough, odd thoughts always popped into her mind.

Feeling their way was slow going, but seemed to be working. After a few hundred steps, the darkness became a murky grey. They could barely make out the walls and each other, but at least it was an improvement. It wasn't long before light, from the opening, bore down the passage meeting them. Grant and Emily both sighed with relief. It had worked; they had returned.

Chapter 25

Not Sure What To Say

Back in the truck, Grant and Emily relaxed each drinking a bottle of water. A rolled up map set on the seat between them.

"I wonder if that water down there is safe to drink. When we go back, we'll have to take a sample." Emily's mind was flittering from one thought to the next. "Hey, who owns the cavern? Is it private, federal, state, city, county, or could it be a non-profit organization, maybe a nature conservatory?"

"I'm not sure, but I need to check my messages real quick, so hold those thoughts." Grant grabbed his cell, hit a few keys, and waited, listening as each caller's voice demanded his time.

Emily picked up the rolled object and uncurled it, spreading it out flat. There was a thick blue line, a few black X's in circles, several black X's not circled, and about five small red X's. One red X, she surmised, was right down from where her apartment was.

Still listening to the voices talking on his cell, Grant reached over, and appended the document. "This is not for you," he chastised. He rolled it up tight and tucked it behind his seat.

It took a few more minutes for all his voice mail messages to run through.

"Okay, done." Grant placed the cell back in its holder.

"I have good news and bad news. What do you want first?" He asked.

Grant's deep blue eyes mesmerized Emily for a second, leaving her unable to decide. "Whatever is easiest."

"Call one... said ...Ria is awake and doing okay."

"When can I see her? When can she come home? I miss her so much!" Emily's sudden joyful shrieks confirmed he'd selected the right one to tell her first.

"I'll drop you by there on my way to the station if you'd like. I gotta be at the station in twenty minutes. Then later, I can pick you up and take you to Dotia's," Grant offered.

Emily nodded, too overwhelmed to speak. She wiped her face with the back of her hand trying to dry the tears wetting her cheeks. Grant reached around behind his seat, grabbed a box of tissues and sat them beside her. Taking a few, she caught her breath and mumbled, "I'm okay... just happy about Ria. What's the bad news?"

"The prints I turned in came back with matches to several crimes and an ID. The guy's a serial rapist and killer. You were very lucky. Good thing you used your head and escaped. I'm afraid he has a long line of victims... not so fortunate." Grant hated to utter this truth.

Emily felt nauseated and weak. Why was it affecting her this much? She had gotten away. She and Ria could go back to the Dorms. They didn't have to stay at the apartments.

Seeing her color pale, Grant tried to reassure her. "It's okay though I have people on the lookout for him. If he returns to that car, we got him!"

"Can you help us move, please? We signed a 6-month lease and don't have any money to get out of it. Maybe if you spoke to the landlord..." She felt like she was asking too much, but Emily was desperate.

"Sure, I think being the circumstance... I mean you're an indispensable eyewitness needing protective services, so I can arrange some things. It'll be done within two days. Until then, you'll have to stay at Dotia's and possibly Ria will too if she's released before then. We'll move your things secretly in case he's watching. Leave it to me."

He cranked up the truck and they headed en route to the hospital.

******

When Emily arrived at Ria's room, she was sitting up eating from a hospital tray. "Emily!" Ria shirked throwing her arms out wide in anticipation of a hug. "Gosh, I've been going crazy here. I woke up a few hours ago. They say they don't know what happened to me."

Emily raced over to Ria's side. Sweeping her long auburn hair away from Ria's food tray, she leaned in to hug Ria. The two squeezed each other tight, sincere in their bond of loving sisterhood.

"I missed you so much." Emily kissed Ria on her cheek. "I was afraid you'd never get well." She released her grip and moved back slightly, to see up close that her friend was indeed well. Tears poured from Emily's eyes.

"Here, have some water. It's helps to keep you from crying," Ria commanded as she thrust a cup of it in front of Emily. It was a technique she had stumbled upon when she was little to keep herself from being beaten more by her cruel grandparents.

Emily clutched it with both hands and sipped. It did help. She sank into the visitor's chair beside the bed.

Ria focused her eyes on Emily's. "I turned on the TV earlier and there's all this stuff about Vampires, Curses, Aliens, Witches... what's going on out there?" Trying to abstract any information she could, her brown eyes intensely fastened on Emily.

Clearing her throat, Emily began, "Yep, you've missed a lot... but I think the media is creating a frenzy. There is something making people sick and a few have died. No one knows why. Anyways, I have so much to tell you. When can you get out of here?"

"This evening. I can't wait to sleep in my *own* bed." Ria complained.

"About that, ..." Emily sighed. This was going to be a long story.

******

Grant parked his truck behind the police station. Reaching behind the seat he secured the rolled up map with the tunnel locations drawn on by Hal. "This is going to be a hard sell to Bill," Grant said out loud.

Bill was acting chief for the time being, till a permanent selection was decided. Grant hoped Bill would get the position. Bill had good common sense, was a hard worker, ethical.

With the treasure in hand, Grant shut the truck door and strolled into the building. Bill's office door was open, exposing his giant desk stacked with papers. Grant respectfully tapped on the door's side as he entered, his rolled up map in hand.

"Bill, I need to go over something with you discretely. You got a sec?"

"Yaaah, close the door." He shuffled the papers he was working on to the side. "I never thought as acting chief I'd have so much paper work to do. Guess someone has to do it," he complained as he rubbed his hairless scalp.

Bill was what most would call a lifer. He had started at the police force forty years ago, when he was about twenty. Being a cop had become, not just a part of his life, but the reason for it. A few years back, after the accident he probably should have retired. But, what else would he do if he couldn't be a cop every day? ... It was all he knew. It was all he wanted. But, he wasn't sure what he had gotten himself into taking over the chief's position.

After closing the door, Grant moved close to the desk and in a low tone implored, "First, I need your word you won't discuss what I show you with anyone, not even other officers. And, then I need you to hear me out before you set on any decisions."

Grant's formidable expression took him by surprise. Wondering what could have turned the young man's disposition this serious and forceful, Bill nodded his acceptance to the terms.

Grant laid the maps on Bill's desk and unrolled them. They were the key to Grant's theory and resulting plan. Bill stared at the images as Grant weighted down the corners to keep the edges from curling up.

"What's these lines?" Bill liked for things to move rapidly.

"I need your patience while I explain the whole thing, or it won't make sense," Grant stressed.

"Here, where the thick blue markings are..." He pointed to the colorations, "...runs a natural underground cave system. It's been kept a secret for particular reasons and needs to stay that way."

"If that's true, it runs over a big segment of the county. How come no one's ever told me about this? Who all knows?" Bill blurted unable to control his need for quick answers.

"Bill, you agreed to wait before interrupting... I'll never get through what I have to say..." Grant's voice was stern like a father talking to a son, but his smile settled Bill.

"Okay... I'll hold it in till you tell me you're done," Bill grumbled.

"What I was saying, you've heard of that Ledniw Corporation ... that owns a huge chunk of the county?" Ledniw backwards is Windel. It's owned by descendants of the Windel's. They own every piece of land over the cave system. It's their secret. Apparently they've gone to great expense to keep the caves a family secret. I got this information from the family and swore never to reveal it. So, I'm entrusting you with my honor and maybe my life by telling you."

Bill started to interrupt again thinking Grant was exaggerating, but the solemn gleam in Grant's deep blue eyes convinced him there was something to this story.

"If you look at the large red X's, those are openings in the system. Now, look at the large thick black circled X's. Those are where the recent deaths occurred, and the non-circled black X's are connected to the episodes of illness or whatever it is affecting people." Grant paused letting the information sink into Bill's mind. Bill nodded his head as the connections formed.

"My theory is whatever is occurring is using or has used a portion of these caves." Grant brushed his fingers over the areas he believed to be involved. "I'd like permission to secretly scout out... investigate the sections."

So intent on the scheme, he forgot their agreement and paused, awaiting Bill's thoughts. The silence ensued for not more than a few minutes. Bill tapped the map thoughtfully and then looked up at Grant. "You done?" Bill muttered.

Grant nodded afraid to utter a sound for fear of ruining his chance of success.

"Thought you were going to *tell* me when you were done," Bill chided.

Trying to fully appraise the situation, he peered up at Grant. Although youthful, Grant's character possessed a solidness and intuition that many three times his age didn't.

"Got to admit, as crazy as it sounds, it seems to have a point." Bill nodded given his preliminary approval. "But, I'm going too... and I'll make Dan go. I know he doesn't seem like it, but he can be dependable when required. Plus, he'll be afraid to tell anyone, if I tell him to keep his trap shut or else.... Oh, but don't tell him about the Windel thing, he's superstitious. Can't have him cracking up..."

"Alright." Grant knew better than to object to Bill's conditions. He was a stubborn old cop. Grant rolled the map back up. "I'll get all the gear. When you want to head out?"

"No time like the present. Holler when you get things ready and packed to go. I'll tell Dan the good news!" With a solid fist he cheerfully thumped his desk and winked at Grant. His lips twisted into mischievous grin imaging the fun he'd have teasing poor Dan.

Grant started towards the door with his treasure secured in his clutch. Bill's voice echoed behind him," Hey, Grant, why Windels sell the old place and let them tear it down?"

"Well, actually, the land still belongs to the Windels. It's on a 100 year lease. As for the house, guess the family decided people would never let go of the tragic story. After all no one would rent it because if you lived there people wouldn't have anything to do with you. The Windel family could never live there either. They'd be targets of the same type of alienation or worse. So, it was time to move on and let go."

"Guess so, makes sense," Bill nodded. The curious thing was how did Grant know the family and obtain the information. He bet it had something to do with Grant's odd little nanny. That sweet looking old woman had scared many strong opponents in her day, maybe even done more than that. Bill had his suspicions, but he'd never waste time looking into it. After all, sometimes something outside the law had to be done to stop evil in its rampage.

Chapter 26

Ready or Not... Let's Go

Brad pulled up to the hospital where the girls were waiting. Ria and Emily eagerly jumped in.

"Thanks Brad. I couldn't imagine where I'd be without you." Ria confessed, her big brown eyes held his gaze adoringly.

Brad leaned over and kissed her lightly on her lips. "Just no more scaring the hell out of me."

She nodded. He put the car in gear and headed for the apartment.

"When we get there, I want you two to stay close to me. No wandering off. We stick together with cell phones ready, right?" His lecturing voice was confident, but stern. "The plan is to get some clothes... in and out."

"It's going to be hard choosing what to leave," Ria remarked.

A few minutes later the car drove up along the entrance to the complex. The odd campers and temporary spectators were still assembled throughout the adjoining land.

"Wow, it is a freak show here," Ria exclaimed. "I'd never believed it. Look there's a tent selling charms. Maybe they have some cool jewelry. Is that a real Indian Wigwam?"

Brad was focusing on driving and didn't see what Ria

was pointing at. Emily was too busy trying to stay calm to be interested in sightseeing.

They pulled into an empty spot marked 613. Emily gave an involuntary shutter. Even with the security of having her friends with her, it was scary coming back. The movement wasn't lost to Ria, who had peered into the mirror to check on her friend, seated in the back.

"Emily, you don't have to come. You can stay in the car, or we can take you over to Dotia's. Brad and I can get the stuff without you," Ria softly offered.

"Thanks, but I'll be okay. Anyways, I need to grab a few things. I only have one change of clothes at Dotia's." The auburn beauty pushed the door opened and climbed out, as did her companions.

"How did you survive with only one change?" Ria's face scrunched up.

Both girls laughed as Brad shook his head in disappointment that such a stereotype would hold true. The laughter was short-lived when Emily spotted the Pontiac. Huddling close to Ria, she whispered, "Don't look or draw attention to it, but the car is over there on the edge of the parking lot."

Ria put her arm around Emily and the pair continued en route up the stairs with Brad.

A new apartment door stood in place of the damaged one. Emily's key didn't work. "Fizzles, they changed the lock. Guess, it was the smart thing to do, but now we'll have to go to the office and get the new one." Her shoulders slumped down aggravated with this new interference.

The trio retraced their steps down the stairs and forged a path to the manager's office. It was a long way from their apartment, on the opposite side of the complex.

Reaching the office, Emily twisted the door knob. The

door opened. A young male who looked like a high school student, sat at a large desk completing what appeared to be his homework. Emily approached and politely began, "Hi. I'm the tenant in 613. The lock was changed due to a break-in, so I need to pick up the new keys, please."

Pushing his papers to the side, the young boy eyed her suspiciously. "Got I.D."?

Emily fumbled in her purse and pulled out a few cards. "Here's driver's license, college I.D., bank card..."

His thin pale hand reached over, flipped through them, then slid them back towards her. Without a word, he rose up from the desk and disappeared through a door at the back of the room. A few seconds later, he returned with two keys in his left hand.

"Okay, that'll be forty dollars, cash." He held his right hand out.

"What! Are you joking me?" Her anxiety caused the pitch in her voice to carry higher than normal.

The boy didn't reply but only yielded a blank uncaring stare.

"There can't be a charge, cause it was a break-in." Emily exclaimed shocked by his demand.

"Break-ins aren't covered by the apartment complex. Take it up with the manager. If you want the keys now, its forty bucks," he smirked, pleased at having authority over someone.

"I don't have forty on me," she cried as she poured out the contents of her purse on the desk. "I can scrape up twenty. Can I get one key and bring the other twenty later? I promise I'll be right back," she pleaded as she stacked the few bills and loose change from her purse into countable arrangements.

"Nope," he sneered.

Brad, who had been causally standing back with Ria over near the entrance door, walked up to the desk. Nervously, the offensive boy stepped backwards. His mouth hung opened, seeing this muscular guy up close. Brad reached into his wallet and slapped two twenty's down inches away from the edge of the desk closest to the boy.

"Give the nice lady the keys *now....* and write a receipt," he growled.

Being of a cowardly nature, the boy only nodded as his shaky hand unclasped the keys, dropping them down within Emily's reach. Still standing, he opened a small desk drawer and removed a receipt book with a pen attached. He scribbled an acknowledgement slip. He nervously held the slip out to Emily.

Snatching up the keys, the slip, and the contents of her purse, Emily spun back towards the exit with Brad close behind. Ria was waiting with the door opened. They marched back towards apartment 613.

"Thanks Brad. I have forty up in my room to repay you with," she confided. "I didn't want to tell the little jerk there was cash up in the room, especially since he had a key."

"Glad I could help." He presented a composed demeanor, but inside he was slightly nervous about the whole process taking so long. The only consolation at the moment was knowing two police cars were not far away, which hopefully meant neither were the officers.

"I can't believe that kid.... I can't believe the management making me pay that much!" In protest of having been treated so unfairly, Emily's stomped hard into each step as she ascended the stairs.

She jammed the key into the lock and angrily thrust the door open. It slammed hard into the wall causing the front windows to rattle.

"Jez girl, you don't know you own strength. I know you're mad, but please don't break the door down, or we'll have to pay out more money," Ria soothingly cautioned. Ria didn't want to upset her friend, but Emily needed to get her temper under control before she did something she would regret.

"I'm sorry Ria. I guess it's all getting to me," she said as she entered the apartment. "I've always played by the rules, been a nice person... maybe too nice, and people walk over me. I guess that guy coming after me like that has really made me angry. What did I do to deserve that pervert?" Her voice quaked with the rage she had been suppressing. Her face flushed, and emerald eyes redden, blurred with tears. Emily retreated into the kitchen and fixed herself a glass of water. With each sip she felt the resentment and pain subside.

Ria came up beside her and comfortingly laid her arm around her traumatized friend.

She exhaled deeply. "I'm sorry, Ria. I'm okay now." "Guess I needed to vent. I realize many people have it worse off than me. I really shouldn't be upset or complain."

"Yes, you should be upset when something wrong happens. You wouldn't be full of compassion if you didn't react to injustice. You have a right to be upset.... Maybe not break the door down though." With Ria's humor, both girls broke into laughter.

Emily shouted over to Brad, who had settled in a chair in the living room to wait for the girls, "Sorry Brad, I'm better now. No more melt downs."

He waved his hand signaling it was okay. "Let me know when you girls are packed and ready to go."

The girls got the hint and made their way towards the bedroom to gather up a few items.

"I'd be a mess if all this happened to me. I mean, I just went to sleep and woke up a few days later. You had to suffer through worrying about me, that creep trying to attack you, and having to relocate. But, it'll get better now. We're together!" Ria's bright smile lightened Emily's spirits.

Each girl disappeared into their respective bedrooms and filled their suitcases and backpacks.

"All done!" Ria proclaimed. Loaded with two suitcases each and a couple of backpacks, the girls lugged their necessities into the living room. Brad looked up from reading a book and shook his head.

"Good thing I don't have a motorcycle. Decide what you want me to carry. Let's try to get it all in one load," Brad stated.

Ria sat one of her suitcases and one of her bags down near him. "Here ya go. I'll volunteer to let you carry these... since you insist." She smiled broadly at him, grateful to have such a wonderful boyfriend.

"Are you sure you can carry the other stuff? After all you did just get out of the hospital." His concerned expression filled Ria's heart with warmth. He did care about her, she told herself. It was so hard for her to truly believe in other people's affection for her, because for most of her life it hadn't been like that.

"I told you two. I feel fine. It was like I had a really good night's sleep. Seriously."

Brad picked up her suitcase and bag in one hand. "Emily, I can take some of your stuff too. I need something in this hand so I'm balanced."

Emily proffered a suitcase and backpack. Then, the trio headed down to the car.

Chapter 27

It's Dark In There

"You want me to go in there? If it's been locked, how can anyone be in there? Sounds like you guys are out there on this theory." Dan was sure they had lost their minds and he wasn't about to join them.

Bill shook his head. "If it's like Grant said, there could be another entrance being used."

"I'll stay out here and stand guard," Dan volunteered. "Plus, if you guys don't come out... how long before I should sound the alarm? People go in them things and never come out. I seen it on TV!"

"Oh no Danny Boy, you're coming with us," Bill insisted. "Do you some good. Facing your fears puts hair on your chest." He snickered knowing that he'd be able to rib Dan the whole time in there. It was too much fun picking on ole Dan. He pushed Dan into the cave's mouth and followed behind him. The cobwebs stuck to Dan's hair.

"Disgusting! I hate spiders," he grumbled swatting at his head to kill anything live that might have been in the web.

"Stop your grumbling. Little spider can't suck much blood. Be surprised if they'd even want your blood, Dan." Bill twisted around to the front of little fellow and looked down into the dark hole. "Come on. Let's get going." With his flashlight out, Bill led the way into the void.

Grant slid in, dropping the camouflage arrangement into place on the outside of the grated entrance. The tight space only permitted the guys to move on their hands and knees.

"Make sure you're behind Dan, Grant. Don't want to waste time finding him later on," Bill chuckled. "Remember Dan, no sissy screaming. We need the element of surprise. Could be a couple of nut cases in here."

Dan hesitated. His eyes bulged and sweat beaded on his forehead. Grant swatted him from behind. "Keep moving. I don't want to look at your behind any longer than I have to."

It wasn't long before there was enough room carved out of the earth to allow the guys to stand. The walls glittered with minerals. But there were no crystals like Grant had seen at the other cave. Maybe the crystals only appeared at a certain depth. Also, they hadn't hit a spot as cold as that one spot in the other cave either. Running these differences around in his mind, Grant continued following Bill's lead, deeper and deeper, silently, cautiously, into the unknown waiting ahead.

******

Once at the car, Brad shuffled the suitcases into the trunk and stacked two of the back packs on top. "The other stuff will have to go into the back seat with Emily," he commented.

"Huh, sorry.. what you need?" Emily asked. She had been scanning the area for sight of her attacker. Instead though, she had potted two police cars at the far end of the complex.

"Hey, I wonder if one of those is Grant's." She pointed towards the vehicles. "His should have a bag of pecans in the front seat."

"I think Emily's distracted," Ria giggled. "After we load our stuff, maybe we could take a look around for him, if Brad has time, Ms. I'm In Love," Ria lightheartedly taunted.

Emily blushed. "Ria, you're sooo mean. But, I did think we could glance down that way for him, if you two don't mind.... After all we are staying at his Godmother's house." She didn't want to admit to herself how much she really wanted to see him.

"I don't have to work tonight, so okay with me if Ria's up to it," Brad agreed.

Ria nodded. "Let's go."

Emily threw one of the backpacks on her shoulder as Brad locked up the car. They walked over to the police cars still parked at the far end of the complex. Emily peered into the front window. On the seat was a bag of pecans. Her heart beat faster. It was his car. He had to be around here someone.

"I think I know where he is. You guys, follow me." Emily tromped off behind the complex and into the thick woods. A few bent tree limbs, broken shoots, and squashed bushes told her that someone or maybe a few people had recently trudged through this area. She followed the vague trail with Ria and Brad closely behind her.

The trio came up to a chain link fence, much like the one she had climbed with Grant. Emily could see the faint temporary path continuing on the other side. Placing her hands up high, she scaled the tall metal fence.

"Emily, do you think this is wise? That's private land. It says no trespassing on the signs. Plus, there may be snakes or maybe bad people back there," the concern in Ria's voice almost made Emily rethink her plan.

"Trust me. If what's back here is anything like Grant

showed me somewhere else, you'll both be amazed. But, you've got to keep it a secret." Reaching the top of the metal obstacle, she swung over, descended a few feet, and then jumped off to the ground.

"Okay, now you're not making any sense. Hope you haven't lost your mind," Ria mumbled.

"What? Couldn't hear you. Come on, hurry." Emily waited for her friends to follow over her the fence.

"Nothing, just talking to myself..." Ria replied as she scaled the fence and landed beside Emily.

Although he thought this was crazy too, Brad was right behind Ria.

Emily trekked further and further into the fenced-in wooded area, keeping her sights on clues to point the way. The same types of large boulders surged up from the downwards sloping ground.

"Bingo!"

From a large clump of boulders, Emily removed some severed tree limbs laid over an old canvas. Then, she pulled back the old canvas to reveal a metal grate closed over a large dark hole about four foot wide and three foot high. The grate's lock was attached to only the grate, not the u-bolt jetting out of the rock. She lifted it open and glanced over at the material that had camouflaged it.

"How did they flip the canvas and the limbs over it?" Emily pondered.

"Are you sure they went in there? What is it?" Brad asked.

"Yes, I know Grant's in there. It's an entrance to an amazing cavern. You've got to see this. I brought a few flashlights, some yarn, a few bottles of water, sodas, and crackers. We'll be fine. Plus, I'll leave a note attached to the front here for Grant in case we miss him."

Her confident manner did not convince him, but Brad was curious. Caves were pretty awesome. With three of them, if there were careful, it could be a great adventure.

"Okay, we can go in, but you girls stay close and we move slow. It could be unstable in areas. I'll lead. You have to test the ground in front of you before put all your weight down. Plus look out for anything that could signal a cave in. You both got it?" Brad commanded.

Ria stroked his arm and gushed, "Wow, Brad, I love it when you take charge like this. It's so sexy."

"Okay Ria, keep focused," Emily teased. Then her voice took on a more serious tone, "How do we pull the canvas and tree limbs back up?"

"I got it. I'll show you. Get inside and hold the grate tilted open, just far enough for me to slide in," he instructed as he began pulling the items closer.

The girls obeyed. Brad arranged the limbs on the canvas and then folded the canvas in half. He placed it right above the grate.

"Okay, now stick your arms though the bars and hold the canvas in place while I slide in."

"This good?" Ria asked.

"Yes. Hold there." Brad released his hold and slipped behind the bars. "Okay now slowly let the bottom of the canvas unfold down. If we do this right, the branches should stack, covering the canvas most of the way."

"That's clever. You are brilliant. I would have never thought of that," Emily praised.

The camouflage plan worked, hiding the trio inside the dim cave's mouth from the outside world. Emily swung her backpack around and pulled out a flashlight.

"Here, Brad."

He took the flashlight.

Digging some more, she produced yarn, paper, and a pen. After scribbling a quick note to Grant, she punched a small hole at the top of the paper with the pen, and then threaded the yarn through the hole.

"Darn, I forgot a knife or something to cut the yarn with," she chastised herself.

"I've got one." Brad pulled out a multi-purpose knife and handed it to her.

"Thanks." She cut about a foot's length and then tied the paper to the grate. "He shouldn't miss this." She beamed proudly. Coming up with the note idea made her feel useful.

"When Grant took me into a different cave, we stuck to the main tunnel. That's probably what he did this time.... Follow the largest, highest opening from the right. We can put a piece of yarn at every spot where there are multiple paths. That way we can be certain which way we came."

Ria pouted. "Okay, now I really feel left out. What other cave... how'd you know about this one?"

"I'll fill you in soon... but let's get going," Emily grinned.

Brad stated, "I don't want to end up in jail." He quizzed her, "Are you sure Grant will be okay with this? We won't get in trouble?"

"I have a good feeling about it. It'll be fine. Maybe we can help with whatever he's doing. "What time is it?" She wasn't sure why she felt pulled to do this. It was unlike her to trespass or break rules, but something was stirring her.

Ria looked as her watch, "Four O'clock."

******

Deep inside the caverns, Officers Grant, Bill, and Dan had paused at a large expansion. It was almost as large as a stadium. The walls were pitted with small holes about the size of a fist. Silky webbing laced the earthen surfaces providing a shimmering effect when the flashlight was cast upon them. Several feet in to the left side, there was a small campsite with a few old pots and pans. There was a stack of fire wood too. Grant strolled over and investigated. Nothing fresh, but without the outside elements at work, it was too hard to tell how long ago it was abandoned. He shook his head negative, to indicate to Bill, it wasn't a lead.

Bill signaled for Grant to check out the left side and he'd take the right. He waved for Dan to come with him. Dan nervously placed his hand on his gun as he trailed a few feet behind Bill.

On the left side further back, Grant spotted a large chest. It reminded him of one he'd seen at Dotia's. After glancing around and making sure the area was secure, he made his way back to the chest. Lifting the lid, he figured it would be empty, but it had clothes, matches, and other items.

"Well, I didn't find anything," Bill said, in a hushed tone, as he walked up over to Grant. "What do you have?"

"Just an old trunk with a few items in it. Looks like stuff from decades ago, nothing recent," Grant remarked. "I didn't see anything either. Maybe further back in the system."

Dan eyed the old trunk. "Do you think there's anything valuable in there?" He reached in and then screamed jerking his hand back out.

Chapter 28

What's Up Ahead?

With the flashlight's illumination, it was easy for Brad to see in the small space. At first it was only conducive to crawl on hands and knees, but a short ways in, the hole expanded, and they were able to stand fully up.

"I'm glad it's bigger here. I wouldn't want to do that for hours. Reminds me of gym class," Ria snickered.

Emily's cell phone rang.

"Yes, this is Emily... yes professor... What did you say? ... the connections bad... What's dangerous?" Emily moved the cell from her ear to check it. It said lost call.

"Guess I lost him. I'll call back later." She muttered.

"What was dangerous?" Ria asked.

"Not sure. All I could make out is the sample results came back. You remember that black thing you found in your hair before you got sick?... Guess he found out what it was. We can call him back later. If it's something dangerous in the apartment, it's not like it can hurt us here."

"Guess not," Ria agreed. "But, maybe it has something to do with why I got sick."

As they descended down the passageway, the cave continued to change. The trio was mesmerized by its beauty and lulled by the almost silent world's tranquilly.

Blamm Blammm. It was an abrupt shock to hear a gun blasting from something further into the caverns.

"What the hell was that?" Brad reacted. "Let's get out of here!"

"What if someone's hurt?" Emily asked.

Ria looked at her watch. "It will take us thirty minutes to run back to the entrance. We'll have to keep trying the cell along the way. Let's hurry." She was ready to get out of there.

Without thinking, Emily grabbed the flashlight from Brad and ran off, barreling down the tunnel. It couldn't be too far up ahead. What if someone was critically hurt? She had to get there in time to at least try to do something.

Darkness engulfed the left-behind pair as Emily traveled further away with the light.

"Damn, guess we'd better follow her. She could get hurt. Plus, she's got the light." Brad took Ria's hand and raced after the crazy girl.

A dim light shined up ahead. Emily slowed down and glanced at her light. Should she turn off her light and creep up? She turned it off, but then decided to turn it back on. Why did she take off and run like that.

"Damn I'm stupid today. What if they think I'm the bad guy and they shoot me? What if it *is* the bad guys?" Emily whispered rebuking herself.

Cautiously, she moved closer towards a dim light up ahead. Brad and Ria caught up to her.

"What are you doing? Are you crazy?" Brad grabbed the flashlight away from her.

"I'm sorry, I just acted. I wasn't thinking. I shouldn't have left you guys, especially without a light...," her voice trembled, "It's just that I...," She didn't know what she had thought.

Muffled voices sounded from up ahead. One was definitely Grant's.

"Okay, I lead. Stay behind me. Got it!" Brad threatened. "Ria, try to keep her inline for her own good."

Embarrassed, she fell in place behind Ria, who was reveling in her take-charge man. Ria clasped Emily's hand firmly in hers and gave a comforting squeeze.

"Hello," Brad called out loudly his voice echoing throughout the underground chambers. "This is Brad Richards. Can anybody hear me?"

The trio stepped into the stadium-sized expanse. The figures wearing police uniforms were over to the far left.

"Brad, this is Grant. Stay where you are. Move very slowly, ... back towards the entrance, and call for an ambulance."

"What's wrong? We brought a few things in Emily's backpack, maybe we have something that can help?" Brad replied. He was confused by Grant's orders.

"Not unless you have a massive amount of spider repellant!"

Emily took out one of the small flood lights she had in her backpack. Turning its strong beam, over to where the three figures were standing, revealed hundreds of baseball-sized black tarantulas poised surrounding the three men. Each man stood holding a gun in one hand and a police baton in the other.

The outer spiders turned to determine what the source of this new intrusion was. Little beady eyes sparkled in the flood light. An eerie scream vibrated through the air as the angry arachnids started separating into two groups, one encircling the officers and the others creeping towards Emily, Grant and Ria.

"Ut oh...." Ria's eyes widened. "Were in trouble."

Emily snatched the other two flood lights out of her backpack. She handed them to Ria, who promptly turned them on and aimed them at the black monsters that were slowly advancing towards them. The spiders scattered back into the safety of the darkness, away from the lights.

Emily fumbled some more in her backpack and pulled out a soda. "Grant, here catch this."

"What are you doing?" Brad asked amazed she would be offering a soda at a time like this.

"Shake it up and spray them. It's cold, wet, and sticky."

In her attempt to hurry, she threw it over to the officers, but missed Grant's opened hands. The soda slammed into a rock, burst out, and started spraying all over the surrounded officers.

The cold sticky liquid hit a few of the six-inch high attackers. The spiders backed away from the trapped men, distracted from proceeding on their attack plan. They jerked their fuzzy eight legs up and down. It looked like they were trying to shake off the substance. Several appeared to be mouthing at the fluid stuck to their hairy bodies. A few flipped around erratically.

"Maybe it's making some of them sick or killing them." Emily shouted. "It might be poisonous to them. Anything that can eat a nail...."

Ria quipped, "I hope so. The less there are the better chances we humans have."

But, after a minute, the dark menaces started herding back around the officers, closer and closer.

Brad looked over to Emily and grabbed at the side of her backpack. "Do you have more?"

"Yes!"

"Give me one! My aims fantastic." His open hand waited.

Emily handed him a can.

"Ready, Grant?" Brad called.

"Throw it," Grant answered.

Brad pitched the can to Grant, who easily caught it. Grant handed it to Bill.

"How many more do you have?" Grant asked.

"Three." Emily pulled them out, ready to hand them one by one to Brad. It had just been that proven he'd be a better choice than her to throw the cans.

"Send them over."

Grant caught the next flying can and handed it to Bill. Two more followed suit.

The tarantulas had regrouped. The charging line was only a few feet from the stranded men. A low eerie noise hummed from the demons, inching forward. Wet liquid was oozing from their fanged mouths.

"Here, Dan, shake this up." Grant handed a can to him. Dan's hand quivered as he took hold of the can. It was hard to keep his balance. The spider's poison, injected into his hand when he reached into the trunk, was all through his body now. His stomach was queasy and he wanted to lay down.

Bill feverishly shook a soda in each hand waiting for Grant's plan to evolve.

Grant pulled his gun back out and readied it as he shook a can in his other hand. He shot one of the spiders to the right of Dan. Spider guts blasted out over onto the arachnid mass behind the hit. The ravenous villains fell upon their shot brethren's remains, stabbing their fangs into any tiny bit of flesh they could. Grant took a few more strategic shots around the circle, loosing spider guts out to distract the approaching mob. The unharmed ones jumped on the chance to suck juices from any tarantula remnants.

"They're getting a little close. Figured it might help us a little." Grant smiled weakly.

The sight of spiders sinking fangs into tiny bits of guts, hissing at each other surely wasn't helping anyone's fortitude. It was too disturbing and disgusting.

Emily ripped open her bag of crackers and spilled them out in front of the opening.

"What's that for?" Brad asked. "Do you think they rather eat crackers than us?"

"I'm grasping at straws," she replied as she empty the other food items the same way. "Maybe it will slow them down or deter them from chasing us. There's salt on them. Maybe they won't cross salt."

"I think that is demons, not spiders," Ria commented. "But, it's worth a try."

Emily sat her flood light down on the tunnel's floor, aimed in the direction of the spider army. The spiders retreated back away from the glaring beams.

"I'll leave this light here. The bright rays seem to detour the spiders. Maybe it hurts all those beady eyes."

Ria followed Emily's lead and did the same with the flood lights she had been holding.

Grant shouted, "Okay, you guys get out of here. We'll follow behind as fast as we can. Run!"

Realizing they couldn't be of more help, Brad, Ria, and Emily raced back out the tunnel. Brad, Ria, and Emily hadn't noticed the webbing before, but it was everywhere. Glancing around as they ran, they all hoped there were none of those things up ahead.

******

"Hang in there Dan! When I give the word, open your can, spray it out to your front and sides ... and run. Run like dam, but be careful and don't slip! You and Bill will go first. I'll bring up the rear." Grant prayed this would work.

The eight-legged mob had devoured all they could of their slain comrades and were refocused on the men. They were inching closer and closer, fangs smacking and oozing.

Grant holstered his gun. "Bill, give me one of your cans, since I'll be last."

"I don't like it much leaving you to bring up the rear. But, I know you're right.... you're the fastest of us." Reluctantly, Bill handed Grant the can he had been shaking with his left hand.

******

By the time Emily, Ria, and Brad reached the area where it was too shallow to stand, all three were panting. But with all the adrenaline coarsening through their veins, none of them were tired. They crawled through the narrow pass in seconds and bolted through the opening, knocking the trees limbs and canvas far away from the hidden entrance.

Emily patted down her body making sure none of the predators were on her. Ria and Brad were doing the same.

******

"Ready, Bill, Dan? NOW!" Grant, Bill, and Dan each opened a can and shot fizzing sprays in a swath. The spiders moved out of the liquid's path. "Run Dan Run!" Grant shouted.

Violently swinging the can from side to side, Dan

focused on the exit, and ran without looking down, stomping on anything under his feet on the way. Right behind Dan, Bill with his gimp leg, sprinted out as fast as he could. Grant hoped Bill could make it. Using his bad leg would cause the older man unimaginable pain.

Within seconds, Dan and Bill cleared the attacking swarm and were entering the exit tunnel. Grant popped the last can opened and ran, spraying the fizzy deterrent out behind him. It didn't take long before he had caught up to his comrades.

"Don't make me leave you guys behind. Move!" Grant ordered. "Those little legs can scurry! They're right behind us."

Nausea surged up in Dan's stomach. Vomit spewed forth, but he didn't slow down. Directly behind Dan, Bill and Grant dodged the putrid substance.

The crawl area was up ahead. Dan dove in scrambling as his mind raced over what it would be like for hundreds of those hairy legs to writhe over him. He frantically scrambled through the low-ceiling area and barreled out the cave's opening. Luckily, Brad had been holding up the grate or Dan, hitting the metal barrier, would have knocked himself unconscious.

Right behind him, Bill and the Grant hastily emerged. Brad let the grate slam shut. The escapees tried to catch their breath as each glance around for any signs of the monsters.

"Where's ... the .... girls?" Grant stammered in between gasps of breath.

"I sent them to the parking lot to meet the ambulance. Do you still need it? We called for one as soon as we cleared the cave," Brad explained.

"Yes, Dan, how are you feeling?" Grant looked over at the wiry man. He appeared okay except for the huge red swollen spot on his hand.

"Too scared to know!" Dan stared down at his hand and then vomited again. "I'm never doing that again. You'll have to fire me!"

Bill laughed, "Me neither! Next time, we'll let Grant go alone with a rope around him. We can pull him out after a few hours. I haven't run that fast in decades. Guess it would be a great boot-camp experience for new recruits."

Grant took the key out of his pocket and relocked the grate. After the canvas was back over the grate and the branches arranged, the guys headed back to the parking lot.

******

The girls arrived in the parking lot both still shaken by the horror scene in the cave. All those creepy spiders. The ambulance was pulling in. The girls still trying to catch their breath walked towards it. The day was fading; the sky was darkening.

"Hi ladies," a voice whispered behind them. "Don't turn around or scream. I have a nice little gun pointed at your backs. I'm sure to get one of you. So, just move towards my car. I know you know which one it is... the yellow Pontiac. We're going to take a harmless ride and if you're good little girls, no one has to get hurt."

They hadn't heard him coming up behind them. Ria glanced out of the corner of her eye to Emily. It was impossible to try anything without one of them getting hurt. If anything happened to Emily, she'd never forgive herself. Emily was thinking the same thing.

The captured pair walked to the car, praying against odds there would be a chance to run. Emily felt a hand twist around her long hair. He led the girls around to the back of the car and popped the trunk.

"Okay, I've got you real tight, so tell your friend to get

quietly in the car trunk and you and I will hop in the front. Got it? Tell her honey, tell her how my hand feels wrapped around your hair, and my gun feels digging into your back," he cackled as if possessed. He bore the gun hard into Emily's flesh.

"His hand's wrapped in my hair and the gun's bearing into my back. I can't move." Emily hated her hair for the first time in her life. If she got out of this alive, no more long hair. She felt like telling Ria to run, but she knew Ria wouldn't. All it would do is make the pervert angry with her.

"Okay, I'll get in, just don't hurt my friend." Ria walked to the trunk and slowly started to climb into the trunk. Her mind screamed not to do it. This could be the last time she would ever see Emily alive.

Chapter 29

Is It Over Now?

The ambulance was parked near the police cars, but the girls were nowhere in sight. Grant approached the EMT who was in the driver's seat reading a book.

"I have a police officer bitten by a spider. I need him to go to the hospital."

"What? ... That's funny dude." The EMT put his book down. "What kind of spider bit him?"

"I think it was a tarantula."

"Well, you're in luck ... tarantula's aren't poisonous. He can drive himself. Is there any other emergency out here?" the EMT remarked snidely. "This isn't a taxi service. I can't be catering to you just 'cause you're cops." He hated cops.

Grant felt like saying, yeah when I get done with beating the crap out of you there'll be an emergency out here but, he composed himself and repeated," As an officer I am requesting that you drive the bitten officer to the hospital now! .. And, you treat him better than you've ever treated anyone. Unless, you don't want to hold the position of EMT any longer."

The EMT stared blankly at Grant. Grant glared back.

"You can't make me... I'll call my boss."

"If you doubt my authority, call the hospital right now," Grant growled. "Tell them Officer Rawles gave you an order from the CEO of Ledniw Corporation and you refused. See what your boss says then."

"Alright, dude. I'll transport him right now." The rude EMT nodded to the other EMT sitting in the passenger side. The second EMT jumped out and headed to the back doors to load their passenger up.

Grant motioned to his comrades. Bill and Brad helped Dan, who was profusely sweating, over to the back of the ambulance. Dan didn't look good at all. His skin color was pale yellowish-green, and the swelling in his hand had increased. The EMT assisted Dan up the steps and sat him on a gurney.

"Never seen a spider bite do this to someone." the EMT remarked.

Grant smiled at Dan, trying to reassure the frightened man. "Okay, Dan, the EMT will take good care of you. It'll be okay."

Then Grant turned to the second EMT and asked, "Have you seen two girls? ... One with long brown hair and the other with short reddish hair?"

"No, sure haven't." The EMT began hooking up an IV into Dan's arm.

"I'm going to look for the girls," Grant told Bill and Brad.

"I'll go to." Brad was concerned. The girls should have been waiting by the ambulance or his car. He hadn't caught sight of them.

******

Emily felt the jolt of the man's body plow into her back. Her hair painfully ripped at her scalp. What had gone wrong? They were doing what he asked. At any second, she expected the gun to go off. The weight of his hand pulled her down to the ground. Emily was dazed. He was lying beside her.

"Sorry lady," a gruff voice said. "I was only trying to knock him out. I didn't mean to hurt you too." Emily felt a hand untangling her hair from the pervert's clasped fist.

"Emily, are you okay?" It was Ria. It was her soft hands, helping Emily up. "Someone get his gun and tie him up." But Ria's plea was late.

The gruff man and the small group beside him already had the gun secured and were tying the man up.

Emily rose to her feet. Her head spun as she glanced around, trying to understand this change in events. A big burly man stood a few feet away from her. There were several other men standing around too.

"You guys helped us?" Emily stammered. A lump stuck in her throat, she couldn't get any more words out.

Focus, she told herself. Get it together. She felt Ria's hand holding her arm. Turning, she met Ria's big brown eyes; tears were glistening down, soaking Ria's cheeks. Emily's face felt wet, warm; she was crying, too. The girls wrapped their arms around each other, too emotional to do anything else.

"You girls will be okay now. Here comes the cops," The gruff man reported. "Hey it's that cop who paid us to keep a look out!" the gruff man chuckled as Grant approached.

"Is everyone alright? Anyone hurt?" Grant asked as he looked down at the guy on the ground and the two weeping girls.

Brad raced over and gently pulled the girls apart trying to determine if they were hurt. Ria threw her arms around him, nodding her head.

"We're okay," Ria sobbed.

Emily's eyes met Grant's. She wanted to rush over and throw her arms around him. But, he was on duty and that wouldn't be right, she told herself. She struggled to gain her composure, wiping her cheeks with the back of her hand.

"These guys saved us," Emily managed to vocalize weakly. "That pervert on the ground had a gun and was forcing us into the car, Ria into the trunk."

"Good job guys!" Grant high-fived the large burly guy. "Come on over to the squad car and I'll get your names. There's a bonus in this for you." Grant knew that was the best way to get an eye-witness list. If you asked people their names they often lied or ran. But offer money, ... it works almost every time.

The small band cheered. He knew he had them.

******

It'd been a long day. Grant, Emily, Ria, Brad, Dotia, and Hal sat around the table in Dotia's kitchen eating pie that Dotia had made. Brad tapped his fingers rhythmically on the table deep in thought.

Ria reached over and placed her hand on his. "What's wrong?"

Brad replied, "It's startling to see all the commotion that those spiders caused. There are 100 or more people camped outside Ria's apartment, all believing strange things like vampires, aliens, witches... How could people be so crazy acting? I mean, I thought it was something weird, but vampires?"

Grant nodded, "Some people are quick to jump to conclusions whether they are believable or not. But, once we expose that it was spiders causing the illnesses and deaths, without letting anyone know about the caves, all those people will go away and things will return to normal."

"Why do the owners want the caves to stay a secret?" Ria asked. "They could open them up and make lots of money."

"From what I understand, there are rare minerals and microscopic life forms in there," Grant explained. "If regular people knew about the caves, many would sneak in and could cause damage to the unique environment in there. Not to mention that people could get hurt. And — "

Dotia interrupted, in a gently scolding tone, "Sneak in like you, Grant? Good thing you didn't get yourself or anyone else hurt."

"Okay, I admit, I didn't have complete permission to search the caves. I just thought ... if someone was in there... I could get the jump on them if I acted quickly. There was no time for a debate." Grant smiled slyly at Dotia.

Hal tapped his pencil on the writing pad in front of him. "The rash actions of youth... You should have waited till that sample from Emily's arm came back. I could have told you that it was from a tarantula. Sometimes, they flick hairs when they are threatened. Those hairs have toxic chemicals in them. Usually, causes a serious rash, or sometimes paralysis."

"I didn't think tarantulas were dangerous or poisonous," Brad commented.

"Most aren't dangerous, but some have poison that they can inject, if they choose to. It usually just causes mild reactions. These just happen to cause serious reactions." Hal replied.

"That's even more reason for me to hate spiders," Ria shivered. "How come I was only bit once, like several of the others, but those two people were bitten all over and died?"

"Guess those two were very unlucky. Usually a dominate spider, like a mother will hunt for a food source by itself. Then, if it is all clear, the babies come out and feast. Those two people who died lived all alone. There wasn't anyone to create an interruption. Once paralyzed from the venom, that was it. One spider can only drink about few tablespoons, but hundreds... well it is easy to see why those bodies didn't have any blood left in them." Hal shook his head saddened over the events.

Brad remarked, "So, I guess, we arrived at the apartment just in time. The noise from us probably chased the spiders off." He smiled understanding that Ria was still alive because of his actions.

Ria reached over and kissed Brad on the cheek. "My hero."

Then Ria looked back at Hal and asked, "But why did I get bitten and not Emily? I mean, I'm glad that Emily wasn't attacked, but Emily was there all alone after I was hospitalized."

"First of, your room had the heater unit in it. The spiders were using the duck work and other holes to run through the apartments. Emily had sealed off her bedroom's air vent because the air distribution made it too cold in her room. Plus, Emily had Jacque sleeping with her. Cats are great spider killers... natural enemies. A spider wouldn't risk getting too close to a cat." Hal's eyes lit up in admiration of the great hunter abilities of the small felines. "Cats love chasing anything that scurries."

"Well, I'm going to be a cat lover from now on," Ria stated.

Jacque jumped up onto Emily's lap as though he knew they had been talking about him.

"And, we could get a cat, like Jacque!" Ria exclaimed. She reached over and patted him gently on the top of his head.

Jacque purred loudly like a cement mixer. Everyone

laughed at the rough unusual sound.

"It may be hard to get a cat like him," Emily cooed as he glanced up at her.

"Well, hopefully, it won't be hard to get rid of all the spiders." Hal passed a paper with a name and address over to Grant. "These are the arachnid specialists lined up to be here two days. They'll capture all the spiders in the caves and apartments that they can. Then, they will set baited traps all around town, continuously over the next year. I'd never thought so many could come from the two females that got loose when my shop was broken into. Guess I'll have to be more careful about the types of pets I carry in the future."

"How did so many come from only two females?" Emily asked.

"Funny thing about some varieties of female Tarantulas... they can hold a male's sperm in a special pouch for years and thus fertilizing eggs when they want. It's not unheard of them having two hundred babies, years after procreating." Hal sipped his tea.

"Damn, that's a lot of monsters." Brad's eye got wide. "How will you know you got them all?"

"Well, we won't, but winter will be here shortly and any left out in the open should die. Fortunately, this particular species is real sensitive to cold. They die when exposed to temperatures below fifty degrees. No one knew they could be so poisonous though," Hal confessed.

Grant added, "Also, the apartments will be tented with poison for 72 hours to kill off any in there. You girls will have to find some place to stay while that's underway, as will all the other occupants. After the tenting, the apartment complex is going to patch all those holes that gave the spiders easy access. Then, traps will be positioned around and monitored over the next year to make sure all the spiders are gotten."

"They can patch the whole building, but Emily and I have decided to move. We're going to find a small apartment far away from there, but still close to school," Ria disclosed. "Maybe you can find something close to us, Brad, since you are moving closer to the University." She gazed hopefully at him.

"There are a couple of small houses about a block away from here. Grant knows the owner, if you want to look at them let me know. She's a real nice older lady," Dotia offered winking at Grant.

"That might work. I could visit you more often, too," Emily smiled at Dotia. She liked spending time with her. Dotia was good at so many things. A thought popped into Emily's head "Maybe you can help me cut my hair short, so no one can use it against me again."

Hal frowned, "But your long hair is probably what also helped to keep them from biting you. Spiders have real weak legs. If one of those legs gets caught in human hair, it snaps off. They have weak teeth too. Can't usually bite through clothes, need open skin. That explains why all the bites were on exposed skin."

"Okay, maybe I'll keep some length to it." Emily shuttered thinking about the black monsters.

A chime went off. Dotia excitedly jumped up from the table. "It's time. The comet's almost here. It only occurs once in a hundred years. Everyone outside now! Hurry! ..." she gracefully dashed out the back door to the garden.

Everyone was confused, but they followed anyways. In the garden, just as the stars aligned, the couples aligned. Dotia and Hal, Ria and Brad, and Emily and Grant. Each pair stood gazing up into the night sky awaiting the mystical passing of the comet. It blazed by magically illuminating the sky with a fiery sparkling tail streaming behind.

Ria and Brad locked into a romantic kiss. No one

noticed. Grant was too distracted gazing into Emily's emerald eyes and she into his mysterious blue eyes. "I've waited so long," he murmured as he embraced her tightly against his body and sank his lips onto hers.

Dotia's heart soared with happiness. Her spell had worked admirably, better than she could ever have dreamed. Must have been the Blood Red roses. Close by, in a freshly cultivated spot, little rose leaves sprang up from the ground. Magic had brought together not one, but three loves. She looked affectionately up into Hal's adoring eyes. He bent close and kissed her lightly.

The End... or maybe just another beginning.....

www.ingramcontent.com/pod-product-compliance
Lightning Source LLC
Chambersburg PA
CBHW061602170626
46811CB00001B/283